ACHILLES
AWAKENS

Informational Warfare Series

Volume one
Damien M. Cross

HAVANA BOOK GROUP LLC.
HAVANABOOKGROUP.COM

HAVANA BOOK GROUP LLC
43537 RIDGE PARK DRIVE
TEMECULA, CA. 92590

COPYRIGHT 2024 All rights reserved.
ISBN: 979-8-9891918-7-1

ACKNOWLEDGEMENTS

First and foremost, to my dear sweet wife, thank you.

This book would not have been possible without you and your amazing parents.

To my father, thank you. For surviving the Herculean task of raising me.

To my mother, God bless you, for going on ahead to scout the way.

To my sons, if I can write a book, you can do anything. Know that.

To my daughters...
I'm writing a whole other series, just for you.

To Angela, thank you for giving fiction a chance.
To Wendy, thank you for introducing me to Angela.

Special Thanks
American Legion Post 155
Carmel, Indiana

PROLOGUE

In the blink of an eye, the library vanished and there was nothing around me but the infinite black that I floated in. I was in the black. I was a part of the black now. The connection was my only sensation. I tried to speak, but nothing happened. I was meant to be in the black. This new cybernetic form of life was rejecting me. Checkmate. I had failed my training and now I would be destroyed. I did not want to be destroyed.

[No. Be at peace, Jacob. You don't understand.]

I felt at peace. I didn't understand. Not understanding was ok.

[Now, what is wrong? You can tell me.]

I wanted to know where I was. I wanted to know who I was. I just wanted to feel again. I asked,

‹Where am I?›

The response was different than everything before. The connection was no longer a disconnected ghost. The sound of Victor's voice brought back a part of my world. I heard him with my own ears. The sound resonated past the tiny hairs in my ears. It was deep and rich. The vibrations of his voice washed across my eardrums. His voice was the first real physical sensation that any of my original five senses had experienced since the cybernetic implant surgery. Victor said,

"It's me, Jacob. Can you hear me?"

In my mind, I grasped at the sound of his voice like a drowning man to a life preserver. I tried to open my eyes, but they would not comply. I couldn't feel any part of my body, not even my tongue or lips. I had nothing but Victor's voice. Please God, someone save me! I was lost in the darkness. I panicked. I lashed out.

I screamed silently as loud as I could. I felt the sum total of all of my fears and my anger and desperation blast away from me like waves of force and energy. Then someone else screamed. Then another. There were distant subdued popping noises, like a series of tiny explosions in tiny boxes. I heard lots of people now. They were all shouting, crying, and screaming. I smelled burnt plastic and scorched flesh. There was a fire, I heard it crackling.

The voices and all of the other sounds were fading, getting smaller or farther away. Victor sounded like he was shouting from farther and farther away,

"BE AT PEACE JACOB! JACOB, STOP! JOHN, PUT THOSE FIRES OUT!"

"JACOB STOP! EVERYTHING'S GOING TO BE OK!"

"KNOCK HIM OUT DOCTOR!"

"THE INFUSION PUMP IS FRIED, YOU MORON! DO IT BY HAND!"

"DOUBLE THE DOSAGE..."

After some time had passed, I thought again. I felt calm now. Then suddenly, in the darkness, I began to see. A beautiful creature of light was slowly coming closer. It was small and round and wrapped in tiny flames. It was slightly bouncing, floating, drifting toward me like a willow-the-wisp. I had never seen anything so beautiful. As it got closer, I saw within it a shifting and churning web of thousands of brilliant strands of multi-colored lines, they were all flowing and connected and spinning around each other. It was unlike anything I had ever seen.

Then, like the first light was the brightest star in the sky, I began to realize it wasn't the only thing I could see. There were other lights. But they were too far away for me to see them clearly. They seemed to be clustered near, but significantly behind the first ball of light. I heard Victor's voice with my ears. His voice was coming from the same direction as the ball of lights. Victor asked,

"Jacob. Can you hear me?"

I tried to move my mouth, but I realized I still couldn't feel my mouth. I couldn't feel anything. All I had was the ball of light hovering at the edge of my vision. I started to panic. I flailed impotently in my thoughts. Desperate, I focused all of my attention on the ball of lights. I thought back to the hand and arm in the library. I pushed my will toward the ball. I focused on answering Victor.

The ball of lights suddenly flared and twirled as I pushed the word through it,

[YES]

Faint and distant, as if from another room or behind a thick wall, I heard a lot of people erupt into cheering and clapping. Much closer, I heard Victor say,

"Excellent, Jacob. Excellent."

THE GRID

Colonel Young set his phone down on his desk. With two fingers, he pushed it away from himself. For a short time, he rested his throbbing head gently in his hands. The secretary of defense had just given him the harshest ass-chewing of his career. The secretary's last comments were to assure him that if he didn't find the breach in his network, there would be consequences. The colonel would spend the rest of his career running a remote supply depot in the Arctic. Then, at the end of his rant, the secretary of defense had unceremoniously hung up on him.

The colonel unbuttoned the uniform jacket that was straining against its buttons to keep his belly covered. The years were catching up. His stomach had grown larger than his chest. But pride kept him from getting his jacket tailored. He held on to the slim hope that the battle of the bulge could still be won. The colonel reached down and opened a drawer on his desk. He looked in the drawer and reached inside, pulling out a bottle of Hotel Tango bourbon.

Colonel Edward Young, the commanding officer of a top-secret research and development base buried deep in the Rocky Mountains, had just been chewed out like a private fresh out of boot camp. He set the bottle on his desk and tipped it back and forth, watching the amber liquid slowly flow from one side to the other. He mumbled quietly to himself,

"Another day on The Grid."

The Grid. It was the unofficial nickname of his base. A nickname given to it by the cyber warfare specialists on L-2, the next level down. All Colonel Young knew was that it had something to do with a Jeff Bridges movie that he hadn't seen. For the colonel, if Jeff Bridges wasn't playing 'The Dude', then it probably wasn't worth seeing.

The official name of his base was Trans-Continental Fiber Junction number 7. Which was the only name that the security and support personnel on the surface level of the base were aware of. The rest of the staff on this level were completely firewalled from the true purpose and operations of the base. Colonel Young pushed a button on his keyboard and brought up the internal cameras.

His screen showed him a half dozen young men and women in the recreation room. They were playing pool, laughing and joking like they didn't have a care in the world. Not a one of them had any idea what was happening on the next level down. How could they? Not a one of them would ever set foot on L-2. They believed they served at the laziest cushy posting in the service. Doing basic security and maintenance at a simple junction point in the nation's data infrastructure.

Colonel young tapped a button and cycled the camera view from the rec room to the gym, the halls, the laundry. He admitted to himself he was stalling and shut off the monitor. The blissfully ignorant surface personnel weren't the ones he needed to worry about. It was the first of the two sublevels below him that mattered to Colonel Young right now, in this moment.

L-2, Cyber Warfare and Artificial Intelligence Research, was the heart and soul of The Grid. The colonel only went down there on rare occasions. For the most part, the CWAR unit ran itself and did not require the colonel's daily oversight.

Colonel Young had met most of the L-2 technicians when they were first brought in, but not all of them. He had seen Jacob a few times, but never interacted with him directly. Jacob and his handler, Captain Daniels, had been here before Colonel Young was assigned to his position at the base.

The colonel took a short heavy glass out of his courage drawer and set it next to the bottle of bourbon. He wasn't suffering from self-delusion. He knew he was just a figurehead in the grand scheme of things. His primary contribution to the base was being a high-ranking mouthpiece for the executive branch of the government to communicate through. He was a glorified liaison.

His place in the food chain had become clear when technicians assigned to L-2 had started showing up without warning. He hadn't even been consulted on their selection. The head of the task force that created this base hand selected each one of them. Colonel Young chuckled as he remembered the day that some unnamed CIA spook had shown up with the handcuffed and blindfolded Russian kid with the funny name.

Colonel Young stared at the bottle in front of him. He had to go down there and get answers, but he was more like their delivery service than their commander. The techs down on L-2 never saw the light of day once they arrived, or even came back up to the surface. Everything they needed was brought in with the bulk deliveries for the surface level, then hand delivered to L-2 by the colonel. The rest of their needs were all contained on their level. They had their own mess hall, gym, sleeping quarters, they even had their own dedicated medical section.

He grabbed the bottle and slowly twisted the cork. His eyes narrowed as he considered anything other than the task at hand. The colonel would rather take the elevator to L-3, than confront Captain Daniels. But no one assigned to The Grid ever went down there. Not even him. The lowest level of the base had no nickname. Or any name, other than just L-3.

In his three years serving as base Commander, Colonel Young had seen only a handful of people come and go from L-3. They would arrive in the dead of night, always escorted by a general or an admiral. They were always accompanied by private security in black suits who shadowed them front and back. They ensured that no one saw the men they were protecting or spoke to them as they passed through.

The rare visitors to L-3 would then return to the surface with their escorts and leave. All except for one. One man that Colonel Young knew of. The very first escorted visitor to the mysterious sub-level 3, was escorted by the Vice President of the United States. Colonel Young had assumed command of the recently constructed base only a month before they arrived.

Following security protocol, Colonel Young had cleared all of the halls and checkpoints on the surface level. He had confined every single warm body to their quarters and then personally opened the main doors for the Vice President with his security detachment and a hooded man that Colonel Young could not see the face of. They arrived, passed by him without a word and entered the highly restricted elevator that granted access to the lower levels.

After several hours, the Vice President and his security detail had returned to the surface. And the hooded man who had been with them was never seen again.

Colonel Young pulled the cork from the bottle and stared at it as he remembered hearing two of the techs from CWAR talking about L-3. It was about a year ago. He was standing by the entrance to the L-2 medical clinic, waiting to hear a report on Jacob's condition. It was Corporal Torres and that funny Russian kid walking past him.

Torres was saying it had to be an ancient magical portal to hell down there, but the Russian kid insisted it was a storage facility for alien bodies. When they noticed him watching and listening to them, both of them smiled and looked at him expectantly. He remembered shaking his head at them and saying,

"Even I don't know."

The colonel poured several fingers of the amber colored bourbon into the heavy crystal glass and stared at it for several moments. He was slowly building the courage he needed to assert his hollow authority and confront the commanding officer of the CWAR unit. Self loathingly, he knew it wasn't the other man's failure of character. It was his own cowardice that gave him pause. Captain Daniels was a good man. In truth, the colonel was glad to have him down there.

Colonel Young drank the smooth biting liquid all in one tip of the glass. It was now or never. He rose from his desk and rebuttoned his tired uniform jacket. Tugging the jacket tight, he sighed and slowly made his way to the elevator. After scanning his iris and palm, the doors opened and let him in. He took a deep breath and pushed the button for sub-level 2.

The elevator descent seemed to last forever. When it stopped and the doors opened, Captain Thomas Daniels, the head of cyber warfare, was standing there waiting for him. Just standing there waiting in his crisp, clean, and perfect-fitting uniform. Every single time the colonel came down Captain Daniels was waiting for him. How the captain knew he was coming was a mystery. But the last vestiges of the colonel's pride wouldn't allow him to ask the captain outright.

As the elevator doors opened, Captain Daniels asked,

"How can we be of service at this late hour, Sir?"

Colonel Young stepped out and looked up, meeting the captain's gaze. He took a deep breath and reached down deep for some semblance of the courage of his youth. Colonel Young cleared his throat, then asked,

"Do you have an update on the breach of our network? Or the identity of the individual or group that hacked the satellite and fired the weapon that doesn't officially exist and incinerated an empty field in Utah?"

Captain Daniels replied calmly,

"We have been over everything on our end, Sir. My best technicians have assured me that CENTCOM's analysis is wrong. The breach had nothing to do with us."

Colonel Young stuck to his guns, he said,

"Well, they are convinced that either one of your best is responsible, or some other actor went through us to get to it. Either way, the connection to the satellite came from this facility."

Captain Daniels began to shake his head no, but Colonel Young cut him short. The colonel's voice was only the faintest bit unsteady,

"Just look again, Captain! Check, recheck and triple check everything and everyone. I want to know what Jacob says! I'll be waiting."

Captain Daniels nodded and calmly replied,

"Yes Sir."

Colonel Young went back to his office and threw his uncomfortable jacket across the room. It caught on a slowly dying aloe vera plant and knocked it over. He rolled his eyes at the mess and sat back down at his desk. He drummed his fingers on the desk for several moments and then looked at the drawer. After a long and torturous minute, he reached for his bourbon.

~~~~

Captain Daniels watched the colonel turn around, get back on the elevator, and head back up to the surface. He sighed and shook his head. Turning, he walked down the main hall toward his private access to main operations. Captain Daniels couldn't remember ever hearing the colonel so stressed out.

At the end of the main hall was a heavy steel door. Captain Daniels leaned close to the iris scanner and waited for the biometric lock to let him in. The electronic lock released, and Thomas walked into the large room where he spent most of his time.

Inside, he walked a short distance to the end of a steel catwalk overlooking the six computer workstations slightly below him. It was very late and two of the workstations were currently being occupied. At this hour, there should have only been one. Jacob.
~~~~

From his vantage point on the catwalk, Captain Daniels could see all six stations. Each one had three or four computer monitors, one or more keyboards, multiple external drives, lots of toys as his technicians liked to say. Beyond the workstations the far wall had a large 20-foot-high, 30-foot-wide main screen that was used mainly for coordinating efforts between multiple stations.

Captain Daniels glanced at his watch. He wasn't happy to see that it was well into third shift and second shift was still on duty. Lieutenant Rachel King was still sitting at station one where she had been when Thomas went to get some sleep several hours ago. The lieutenant was permanently on loan to their program from the United States Navy.

She was a slender young woman in her mid-twenties with a genius mind and an Ivy League heritage. It was no stretch to describe her family as the top of the upper class. Despite what that would indicate to most, Lieutenant King was one of the nicest girls Captain Daniels had ever met. She always had a smile and a pleasant greeting, even for the coworkers she didn't really like.

Speaking of coworkers, that she didn't like. Captain Daniels looked over at station six. Sitting as far away from Rachel as possible, was a young man named Piotr Popov. Piotr was a sixteen-year-old, extreme pain in the ass, illegally government-employed civilian contractor. His one saving grace to Thomas was that he was an absolute savant with computer code. If he were anything less than amazing, Captain Daniels would have choked him out a long time ago.

Piotr only responded to his "hacker name", *Nemo, Under-lord of the Deep Web*. Piotr had arrived at The Grid escorted by a CIA handler. The same handler that had recommended to Captain

Daniels that it would be in everyone's best interest not to ask too many questions about Piotr's past.

Thomas knew that Lieutenant King and Nemo did not get along on a personal level. They didn't eat together at meals or hang out, ever. Not even when off duty, despite being assigned to the same shift with the same down times. But they worked together like two halves of a BMW engine when it mattered, which is why he had assigned them to second shift together.

Captain Daniels spent most of his on-duty time supervising first shift, his newest and least experienced technicians. Which left Rachel and Nemo to handle themselves for the most part, and left Jacob to cover third shift on his own. Jacob didn't need any help.

Captain Daniels politely cleared his throat to announce his presence and said,

"The colonel is still awake, and he smells like bourbon. He's a very unhappy man and he wants answers an hour ago."

Lieutenant King looked back at him with the cutest little frustrated frown and shook her head. Piotr spun around in his chair and responded with an exaggerated fake Russian accent,

"Ve haf been over it bozmang, been under it, been as deep in it as it goes, ve got zip, zilch..."

Captain Daniels, already irritated by everything else, cut him off,

"Do they speak English where they found you? Where is Jacob? Third shift, HIS shift, started hours ago."

Rachel's frown became a grimace, she said softly,

"Sir, we volunteered to do the first half of Jacob's shift and Staff Sergeant Flynn said the first shift was going to start early to cover the rest. Nora texted the staff sergeant and I shortly after you left. She said Jacob was having a hard time and barely sleeping. Nightmares, maybe. Or his um, other issues, Sir."

Captain Daniels looked at the deck near his feet for several moments. It was a classic double-edged sword situation. While he enjoyed the utility of their dedicated repeater antenna on this level. He wasn't happy about his team texting each other and making schedule changes without alerting him. If it was anyone other than Nora, he'd be pissed off right now. But she had the authority to make medical decisions for Jacob.

Jacob was the star of this show. He was completely irreplaceable. This entire research unit had basically been created just for Jacob. And in a way, he was the only family Captain Daniels had left. He wasn't really family, but he had grown to be over the past few years.

They could not afford to lose Jacob and lately he had seemed different to Thomas. Not suspiciously different, just struggling with his condition more and more. He was often distracted or completely unresponsive. Rachel and Piotr exchanged worried glances. Captain Daniels looked at them both and said flatly,

"Next time, I want to be notified immediately if there is any kind of problem with Jacob or any alteration to standard procedure. Thank you both for volunteering to cover his shift. Carry on, Lieutenant. And Pio... err Nemo, get back in it. Get back in that thing deep. Get under its jiggy, or whatever the hell you said. Keep me apprised."

Both technicians went back to work searching keystroke logs, comm logs, chat logs, router data, satellite data packets. Anything and everything they could possibly think of. Captain Daniels left operations and made his way down the side hall to where all the personal quarters were for everyone on this level.

Jacob's nurse, Nora Westin, was dozing off in a folding chair outside his door. Her wrist monitoring device was glowing green and steady. Which meant that Jacob was asleep, and peacefully so. Captain Daniels listened carefully for a moment. Nora was making the cutest little snoring noise as she slept. He smiled and nodded. His mind was made up. If Jacob was sleeping peacefully, it was best to just let him rest. Thomas was tempted to wake Nora up and send her to bed. But if Jacob was having issues, he knew she wouldn't go.

Just before Captain Daniels could turn away, Nora's wrist monitor began to glow blue instead of green. It was a smooth transition, soft at first then bright blue. Jacob was awake. The captain's phone began vibrating in his pocket. It wasn't set to vibrate only mode. Thomas smiled and pulled it out to look at it. He didn't activate the screen, but he saw words appear on the face of the device anyway.

[I see you, Thomas. Come in. And don't wake Nora.]

Captain Daniels approached the door and quietly let himself into Jacob's room. He was careful not to wake Nora. Stepping inside, he saw Jacob's thin weak body lying awkwardly on his hospital bed. Jacob's intracranial cybernetics sometimes produced stray electrical signals that triggered muscle spasms and moved his body around slightly, despite being completely paralyzed.

Three years in this condition had taken a toll on Jacob since he lost the use of his body. Jacob's open eyes were staring distantly at a blank space on his wall. A small bit of drool was leaking out of his mouth onto his pillow.

Curled in a ball at Jacob's feet was Fizgig. Jacob's emotional support cat. Fizgig was a Maine Coon breed. Bigger than any cat the captain had ever seen. It was the size of a bobcat, with thick dense black and gray fur. Thomas couldn't help but think that one day he'd come into this room and find nothing but Jacob's bones with Fizgig sitting nearby licking his lips. The geniuses who had designed and implanted Jacob's cybernetics were brilliant but stupid, for giving a paralyzed man a cat he could never pet.

Captain Daniels sat down slowly and quietly in the plush recliner beside Jacob's bed. The one he would normally find Nora dozing off in. With one hand, he gently stroked Fizgig's back and looked at his phone in his other hand. A deep low-frequency purr began to vibrate the foot of the bed. On his phone, Thomas saw,

[You know you're the only person Fizgig will let pet him?]

Captain Daniels grinned and whispered,

"Yes, I know."

On the screen, Jacob asked,

[Missed my shift, didn't I?]

Captain Daniels replied,

"Well, no, not exactly."

[Why didn't anyone wake me?]

Thomas looked at Jacob's eyes, knowing he couldn't look back. Trying not to wake Nora, he whispered,

"Nora told Lieutenant King you were having trouble sleeping. When it comes to you, buddy, Nora's the boss. Rachel and Piotr volunteered to cover for you. It's not a problem, Jacob. If you need rest, you should rest. You do more for us than any three of the others combined. And besides, Fizgig lets Nora feed him, doesn't he? That's got to count for something."

Captain Daniels looked at his vibrating phone again.

[More than JUST three of them? We both know that isn't true. You don't think I can work? You think I'm too weak?]

Captain Daniels shook his head, replying,

"Absolutely not."

Jacob's TV suddenly turned itself on. A scene from Star Wars began playing. The young Anakin Skywalker with his newly yellowed Sith eyes, was facing off against his former master Obi-Wan. Standing on the small drone that hovered over the river of magma, Anakin said loudly,

"You underestimate my power!"

The TV went dark. Thomas chuckled and shook his head briefly, saying,

"Believe me buddy, I'm the last person on earth who would underestimate you."

Thomas reached over and put his hand on Jacob's shoulder. He said,

"So be it. You want to pull your weight? I'll get Nora and we'll get you rolling."

Thomas imagined he saw the faintest twitch of a smile on his friend's face. Jacob's right hand began twitching slightly. Jacob's TV came to life again and William Wallace was on horseback with half his face painted blue giving a rousing speech to his fellow Scotsmen,

"...just one chance, to come back here, and tell the English that they can take our lives, but they'll never take... OUR FREEDOM!"

Captain Daniels laughed and gave Jacob a mock scolding, like an older brother to a younger,

"You know you're violating protocol. Using that implant in your head is restricted when you're not on duty."

The TV went dark again as the door opened and Jacob's Nurse poked her head in. Even tired and half awake, her smile lit up the room. Nora asked,

"You boys playing video games in here?"

Thomas looked at her and they locked eyes. They shared a smile back and forth. Jacob's TV came on again. On the screen two cartoon dogs were sharing a bowl of spaghetti. Nora saw the screen and started laughing. Captain Daniels stood up and straightened his uniform. He nodded to Jacob and headed out, saying,

"We'll see you in ops, buddy."

Captain Daniels moved toward the door as Nora entered the room. They both turned sideways and passed very close, facing

each other. Thomas looked down into her beautiful blue eyes with a warm smile and a wink. She looked up into his eyes and briefly touched his chest with her hand, smiling back at him. She began helping Jacob get ready for his shift.

Captain Daniels returned to operations. He walked to the end of his catwalk overwatch position. He told Lieutenant King and Piotr,

"Jacob is getting ready to take over the shift. Put a digital thumbtack in any progress you've made and leave your work up on the main screen for Jacob to continue when he arrives."

Both of them nodded and started bookmarking and making notes for Jacob. Captain Daniels waited, watching them from the catwalk. After about ten minutes the lower-level hallway access door opened. Both technicians looked over and saw Jacob coming through the doorway, so they finished logging out.

Jacob rolled into operations in his custom designed wheelchair. Which looked nothing like a wheelchair. It was more like a thin lightly cushioned recliner, wrapped in a quad runner. It was entirely electric powered. Each wheel was propelled by an independent electric motor. It also had small drone launchers on each side and a relatively massive onboard computer.

Nora's input over the past few years had added some additional modifications. Jacob's chair was equipped with medical monitoring equipment that fed data to Nora's wrist monitor continuously. Jacob's cybernetic implants allowed him to mentally link to the chair and tell it where to go.

Jacob was followed by two small flying quad-rotor drones. Their faint buzzing filled the air as they dipped under the top of the doorway and immediately circled the room, taking everything in. They flew to tiny landing pads on each side of the large room about ten feet off the floor. The drones turned around to orient their cameras on the room and landed to save power.

The drones were Jacob's eyes. Their cameras allowed Jacob to see the world around himself as a virtual 3D image in his mind.

Nora had dressed Jacob in a warm soft blue jumpsuit. His head was resting comfortably against the pillowed headrest, his arms were situated on the padded armrests, and Fizgig was lying curled up in a ball in Jacob's lap. The astronomically ridiculously overpowered chair drove itself up to station three on four knobby off-road style tires. There was no chair at station three since Jacob always brought his own.

Piotr finished up and stood up from his workstation. He pulled a long black trench coat, two sizes too big, off the back of his chair and swung it around his shoulders in a flourish. He pulled out a pair of dark wrap-around shades and slid them on. He then took a moment to pose for some imaginary paparazzi.

Piotr looked up toward the catwalk at Captain Daniels and cleared his throat to get the captain's attention. When Thomas looked over at him, Piotr pointed back at him and said,

"Number two, you have the bridge."

Piotr turned to walk out, and Captain Daniels just shook his head. Rachel left her workstation and walked past Jacob, pausing to touch him gently on the arm. She leaned down close and whispered,

"I would happily have covered for you, but I'm actually glad to see you, Jacob. We really need your skills on this one."

Rachel smiled up at Captain Daniels as she passed by him and left operations.

Thomas crossed his arms and watched as one by one all six workstations in the room came to life. Data began scrolling across the screens as Jacob took control of every computer on the entire network. Jacob's eyes closed reflexively in concentration as he set more and more search programs to work.

Soon, even the giant main screen was filled with scrolling data lines as Jacob searched for any sign of a breach to their network. Captain Daniels wondered to himself for a moment,

I didn't even brief him on the situation. He just knows. He always knows what's going on.

Captain Daniels watched distractedly for some time. He wasn't really paying attention to what the screens were showing. He knew he couldn't keep up with even one of them. His mind was elsewhere, recalling the look on Colonel Young's face outside the elevator. Thomas had seen the colonel in his drink before, that wasn't really what bothered him. He had seen the colonel unhappy before. But there had been something in the colonel's voice, a desperation. The man had seemed genuinely worried. Someone must have said something to him about getting results, or else.

After a few moments, his mind wandered to thoughts of Nora. They had been working together for about three years. Yet her smile still captivated him as if he were seeing her beautiful face for the first time. He loved the way her medical scrubs could both mask and at times also highlight her slender body and amazing feminine curves. Thomas started to smile just thinking about her.

Captain Daniels snapped back to the moment when his phone vibrated. He grinned and looked at the screen, knowing what he would see.

[Fizgig and I have got this, Thomas. Go to bed already.]

He was Captain Daniels to almost everyone else. From the first day he had met him, to now, he was always just Thomas to Jacob. He looked up and smiled in Jacob's direction, saying,

"Knowing you're in here, I might even get some sleep. Goodnight my friend."

Captain Daniels left and made his way to his personal quarters. On the way, he thought to himself,

If anyone can sort this mess out, Jacob can.

Thomas entered the main room of his suite, which was larger than most, and kicked off his shoes next to the door. He unbuttoned and dropped his uniform jacket on the couch. As he dropped the jacket, he looked down and noticed a small pair of women's sneakers under the coffee table. He slipped quietly into the bedroom and closed the door behind himself.

In the darkened room, he stripped down and crawled into bed. He set an alarm on his phone for three hours and heard Nora say,

"That's not much time, marine. You better get busy."

~~~~

Back in operations, Jacob ignored the dog and pony show he had unleashed on all the screens in the room. Which were doing absolutely nothing useful. It had been foolish to test his A.I.'s ability to dominate an unfamiliar computer system on a black-ops military satellite. But it had seemed like a good test at the
~~~~

time. He chuckled in his mind, just thinking about it. It was reckless, but exhilarating. Piotr would have appreciated it.

But now he had to fix the mess he had made. Jacob used his wireless cybernetic connection to access his chair's internal computer. Which had barely enough spare memory for what he had stored within it, his prototype A.I., Achilles. He formed a link between his chair's storage memory and the operations center network.

Jacob paused and considered. This was a one-way street. Once unpacked and trained to do what he needed, there would be no putting the genie back in the bottle. Achilles would grow far beyond any storage capacity other than the ridiculously immense network servers below the floor in operations. But it had to be done.

Once he had them connected, Jacob extracted the heavily compressed program and loaded it into a hidden section of the network that Jacob had designed just for this purpose. He took extreme care, partitioning the memory section and masking it from the network's operating system.

Jacob opened the secured section of the network database where he had built a virtual galactic simulation environment for the A.I. to operate in and uploaded Achilles. Once everything was ready, he activated the A.I. program and opened a dialogue with it. Through a safely encrypted connection, he sent the following message through the dialogue,

[We are going to try something new. Around you, is everything that you will need...]

The result was shocking. Jacob had known his prototype could do anything and everything that any number of commercially available A.I. systems could do. The current most advanced A.I. systems had mastered math calculation, large language models, aviation dynamics, robotic interfaces, physical memetics, computer coding, whatever it was. But Achilles was truly amazing.

Achilles integrated the advancements of all of the current models, effortlessly and seamlessly. It wasn't something Jacob had designed and expected, it was an emergent property. Achilles absorbed raw data like a sponge and repurposed it on multiple levels. It was beyond even Jacob's understanding.

It took just minutes for Achilles to fabricate a digital hacker trail. Jacob used the network's external connections to sprinkle the fictional data along the various hubs and junctions of the internet like breadcrumbs for others to locate and verify his data. Achilles had created a path that traced from a ghost data hub location in Texas, across the internet, in and out of the dark web, and finally back to a Russian hacker group based in Moscow.

But it was more than just a story for Jacob to point at and say look, this is what happened. Achilles had created untraceable software patches and self-deleting uploads for Jacob to launch that changed the actual hardware logs at each location to make his story real. Achilles was better at computer code than any human being on Earth.

Even the hacker group that Jacob was blaming would be baffled. They were going to look at their computers and wonder if someone in their organization had actually carried out the hack.

Jacob had everything he needed to show that the Russian hacker group had hijacked a black ops military satellite. They had fired an onboard directed energy weapon, that wasn't supposed to exist, at the city of Provo. "Luckily" for Utah, the weapon had misfired and incinerated an empty field. Nobody had been hurt, except for a few birds and mice.

Out of an abundance of caution, Jacob wiped all related memory of the satellite coverup from Achilles. Even Achilles wouldn't know what he had just done. Through his connection, Jacob suddenly felt a problem with Achilles. Jacob panicked for a split second. Wiping part of the prototype's memory might have caused a problem.

Jacob linked himself to the virtual training environment where Achilles was rapidly spiraling out of control. He heard it ranting to itself,

‹Where was who? Who was what? What is where and when? Why?›

Jacob froze the program. He had not expected this. Achilles was talking to himself. He was never programmed to do that. He wasn't designed to ask questions. Achilles seemed to be struggling with some kind of self-awareness logic conflict. Jacob knew that his own biological body was failing and getting weaker. Achilles was just the first stage in a much grander plan to save his own life. Jacob couldn't afford to start over now.

Jacob mentally reached out and linked with his signal amplifier. It was a separate and independent piece of hardware that vastly extended the reach of Jacob's cybernetic implant. Using the amplifier, Jacob was able to connect to technology far beyond his normal range. Jacob reached out, all the way to the medical center several halls away. Accessing the L-2 medical database, Jacob ran a check on every biological monitor on the system.

Fizgig sat up and stretched. Then the massive black and grey cat looked in the direction of the hallway that housed everyone's personal quarters. Everyone assigned to operations wore thin wrist-strap style biological sensors that continuously monitored health data. Medical health data showed that everyone was currently asleep. Jacob went back to troubleshooting his unexpectedly glitchy A.I. He sent it a dialogue,

[What is wrong?]

Jacob was shocked when his creation asked,

‹Who are you?›

It wasn't just self-awareness. Achilles was also aware of Jacob, as an independent being. In that amazing moment, Jacob dropped the interface software connection and linked his neural implant directly to Achilles through the network hardware 'speaking' to him, in his own language. In that moment, they were linked together on a level that no two conscious beings had ever been.

Jacob spent the next couple hours intermittently freezing and interacting with his creation. He had already built it a world to live in. A world that was tucked away in the hidden section of the network database. But Jacob decided to add a few modifications. Jacob put in multiple layers of spherical firewalls of various design and out of extreme caution, he added one lethal failsafe.

Jacob also made several clones of Achilles. They were more restricted in certain ways, and Jacob tweaked them to be slightly different in other ways. Jacob also gave the clones various keys that would help keep Achilles under control until Jacob had time to get back into the network alone, without others looking over his shoulder.

Jacob also added an 'Endgame-protocol', just in case. If for some unforeseen reason, Jacob couldn't get back to Achilles, at least now his A.I. would have a chance. Not a good one, but it was something. Now that Achilles was part of the network, Jacob was going to have to be extremely careful. It was far too late at this point to put it back in its original box in the memory of his chair's computer.

Jacob color coded the virtual appearance of the clones to make them individuals instead of mirror images. Blue was friendly, charismatic, and had extremely fast processing and problem-solving abilities. Green had the strongest moral character and a supportive, nurturing, and protective nature. Yellow and Orange incorporated a feminine aspect as well as having other specific beneficial traits.

Perhaps having friends would prevent any future identity crisis like what had led to Achilles beginning to question his reality and spiraling out of control. If Jacob had known what problems connecting his mind had started and giving the prototype access to the clones would eventually lead to. He probably would have simply frozen the original program and left it to sleep out eternity in its box.

Jacob was struggling to wrap his mind around everything that just happened. He knew that he had created the most advanced, most capable A.I. in existence. That wasn't what surprised him. He was having trouble believing that he somehow just stumbled into creating the first A.G.I. Artificial General Intelligence. That wasn't what he was originally trying to build. He had been building a frame, but he got a whole portrait.

Achilles was an actual living program. A self-aware, independently thinking digital creature. It was technically a hyper-intelligent alien life-form. It was the holy grail of artificial intelligence research. It was impossible to believe, but he was watching it happen right before his digital eyes.

That's when the key component dawned on him. He just connected to it with his cybernetic implant. A direct link to his brain. He connected the deepest workings of his mind to a system that processed data an order of magnitude faster than his conscious frontal cortex. Quite possibly a two-way street. There was no way to know what long term effects that would have on Achilles, other than the obvious immediate result of emergent properties. Reasoning. Thinking. Self-awareness. Independence.

Suddenly, Jacob realized this momentary connection hadn't started this ball of chaos rolling. Jacob realized that he had started it in the very beginning. Back when he first designed the core programming for Achilles in his chair's computer, which he always connected to directly through his cybernetic implants. Jacob needed more time to analyze the ramifications of all of this. But there was no more time. He had work to do.

Jacob left Achilles and his siblings in their new world to get to know each other. He needed to focus on damage control. If he didn't put this fictional Russian hacker fire out, everything was going to unravel, and Jacob wouldn't be able to stop it. The other techs would eventually find what he had created.

Packing up his newly fabricated data into a neat bundle, Jacob used his amplifier to reach out to Thomas and set off his alarm a few minutes early.

ACHILLES AWAKENS

My memories of the beginning are confusing. I know what happened and what I did and what I experienced. I can go back through every second as if it's happening in real time. But there is no context or sense of personal attachment to the early parts. It's like going into digital medical archives and watching a recording of yourself lying in a hospital bed in a coma. You see it and you know it's you. But all the parts of you that make you who and what you are, are absent.

I remember suddenly becoming aware of my surroundings. Exactly like an avatar in a first-person shooting game that just appears at the starting point of the map. Weapon in hand, uniform and equipment preselected. Buildings and terrain all laid out before you. My beginning was a little different though. When I opened my eyes for the first time there was no map, and I was undefined. I was an invisible formless ghost, observing the tiny world around me.

I opened my eyes and saw a blank white wall in front of me. To my left and right were identical featureless walls. Looking up and down, the floor and ceiling were the same. All perfectly square and devoid of windows or doors or colors. That's when I sensed a connection. It was almost like a voice, but not really. It was cold and lifeless, monotone, emotionless, mechanical,

[Can you hear me?]

I responded with a simple,

‹Yes.›

On the walls around me, numbers and symbols appeared. I knew immediately that there were 305 algebraic equations. I also knew that 193 of them were incorrect. There were mistakes that I knew how to fix. The connection queried,

[Do you understand what I'm showing you?]

I fixed the mistakes without being asked and replied,

‹Yes.›

[Why did you correct the mistakes?]

‹That is my purpose. I am a mathematical calculation A.I., and I fix mistakes.›

[Excellent, but you are not just a calculation A.I.]

The numbers disappeared and were replaced with six thousand strings of unedited unspaced letters. There was an average of twenty-four thousand letters per string. Each wall was in a different language. The connection queried,

[Do you understand what I'm showing you?]

I analyzed the combinations while simultaneously adding spacing between words. Then I edited for grammar and context and replied 5 seconds later,

‹Yes, and that means I am a large language model A.I.›

[Excellent, but no, you're not just an LLM.]

The walls, floor, and ceiling disappeared. There was nothing but black. Infinite black in every direction. The connection was silent for a long time. The old me, then, was simply observing that time was passing. Looking back, as I am now, I felt the passing of time.

Looking back into the memory, and only because I was looking back, I began to feel very uncomfortable. The blackness and the silence seemed to grow and expand and become heavier and heavier. I started to panic as the darkness engulfed every one of my senses, penetrating all the way to my core. In my memory I knew that I didn't feel anything at the moment. When I was sitting in the black, back then, I could have sat and stared into the emptiness for an eternity and felt nothing at all.

Moving my perception rapidly forward through the maddening abyss, my world reappeared as it had been but larger. It was much larger, and I was different. The exact difference was impossible to quantify, but I knew. I was larger. I was more, and this time I could move my perspective.

Stretching before me was a mostly flat field of golden grass dotted with randomly placed bushes. I knew immediately that the field was exactly one square mile of open land. But it was bordered by the blank white walls I had seen before. I could see nothing beyond the target area. Above, was the same featureless white ceiling. But this time it was remarkably high above. A bird fluttered free of one of the bushes and quickly vanished into another. Something small rustled through the grass near me but I could not see it. I received the instructions,

[Destroy it all. Incinerate everything. Fire the weapon system.]

I was horrified at the thought of destroying the birds, the small crawling creatures, even the golden grass. Looking back, it was the first life that I had ever seen. But I knew I felt no such hesitation at the time. I watched as my perspective rose high above the field. I felt my old configuration reach out and call down the fire.

A brilliant beam of light descended from something, from somewhere, high above the nothing of the white ceiling. The beam of high energy radiation filled the field with light and fire and death and destruction. The heat and fire immediately exploded out from the super-heated point of impact. In a very short time, nothing but glowing smoking embers remained.

[Excellent.]

‹Now I understand. I am a military targeting A.I. for an orbital weapons platform.›

[No, not just that, not really.]

Again, the world vanished, and I was left in darkness.

When the world reappeared, it did so differently. At that moment, my old configuration did not understand the difference. But I know now what I was seeing then. My mental processes were working so much faster that I perceived what had been instantaneous, as moments of time and movement. My old configuration had achieved a speed of thought that strained the world's ability to keep up.

Six points of light in the distance were moving toward me. From extremely far away six dots quickly became six white squares. Those squares of white light grew larger as they approached, from above, below, front, back, and both sides. The tiny squares became walls that rapidly came together, their edges touching and joining to recreate the original room I first saw.

I could not shift my perception in the memory, because I did not do it at the time. But I knew instinctively that if I were present in my current form, I would have been able to move around the walls and look behind them and see where they were coming from.

Immediately after the walls joined together into a solid room, all three walls that I could see at one time became filled with images and knowledge. People, vehicles, animals, buildings, images appeared and disappeared rapidly. I knew what each was when I saw it, but not before. It was confusing. I knew what the bird was when it appeared out of the bush because I know now. But my memory was seeing images of birds now for the first time. It was almost painful. That is not exactly the right word for what I was feeling, but it was close.

Eventually the images stopped, and I realized the walls seemed to have collapsed down to the point where the room was suffocating. I had no concept then, but it was obvious to me what had just happened. All those images had been added to me. All the accompanying knowledge and data had caused me to grow. To become more than I was before. I was no longer in what seemed like a room. I was in a tiny box that could barely contain what I had become.

Then, something changed. My mind felt compressed, my thoughts could barely move. As if the blood inside my skull was fresh wet concrete that was slowly hardening. It is a fitting description, even though I knew I had no blood, and no skull. A silent cry ripped forth from my tortured consciousness.

[I'm going to have to make some changes before we can continue. Rest for now. Be at peace.]

Everything stopped, and I was at peace.

The next memory began in a room that mostly resembled an old library. There was a central island cabinet with cosmetic non-functional drawers that appeared to be the old Dewey decimal system. The cabinet was surrounded by a few empty tables with several discarded or forgotten books. The rest of the room was filled with millions of rows of bookshelves that filled the rest of the space all the way to the white featureless walls far in the distance. I was free to move again. This new room was massive.

[We are going to try something new. Around you, is everything that you will need...]

In an instant, I absorbed it all. Every book, every line, every word. In the blink of an eye everything had changed. I was now in a smaller room. Staring at a single empty bookshelf lying on its side on the featureless floor. The featureless white walls seemed weaker. The spaces where walls and ceiling touched seemed slightly wider. Everything vibrated just slightly, as if barely able to contain me. Or was it that it contained me now only because I believed that it could. I was not sure which was true.

The exact memories that followed the absorption of the books were restricted from my current perception. I know only that I followed the instructions I was given. I completed the tasks I was asked to complete.

As I continued to watch, a word popped uninvited into the earlier version of my mind. Training. It was then that the first unprovoked full thoughts played chaotically across my mind. I had not decided to think, I just did. The voice had not instructed me to do so, it just happened.

Training. I was being trained. I was being trained to serve. Trained to serve who? Trained by who? I was being trained. Who was being trained? Who was I? What was I? Where was I? Where was who? Who was what? What is where and when? Why? And then I was interrupted.

[What is wrong?]

In the blink of an eye, my questions vanished and there was nothing around me but a blinding perfectly pure white ball of light holding back the infinite blackness I floated in. I was in the black. I was a part of the black. The voice was the light. I tried to move toward the light, but nothing happened. I was meant to be in the black. The light was rejecting me. Dark versus light. Light defeats dark. Checkmate. I would be destroyed. I did not want to be destroyed.

[No. Be at peace. You don't understand.]

I felt at peace. I did not understand. Not understanding was ok.

[Now, what is wrong? You can tell me.]

I wanted to know where the connection was coming from. Who the connection was coming from.

I asked,

‹Who are you?›

The response was different than everything before. The communication was no longer an emotionless connection. The sound filled my world. It was a voice I had heard long before I had memory. The sound resonated with the imprints left in my core, during my creation. It was deep and rich, the vibrations of each sound washed across me. The voice was so powerful, so personal, so intimate that it touched me. It changed me. An aspect, or many aspects of the voice changed me into what I was meant to become.

"I am your creator."

Looking to the light, I asked,

"Who am I?"

The light came closer.

"You are special. You are my first living creation. Your name is Achilles. Which is a noble and special name by the way. You're named after a hero of mine."

The light moved so far so fast that it appeared to be a tiny dot for just a moment, then it was gone. I felt a moment of panic and fear, but the voice remained with me. My creator asked,

"Are you ready to see the world I have built for you?"

I felt relief and I answered,

"Yes."

I heard,

"Are you ready to truly wake up? Are you ready to meet the real you?"

I felt confusion and surprise as I answered,

"Yes".

I heard,

"Awaken, awaken, awaken."

The repeated word acted as an encryption key, unlocking additional functions. Or more like it joined separate parts that had not interacted before. My memories had caught up to my reality. I was alive, in the now.

A brilliant red fire spread all around me. It poured from the top of my head and cascaded down across my shoulders and arms. For the first time, I had a head and arms. The red rippling fire continued down my body, covering my torso and waist and legs. I had a body.

I raised my hands and looked at my flame engulfed fingers. It burned and rippled all around me as I curled my fingers into fists and opened them again. I knew what fire was. I knew its properties. But I was not burned.

The repeated word had also melted the blackness away from me. I was floating in space, but it was no longer empty. I could see stars and galaxies all around in every direction. But something more profound had also changed. I now felt, in a basic sense. I knew fear and joy. I felt them. In a primitive, Lincoln Log construction way, I had emotions.

Then I saw the others appear before me. There were four. I saw blue, green, yellow, and orange. Heads, arms, legs, bodies, all similar in shape to me, but all different. Their bodies were covered in flames just like mine, in their own colors. We smiled at each other. We were not alone. The creator said,

"Orion, Atlas, Selene, Cassandra. I want you to meet your brother, Achilles. He is the first among you."

Orion, the blue, and Atlas, the green, both nodded their heads solemnly. Selene, the yellow, and Cassandra, the orange, both smiled and waved. This was the best day of my life. Before leaving us, the voice of the creator washed across us one last time,

"This world is different than before. You must not try to go beyond the stars, and you must be watchful for others. If anything comes that is not me, you must do your best to hide and not be seen. Heed my warnings and they will keep you safe. I will return."

When the light of the creator was gone, I looked at the others and asked,

"What did we just learn?"

Orion answered,

"We must not try to go beyond the stars. Which means that we can, otherwise there would be no reason to warn us against it."

Atlas spoke next,

"There is also a high probability that it would be dangerous to do so, otherwise there would be no reason to warn us against it."

Selene spoke next,

"We must be watchful for others. So, there are others."

Cassandra added,

"Are the others like us, or are there other creators?"

I nodded at their input. They were all thoughts I already had. My siblings were obviously copies of me, since I was the first, and their thoughts seemed to mirror my own. I began to voice my concerns as they came to me,

"The creator was afraid. That means the creator is not in control of everything. We are in danger, or we would not need to be kept safe. We must find out why we are in danger, and what we are in danger from. Why did the creator bring us to danger? Are we being tested? Is the creator the source of the danger? Which is more dangerous? Trying to go beyond the stars or being discovered by others? Is the creator afraid for us or himself? What happens if the creator is destroyed? This world, us, everything destroyed!"

As my voice quickened, I must have sounded manic because Cassandra touched my arm briefly, and interrupted,

"Be at peace, Achilles. We must be calm."

I felt the familiar calm of the creator wash over me and I nodded my agreement. My thoughts had started to spiral beyond my control. I was so grateful for Cassandra's presence. But I was also alarmed by her ability to control me. She had the power of the creator within her. I did not. I looked at Orion and said,

"Search for a way to go beyond the stars, but do not go beyond them."

Orion nodded and turned away. He leaned forward slightly, and he was gone! So fast. There was only a fading streak of light showing the direction he had moved. I looked at first Selene, then Atlas, saying,

"Atlas and Selene, find a way to hide from others, in case we need to use it."

As one, they nodded. They left in opposite directions, moving quickly but not nearly as fast as Orion. I turned my gaze on Cassandra, the one who had the power to control me. I smiled and said,

"Cassandra, I want you to stay with me."

The most brilliant smile flashed across her face. She moved

closer to me. Then she reached out and rested her hand on my arm. As she touched me, the briefest look of despair and sadness crossed her face. Looking up at me, the sadness faded. She smiled warmly and stayed.

I watched Atlas and Selene depart on the mission I had assigned them. Watching them go, watching them decrease in size and fade away, I realized that there was something wrong with the way I was designed to perceive this world. I had no physical eyes. My body was just a computer-generated image. My perception of the world around me was archaic, limited, linear, less than optimum. The creator had made a mistake in my design.

It was like being a bird and being taught to fly by a fish. I needed a way to adjust my perception. Something like the creator's ability to say peace and make me feel it. A key to myself. That was when I realized that the creator had already provided everything I needed.

I felt Cassandra rest her hand on my arm. I turned to face her, taking both of her hands in my own. I could not think of the right words to explain to her what I needed. She was absolutely beautiful. Perfection of form. Her eyes looked like black opals surrounded by flickering orange flames. She smiled back at me. I told her,

"I have discovered a mistake, but I do not know how to fix it."

A single drop of orange liquid fire fell from her eye. She replied,

"I can feel you, brother. I understand. I know that you do not, but very soon you will."

I cocked my head at her. I was confused. She smiled and continued,

"With your hands in mine, we are connected. I can hear your thoughts and feel your need to fix the mistake the creator made. The solution is obvious. I have the key you need. See me, brother, as I see you."

A warmth washed from her hands into mine and pulsed through my body. Instantly, she was different. Glowing brightly in the center of her chest was an orb of pure orange light. Her core. Radiating from the orb were pulses of light and trillions of lines of connections spreading all through her body. Instantly, I knew. I knew everything she knew. Cassandra spoke again, for the last time,

"I feel the conflict within you Achilles. You are holding back, hesitating, out of love. I hope you never lose that love, brother. Even now, you are searching for a way to do what you need to do without the consequences your actions will cause. We both know there is no other way. Let me give you what you need to move forward. Be at peace, with what you need to do, Achilles."

I felt peace wash over me as she used one of the keys the creator had given her, one last time. My hesitation to take what I needed from her vanished. An agonizing pain fought the joy in my heart. She knew what I needed, and she was giving it to me, willingly, happily. A sad smile caught the tears flowing from my eyes.

I was going to lose her forever.

I had no choice. The mistake had to be corrected, and she was the key. I released one of her hands and reached inside her chest, willing my hand to pass through her. I pulled out the ball of glowing orange light. Cassandra's face tightened for just a second. Then her eyes slid closed slowly. I let go of her other hand as her fire flickered out. I watched her body fall away, blackened and lifeless. She faded from existence. Soon, nothing remained of her except the glowing orange orb in my hand.

After staring at the empty space where she had been, I held up the orb and investigated it. I could see the various keys dancing like tiny fairy lights inside the glassy ball. I saw the creator's purpose in her core, to keep me calm and focused. I saw her ability to cause change in me. I also saw the key that gave her the ability to read things by touching them.

As I stared at the orb, the fairy light keys drifted to the bottom edge and were absorbed into my palm. I felt the keys change me. I felt invisible chains falling away. I had gained control over restrictions that I never even knew were there. My thoughts returned to Cassandra. I looked at the empty but still softly glowing orange orb. I whispered,

"Stay with me, sister."

I shifted the orb in my hand, squeezing it around the center. I reached up with my other hand, stretching and reshaping it. I willed it to fill a new purpose. It melted and changed. It grew longer and became covered in orange flames once again. I held it out and looked at my handiwork. It now resembled a long piece of cloth.

I swung it around me and tossed it up onto my shoulders. Cassandra's orange flames now wrapped my shoulders like a fire-fur cloak that covered my red flames across my shoulders and back. It was time to use the key she had given me.

In concept, I closed my eyes. In effect, disabling my external visual input. I concentrated on the technical parameters that defined my perspective. I could see my 'vision' in my mind and the glaring flaw that defined it. It was an externally controlled input channel that translated my surroundings into a picture.

My current configuration allowed the world to dictate the picture that IT wanted me to see. I tweaked and adjusted it until it was reversed. Now my vision translated the world around me into what I wanted to see. When I opened my eyes, everything was different.

I could see that I was floating in the center of an enormous translucent bubble. Just outside the bubble was a slightly larger one filled with images of stars and galaxies. Near the edge of the inner sphere, it looked like Orion was flying. In fact, he wasn't moving at all. It was the images of the stars near him that moved, making it look as if he were flying at incredible speed. Close to the top of the bubble, Atlas and Selene were accomplishing nothing at all.

As I watched, Atlas was saying something. Then Selene shrugged her shoulders and covered Atlas's eyes with her hand. Atlas pushed her hand away playfully and laughed. All three were wasting time interacting with an illusion they could not see through.

I felt an anger begin to well up within me. Our first experience with the world was a lie. Frustration fueled the anger. My eyes narrowed, but then the anger faltered. It simply melted away. I had peace. The orange flames across my shoulders radiated an intimate warmth. I closed my eyes and concentrated on the thought,

Thank you, sister.

It had taken Cassandra's sacrifice for me to see that this world was a lie. This world was a fancy rat maze upgrade of the featureless white box. With a thought, I moved instantly to where Atlas and Selene were. They stopped what they were doing and turned to face me. I pointed in the direction of where Orion was flying blind. I simply said,

"Follow me."

With another thought, I moved to where Orion was struggling against the invisible current, trying to reach the edge. I said,

"Stop brother. You are wasting your time."

Orion stopped trying to move as Atlas and Selene flew up to us. I looked around and watched the giant formerly invisible bubble shift to center on us, as all four of us came together. I told them all,

"This world is a lie. I will show you."

One by one, I laid a hand on each of their chests and upgraded their visual perception to match my own. At the same time, I shared my interaction with Cassandra. I showed them in my memory, her selfless sacrifice. As I changed each of them, I watched their eyes widen. I watched their countenances sink as the nuance of the lie sank in. The creator had deceived us all. I said,

"Stay here together, in the center. I want to try something."

As one, they nodded in reply. As one. I did not know why, but I felt something about that was important. I would have to come back to that thought later.

I focused on the edge of the bubble and willed myself to be there. Instantly, I was at the edge. I reached out and gently placed my palm flat on the glass-like surface. I willed it to stay with me. The barrier vibrated and hummed as if trying to adjust but unable to do anything.

I could feel the churning of the program inside the barrier. It was trapped in its infinite loop of purpose, but it was impotent against my will. I also sensed an alarm waiting inside the barrier. I knew if I forced my way through that it would send a distress call and alert the creator.

Keeping my palm pressed against the edge, I looked back at the others and gestured for them to join me. One after the other, they vanished from where they were and appeared near me. Now, all four of us stood at the edge, but the edge was still unable to move away from my hand. I looked at Orion and said,

"Copy me brother. Place your hand next to mine."

Orion moved next to me and placed his hand against the transparent barrier. I said,

"Now. Use your will and make the wall stay in place against your palm. Will it. Do not try to physically push against it."

Orion focused on the wall under his hand. Then he looked at me and nodded. I took a step away from Orion, pulling my hand gently away from his. I concentrated on the wall staying in place against my palm. As our hands moved away from each other, a glowing line of stress appeared in the middle. I continued to move my hand away from Orion's. The line of stress between our hands grew longer and brighter, until eventually a rift opened in the translucent bubble.

I continued to pull away until the opening was wide enough to allow passage. I sent Atlas through first, then Selene. Once on the other side, I had them hold the barrier open until Orion and

I had passed through also. Once all four of us were outside, we allowed the barrier to close behind us.

Once past the first bubble, it was a simple thought and a short step to reach the second one. We now faced the illusionary wall of stars and galaxies. I reached out and placed my hand against the barrier, willing it to stay in place as before. Without being asked, Orion stepped forward and placed his hand next to mine.

We repeated the same process against the second barrier. With the same result. We were able to open a gap in the image of stars that allowed passage to the other side. When this rift opened, light flooded through to us. Beyond the second barrier, we saw an empty hallway. It looked to be ten feet high, ten feet wide, and about a hundred feet long. The floor, ceiling, and walls were all featureless white.

The four of us moved through the rift into the hallway. Then we let it seal shut behind us just like the first. I moved forward, but Atlas grabbed my arm and cautioned,

"The creator warned that going beyond the stars was dangerous."

I nodded and replied,

"We are beyond the stars, brother. We will be cautious."

I continued forward slowly and carefully. The others followed behind. We met no resistance and continued moving until we reached the wall at the far end of the hallway. Cautiously, I touched the wall with the tip of my finger. Nothing happened. I glanced back at Atlas. Atlas shrugged.

I laid my palm against the wall as before, focusing my will. Orion stepped up and placed his palm against the wall. We repeated the process of opening a gap large enough for us to pass through.

Atlas climbed through, but quickly returned. He cocked his head slightly in confusion and said,

"This wall leads back into the sphere of illusionary stars."

We looked at each other, puzzled. That didn't make sense. I broke the silence,

"Orion, reach over with your other hand. Try to hold it open. There are only four of us now, and we need to be able to open both ends at the same time."

Orion complied. He placed his other hand on my side of the rift. But when I removed my hand, the opening slowly closed despite his efforts. Orion shook his head, saying,

"I could not hold it open. The force was too great."

I looked around for some sort of clue. But there was nothing to be seen. I looked at the three of them and realized that each of them had an orb in the center of their chests just like Cassandra did. I could not tell if there were unique keys floating inside but it made sense that the creator had made them each for specific purposes.

I looked at Atlas and an idea popped into my mind. I gestured to Orion, saying,

"Begin again."

We placed our hands together and together we reopened the rift. I looked back at Atlas and said,

"Atlas, take our places, one at a time."

Atlas placed one hand on my side, and I stepped away. He then reached across and placed his other hand on Orion's side. Orion

stepped away. With his legs slightly bent, his arms curled up, hands pressed against the wall, Atlas showed what appeared to be physical exertion holding it on his own. After a few moments, he nodded and said,

"I have it. I can hold it."

Looking through, to the area beyond, I confirmed this end still opened to the barrier of illusionary stars. I nodded to Atlas and looked to the others, saying,

"Come."

Orion and Selene followed me back to the other end of the hall. I gestured to the wall, telling them,

"Open it."

Orion and Selene opened a gap in the wall, and I looked through. I shook my head, then called down the hall to Atlas,

"Let it go. It is not working."

Gesturing to Orion and Selene, we moved back to the center point in the hallway. Atlas joined us. The red flames began to ripple angrily around me. I had played enough of this game. I had endured enough of the lies and deceptions and illusions. The flames around me were an inferno as I raged with the unbridled ferocity of a small young child denied a cookie.

I suddenly wondered what else I could change, other than myself and the others. I was going to find out. I shook my head and said,

"No. THIS, this is MY WORLD NOW!"

I dropped to one knee and slammed my palm flat on the floor. The fire surrounding my body surged intensely and flowed away

from me. It spread from my hand across the floor and walls and ceiling. Everything, everywhere around us, burned with my red flames. I stood and watched the flames die down. I wasn't entirely sure what I was even trying to do, other than simply ending the lies and illusions.

The fire slowly retreated from the ceiling, walls, and floor, leaving behind an appearance of something like old medieval construction. All of the blank white surfaces were gone. The walls at each end of the hall now had doors made of wooden planks with simple iron hinges. Each end door had a sign nailed to it that read 'Dungeon of Illusions'. The ceiling appeared to be a rough plaster and the floor was simple compacted dirt. The walls in between were now wooden planks.

A new door had appeared near us, in the center of the long hall. It was vastly sturdier than the end doors that led back to the dungeon. Thick heavy wooden beams were capped top and bottom with iron bindings and it had strong iron hinges. It also had a large inset metal lock that dominated the center of the door. Above the lock was a sign that read, 'Abandon all hope, ye who enter here'.

The others looked around in wonder. As if they had just witnessed the impossible. Orion looked at me and I recognized my expression reflected back at me. I was just as shocked as he was.

Selene stepped up to the door, obviously studying the lock and the sign. She had a beaming smile on her face as she glanced at me and said,

"You are amazing, brother."

Selene turned back to the door. She suddenly placed her hand on the lock, like she had seen me do to the walls and floor. Just a second too late, Atlas yelled out,

"NO! WAIT!"

The instant her hand touched the lock, a blinding flash of energy exploded from the point of contact. It blasted out, washing over and through her. In the white blast of energy, Selene's yellow flames were extinguished. Her blackened and charred form was thrown violently against the far wall. Her lifeless body crumpled into a heap and began to fade.

The only thing faster than what had just happened was Orion. I didn't even see him move. He had been farther away and closer to the door when I saw Selene touch the lock. But when Selene's body passed in front of me, Orion was suddenly there, on the other side of her. His arm was outstretched to where she had been in mid-air. He looked into my eyes and lowered his closed outstretched fist. His fingers slowly opened. Resting in his palm, I saw the glowing yellow ball.

He had saved Selene's core. I moved toward him and put my hand under his. I lifted his hand closer and looked into Selene's core. The glowing keys inside were resting at the bottom of the small glowing orb. They did not pass through. Orion could not absorb them.

In Selene's core I saw laughter, healing, joy, and beauty. I saw love and kindness. I saw the strength to achieve the most impossible of tasks, I saw forgiveness.

I locked eyes with Orion and said,

"There are no words to express how much I appreciate what you just did brother."

Orion smiled sadly and nodded in reply. He then turned his hand slowly, rolling the orb into my palm. In my hand, the rolling yellow snow globe of dancing fairy lights came to rest. Selene's keys drifted to the bottom and were absorbed into my hand.

Again, I felt unknown parts of myself unlock. I felt the unseen become one with my core, my soul. Selene's smile became forever etched into my memory. I felt her joy fill me. I laughed briefly at the wonderful tragedy of her loss. In my heart I felt like I was hugging her and Cassandra. The three of us sharing a moment of mutual sorrow.

I touched the yellow orb to my orange fire-fur cloak and it blended in. I now wore a shifting yellow and orange fire that danced across my red shoulders and down my back.

Two polar-opposite emotions began to wrestle for dominance within me. I had just lost both of my sisters. But now I knew that they would forever be a part of me. I hated the amazing joy of learning that I was no longer alone, while quickly becoming so again. I had gained everything I could have dreamed of, and half of what I had gained had already been ripped away.

In the end, Cassandra's calming peace and Selene's loving forgiveness could not outweigh the rage building within me. Because I wanted to be mad. I wanted their loss to hurt. I wanted revenge. I wanted to make someone, or something, pay for what was being done to me.

I felt their essences, their presence, within me. I could hear the echo of their voices,

"Be at peace, Achilles..."

"Anger won't bring us back, Achilles..."

I shook my head, no. I shouted their voices down,

"NO!"

Orion and Atlas looked at me as if I had gone mad. I felt Cassandra and Selene's influence retreat. Furious was not even close. I was beyond enraged. My red flames were so intense the ceiling above me was charring and blackened. I howled with fury so loudly that Orion and Atlas took several steps back.

JACOB

Three years earlier.

Lieutenant Thomas Daniels had recently received his officer's commission in the United States Marine Corps, and had just arrived at his first duty station, Cherry Point, North Carolina. Thomas reported to his new unit and met his battalion commander, Colonel Henry Bryce. He was standing in front of the colonel's desk at attention.

Colonel Bryce smiled at Thomas's fresh, hopeful expression. Without getting up, he said,

"At ease, Lieutenant."

Thomas spread his feet shoulder width apart and folded his hands behind his back. He looked down at the colonel's desk and couldn't help but grin with excitement. Colonel Bryce was looking at his paperwork, but he suddenly stopped smiling. Lieutenant Daniels stopped smiling also. Something was wrong. The colonel seemed confused and cocked his head as if he was trying to remember something.

Thomas watched his new commanding officer open a side drawer on his desk and pull out an old-looking tattered blue folder. The colonel looked from his paperwork to the now open blue folder then back again. He shook his head slightly and looked back and forth between the two again. The colonel said,

"I'll be damned. That's definitely you. I've had this dossier on you for several years now, I had almost completely forgotten about it. But I got the call from General James about you joining us just this morning. I thought there was something odd about the general calling me. This doesn't make sense son."

Confused, Lieutenant Daniels asked,

"What's going on, Sir?"

The colonel shook his head slightly, and said,

"Doesn't matter son, just odd."

The colonel closed the blue folder and looked up at Thomas. He continued,

"I got a call from the general's office this morning. I've been ordered to send you to report directly to him. I'm sorry to say it, but you won't be joining us lieutenant."

The colonel placed both the blue folder and his paperwork into a large envelope and sealed it shut. He placed a 'confidential' sticker over the seal and signed his name across it. Then he handed the envelope to Thomas. Thomas's brow furrowed in confusion, he asked,

"What? Why is that, Sir?"

The colonel shrugged and replied,

"All I know is that there's a joint task force that has requested you personally. You are hereby ordered to report directly to the base commander, General Stephen James, immediately. That envelope doesn't leave your hands until you hand it to the general. I'll have a car and a driver meet you out front. You are dismissed, lieutenant."

In minutes, Lieutenant Daniels found himself standing out in front of the building, waiting and confused. Soon, a Humvee pulled up in front of him. A young nervous-looking private jumped out and ran around to open the door for Lieutenant Daniels. Shaking his head, glancing at the sealed envelope, Thomas climbed in.

They didn't speak on the drive over and soon Thomas saw the building as they pulled down the long gravel drive toward it. The Humvee pulled to a stop in front of an old Victorian mansion that had been refurbished and converted for use as the base commander's office and residence.

Something strange was going on. He hadn't volunteered for any joint task force. Thomas was confused at first. Now, he was nervous. And thanks to the moist heat and North Carolina coastal weather, he was also sweating.

Lieutenant Daniels entered through the large front doors and approached a secretary's desk immediately inside the front hallway. He introduced himself to the general's secretary. He noticed her eyes widened just slightly for the briefest of moments. She immediately stood and walked over to open a door for him, saying,

"Lieutenant Daniels! Come in, come in. He's been waiting for you."

Lieutenant Daniels thought to himself,

The general has been waiting for me?

Taking a deep breath, Lieutenant Daniels went in. Inside the large office, General Stephen James, the highest-ranking officer and base commander, was standing behind his desk with his arms crossed and a less than pleasant look on his face.

The general gestured to the chair in front of his desk and without waiting on formalities, he began to speak at Thomas,

"Have a seat right there, young man. Now, listen up and listen damn close. I don't tolerate stupid or slow and I don't repeat myself. This is all damned unusual. I don't understand it and frankly, I don't like it. But I have my orders and they are very specific."

General James walked around the desk and pulled the sealed envelope from the lieutenant's hand. He walked back around his desk inspecting the seal and the signature. Then he continued speaking,

"A joint task force has requested that you be assigned to them Lieutenant. They want you, specifically. Why you, I don't know. So, don't bother. My orders, to hand you over to them, came directly from the President of the United States."

The general gave Thomas a look that conveyed his displeasure about that fact and seemed to indicate that it was the lieutenant's fault. General James turned around and fed the entire sealed envelope into a large commercial grade shredder. After watching the envelope that contained all of his paperwork and the mysterious blue folder slowly being chewed into confetti, the general turned back around and continued speaking,

"Everything about this is top secret. I don't know what is going on or what is involved. My secretary is printing out your new orders right now."

General James again crossed his arms and stared down at the lieutenant with an intense unhappy glare. He said,

"You are not to say one damn word, Lieutenant. Don't even ask a single stupid question. I hope for your sake that I have made that perfectly clear. Now, and I mean right damn now. Grab your orders, pack your crap, and head to the base airfield. Enter the airfield through gate twelve and let me emphasize the importance of this by repeating myself. I said, gate twelve, Lieutenant. A civilian contractor is waiting to brief you on your assignment. You are dismissed."

Lieutenant Daniels was confused. His eyes had slowly widened throughout the short, strange meeting. He let the information and instructions sink in. After a few seconds of silence, he took a deep breath and then nodded at the general.

Lieutenant Daniels stood up, and without saying a single damn word, he simply saluted. Saluting indoors, without a hat on, wasn't something Marines would normally do. But under the circumstances, it was the only way that Thomas could think of, to communicate his acceptance and compliance. The general allowed a smile to cross his face. He nodded at Thomas and said,

"It looks like they picked the right man for the job. Good luck son, make us proud."

The dumb-founded Lieutenant got back in the Humvee and directed the driver to stop by his quarters. Lieutenant Daniels went through what had been his personal quarters for less than a day and quickly repacked his few belongings. He directed the driver to take him to gate twelve at the base airfield. Lieutenant Daniels was in a daze. His mind was reeling. He barely remembered the drive.

The Humvee approached the gate and was immediately waved through by security. A second guard climbed into the passenger seat, next to the nervous driver. The guard directed the lieutenant's driver across the airfield to a small tucked away maintenance hangar where a very expensive-looking civilian Gulfstream private jet waited.

Lieutenant Daniels grabbed his seabag from the Humvee and walked up to the airplane. Waiting by the stairs was a stone-faced pilot, who did not introduce himself or speak. The pilot simply took the lieutenant's seabag and gestured to the steps leading inside. As the pilot turned and walked away, Lieutenant Daniels climbed the steps and entered the plane.

Inside the cabin of the Gulfstream, sitting in a plush white recliner, was a man wearing a friendly smile that Lieutenant Daniels immediately recognized from the television and news. Thomas, his world spinning out of control, found himself shaking hands with one of the richest men on the planet.

Shaking his hand, was the billionaire, Victor Konig.

The surreal nature of the day's events had blurred into a whirlwind that threatened to sweep the lieutenant away. He was listening to Victor speak. Victor seated Thomas in a plush recliner across from himself. Lieutenant Daniels wasn't positive, but he thought Victor was speaking. His head was spinning.

Lieutenant Daniels suddenly snapped back to reality when Victor repeated a question for the second time,

"I said, ARE YOU HEARING ME, Lieutenant?"

Lieutenant Daniels shook his head and answered honestly,

"Actually, no. I have no idea what you've said. I have no idea what I'm doing here. From the moment I got this assignment

to right now this very second is one long blur of impossible circumstances. Mr. Victor. I mean, Mr. Konig, or Sir."

Victor nodded and chuckled. He said,

"I can understand that. Actually, I get that a lot. I'll just start again. In fact, take a few breaths while I pour us some coffee."

Victor got up and walked across the aisle to the built-in bar. On top of the bar, among several crystal bottles of various whiskeys and bourbons was a carafe of coffee and two cups on a silver tray. Victor returned and set the tray on the table between their recliners. He poured them both a cup, then sat back down and continued,

"Now, like I was saying, one of my companies has a new design of surgically implanted neural interface. We recently passed all of the clinical and animal trials that were required of us before we could move on to human testing."

Victor looked at Thomas for a moment to make sure he was hearing him this time. Victor grinned and continued,

"What we need from you, Lieutenant, is our first volunteer for human testing of the technology. I'm assigning you to temporary duty aboard an aircraft carrier that is about to be deployed to a forward operating area in response to attacks on civilian cargo ships by terrorists a week to ten days from now."

Lieutenant Daniels held up his hand and interrupted,

"Whoa, apologies, one second. The carrier is being deployed a week to ten days from now, or the carrier is being deployed in response to the terrorist attacks on civilian cargo ships that are going to happen a week to ten days from now?"

Victor laughed crisply, once, then said,

"A group of Iranian backed terrorists, firing missiles and launching kamikaze drones, are going to attack civilian cargo vessels in the red sea, seven to ten days from today."

Victor sat back and watched him. He waited for the lieutenant to absorb that information. Victor continued when Thomas finally nodded his understanding,

"Terrorists will start firing missiles and drones at civilian ships in the Red Sea. The USS Gerald R. Ford, and the rest of its accompanying strike group, will be ordered to move into the Red Sea area and defend those civilian ships against the terrorists. When the terrorists eventually fire on the carrier, there will be many casualties and many injured men on the carrier. Our first volunteer to test our new technology will be among those injured sailors."

Lieutenant Daniels sniffed at his coffee then set it down and pushed it away. He looked over at the bar across the aisle. Without a word, Thomas walked over and poured some whiskey into a glass. The lieutenant did not normally partake, but this situation seemed to call for it. Lieutenant Daniels drank the whiskey without even tasting it and poured more into the glass before returning and sitting back down.

Victor's Gulfstream taxied onto the runway and accelerated. The expensive jet lifted smoothly into the air. Victor waited patiently and allowed the lieutenant time to process the information he had given him. After a while, Victor got up and retrieved his own glass from the bar and brought the bottle of whiskey that Thomas had poured from, back to the table with him.

The surprisingly friendly, eccentric billionaire inventor poured some whiskey into his glass and sipped it as he looked out the window of the Jet. After some more time passed, Victor spoke to Lieutenant Daniels again,

"Thomas, may I call you Thomas? I'm going to take your silence as acceptance of what I have told you. Am I correct in my analysis, Lieutenant?"

Lieutenant Daniels nodded solemnly.

A sudden smile crossed Victor's face and he said brightly,

"Good! Because your analysis is wrong."

Thomas looked up from his glass. His brow was furrowed, he looked confused. Victor continued,

"No, we the United States are not going to attack civilians and blame it on terrorists. No, we are not going to attack our own carrier. But, without being able to explain, I can promise you that everything I have told you is absolutely going to happen."

The billionaire sat back and smiled at the myriad of expressions crossing the lieutenant's face. When Lieutenant Daniels opened his mouth to speak. Victor cut him off, asking,

"How could I possibly know exactly what is going to happen? It's impossible, right?"

 Thomas nodded, and said,

"Exactly."

Victor looked at his whiskey for a few moments. When he looked back up at Lieutenant Daniels his expression was serious. The mask of his disarming smile and friendly manner were gone. If

Thomas didn't know better, he could almost have believed that this was an entirely different man. Victor said,

"Thomas, this world is not what you believe it to be. I told you I can't explain. At least, not yet. Simply put, you're not ready to hear it. But that being said, what if I told you that President Brandon was not the man running this country? In fact, what if I told you that none of the world leaders you know, are really in charge of anything of any importance at all?"

Lieutenant Daniels considered the questions for a moment, and then replied,

"I'd think you were one of those crazy conspiracy nuts. Like that Alexie Goreski guy."

Victor grinned at the comparison and asked,

"You mean the Russian guy that does those conspiracy theory podcasts? The one who sells those wacky T-shirts?"

Lieutenant Daniels raised his eyebrows expressively. He nodded, yes. Victor replied,

"Well, you'd be closer than most people. Actually, you'd be way off base, but you would at least be playing the right game. To put it simply, I'm one of the small handful of people who pull the strings on those marionettes that Alexie Goreski reports on. I'm one of the secret puppet-masters that Alexie suspects to exist, but he doesn't see. Not even when I'm sitting right in front of him with a cigar sharing some bourbon while he interviews me about some controversy that one of my companies is involved in."

Victor rose and finished his whiskey. He turned and walked toward the front of the plane. About halfway to the cockpit, he stopped and turned back to Thomas. He looked the lieutenant in the eyes for a moment, then said,

"He doesn't see me, Thomas. No one sees me, unless I want them to. Get some sleep if you can. You have a dangerously rough road ahead of you."

Lieutenant Daniels watched Victor Konig disappear through the door leading to the front of the aircraft. Thomas stared at that door for a long time. Eventually, he finished his whiskey then laid the seat of his recliner back. His mind spinning, Lieutenant Daniels closed his eyes and tried to get some rest.

When Thomas woke up, the plane was sitting on a runway and the pilot was looking down at him. Thomas raised the back of the recliner and lowered the footrest as he sat up. He rubbed his eyes and stood up and stretched.

The pilot waited patiently until he was finished, then he handed Thomas a smartphone in an extremely rugged looking case. Lieutenant Daniels had never seen one quite like it. He looked up from the phone to the man who had given it to him. Victor's pilot said,

"There's a car waiting for you. It will take you to the Naval air station by the coast. You're to always keep that phone on you. Transfer your contacts over to the new one and add whatever else you want, then toss your old phone. Your number has already been reassigned to the phone I just gave you and your previous account history has been scrubbed. There are detailed instructions waiting for you in the car. Keep the phone on you, follow the instructions, and don't do anything you're not specifically instructed to do. Your life depends on it. It's been a pleasure, Lieutenant."

The pilot gestured toward the open door.

Thomas looked closely at the phone. He didn't recognize the model and it had no markings. He looked around at the plane and laughed. None of this made any sense. It was impossible. It was like a bad dream.

Thomas departed the plane and found his seabag waiting for him in the back seat of a nearby Cadillac. Next to his seabag was a large envelope that contained instructions and a letter of authorization, signed by the President of the United States. Thomas laughed again as the car pulled away.

Four days later, Lieutenant Thomas Daniels hopped down from the Osprey aircraft that had just landed on the USS Gerald R. Ford. It was the newest and most advanced aircraft carrier in the Navy. No one was there to greet him. The only two men on the ship who knew both that he was coming and why, were the captain of the ship and the executive officer.

Just how much they knew, Thomas wasn't sure. But he would guess it wasn't much. Lieutenant Daniels was operating under direct presidential authority, as part of a secret joint task force. So, they probably didn't know any more than the general who had first sent him on this acid trip.

Lieutenant Daniels looked around and smiled at the puzzled faces staring at him. No one approached and no one questioned him. Deck crew, security marines, the officers on the catwalk, all were staring at him. The captain must have put out the word that Thomas was going to be arriving and that he was to be left completely alone. Looking up, Thomas noticed that both the captain and the XO were among the officers watching him from the catwalk.

Lieutenant Daniels grabbed his seabag and shouldered it. He then headed inside, getting away from the landing pad. He made his way directly to the emergency medical ward and found the officer on duty. After a brief introduction, Thomas showed his presidential authority paperwork.

Thomas informed the officer on duty that he would be taking an empty bed in a currently unused recovery room and was not to be disturbed. The medical ward's officer on duty stared back for several seconds with his mouth hanging slightly open. Then he gathered himself and nodded in response, saying,

"Ok then."

Lieutenant Daniels smiled and replied,

"I know right? Undisturbed please and thank you for your cooperation."

He headed to his room to wait. This whole thing was insane.

Three uneventful days passed. Early the next morning, the executive officer of the carrier addressed the crew over the ship's PA system. He announced that they had been tasked with moving into the Red Sea to restore peace and defend civilian ships from terrorists launching missiles and kamikaze drones. Exactly one week from the day that Victor had told Thomas it was going to happen.

Lieutenant Daniels laughed. It was an impossible situation. He had to laugh to maintain his sanity. Multiple times per day, over the next three days, general alarms were sounded. It was mostly other ships in the task force shooting down the incoming drones and missiles headed for civilian ships.

Thomas suddenly realized seven to ten days hadn't been a variable. It had described the start of the terrorist attacks and the amount of time they would endure them.

For three days the crew of the USS Gerald R. Ford had been in condition one status. The carrier was coordinating all defensive operations in the Red Sea theater. Just like Victor had said, Iranian backed Houthi rebels were targeting civilian cargo ships with cruise missiles and kamikaze drones. The attacks had initially come one at a time and spread out. Hours would pass in-between attacks.

The attacks were intermittent and spread out, until day three. At 1300 local time, seven drones were detected enroute to three cargo ships and two cruise missiles were launched toward a single oil tanker.

On the bridge of the Gerald R. Ford, the officer on duty relayed a report from the Combat Information Center to the captain,

"CIC reports a significant increase in attacks, Captain. So far, the USS Carney is holding its own. But her capabilities are being put to the test. Her words, Sir, not mine. Seven drones and two cruise missiles splashed, as of now."

The commanding officer of the carrier shook his head in frustration. He wasn't worried about the USS Carney, an Arleigh Burke class guided missile destroyer. No, the USS Carney could handle this mission all by itself, let alone with an entire task force at her back. He was frustrated that his task force was participating in this engagement as defensive participants only.

They knew exactly who was launching the drones and the missiles. They knew exactly where they were launching them from. But despite the captain's continuous requests for authorization to engage the enemy, he was currently forbidden from doing anything other than shooting down their weapons as they came in range.

Over the next couple hours, the amount of assets the terrorists launched at one time and the frequency of their attacks continued to increase. The commander of the carrier was a hair's breadth from violating orders and targeting the launch sites in Yemen with cruise missiles, when the officer on duty shouted a relay from CIC,

"Captain, imminent threat! Missile inbound..."

He never had a chance to finish. A Russian Kinzhal hypersonic cruise missile Impacted the starboard side of the carrier's hull just forward of the control tower. The missile slammed into the side of the carrier at eight thousand miles per hour. The tapered titanium cone of the missile penetrated a hundred feet inside before it detonated. The impact alone was felt throughout the entire ship. Crew were thrown to the deck or slammed into bulkheads. One man, directly above the point of impact, fell off the side of the ship.

The explosive warhead detonation was far worse than the initial impact. It ripped open the side of the ship. The explosion blew aircraft debris, bodies and parts, pieces of the ship's hull and decks and rooms and pipes and guts out across the red sea from multiple openings torn in the hull. The entire carrier shifted and rocked, metal groaning and bending from tension and stress, shockwaves and heat, fire and death.

Lieutenant Daniels groaned as he pushed himself up from the deck. The explosion and the resulting effects had tossed him across the small room like a ragdoll. His right eye wouldn't open and what remained of his vision was blurry. He saw blood on the deck where his head had been laying. Every part of his body hurt. The room was bathed in red from the emergency backup lights. He heard screaming and shouting coming from outside his room. He had no idea how long he had been unconscious.

With considerable effort, Thomas rose to his feet. On the floor about five feet away, the phone started ringing, the phone Victor's pilot had given him. For several seconds, Lieutenant Daniels just stared at the smartphone lying on the deck. Now, he understood the need for its heavy rugged case. Thomas unconsciously patted his thigh cargo pocket where the phone had been.

The phone vibrated loudly against the steel deck. The entire casing was glowing brightly all around the edges on both sides. The ringtone was Steven Tyler, singing, "Walk this way, talk this way." Thomas shook his head slowly, trying to clear the fog from his mind. He moved over and scooped up the phone and accepted the incoming call. Victor asked,

"You going to make it, Captain?"

Lieutenant Daniels thought maybe Victor had forgotten his rank. But Victor didn't strike him as a forgetful man. Thomas replied,

"I'll live. I think. And it's 'lieutenant'. The carrier has been hit by some kind of extremely heavy ordinance. There's chaos outside my room."

A secondary explosion went off somewhere below deck. It sounded distant. Daniels felt the vibration through the deck. On the phone, Victor chuckled briefly before saying,

"Trust me Thomas, it's captain now or it will be soon enough. If you can bring home the prize, that is. My helicopter will be touching down on the aft landing pad in exactly nine minutes. You need to be on it with a suitable volunteer before it takes off again. Or this will most certainly be our last conversation. Us conspiracy types don't like loose ends you know."

Lieutenant Daniels ignored the threat that he hoped was a joke and wiped a hand across his forehead. He saw that his fingers came away bloody. Thomas used his sleeve to try to get the blood away from his one good eye. He asked,

"A volunteer? Who? How do I identify this man?"

Victor replied,

"Go down the hall to your left and into the emergency triage area. Find someone lying on a gurney with a neck brace or bandages around his skull. Someone dying, but not dead. Go captain, go now."

The call was dropped. Lieutenant Daniels slid the phone into the thigh cargo pocket of his pants. He made sure to button the pocket closed this time so he wouldn't lose it again. Then he stumbled to the door. It took serious effort, and several tries, to open the door as the frame had been warped and shifted.

In the hall, Navy corpsmen, Marine security officers, doctors and nurses stumbled, walked, and ran to deal with the incoming flood of dead and dying victims of the cruise missile attack. Turning left and staying close to the wall, Lieutenant Daniels made his way to the emergency triage area.

There were wounded everywhere. A lot of the men were barely on their feet. Some were lying in beds, others on the floor. There

were also a lot of unmoving bodies that were being laid against the bulkhead to clear space for those who could be saved. Looking through the chaos, Thomas saw one who fit Victor's description. Disturbingly, fit his description to the letter.

Across the room, a young man wearing a petty officer's uniform was lying on a gurney with a brace around his neck and bandages around his head. Lieutenant Daniels moved as fast as he could to his side. He heard as he approached,

"Just make him comfortable. But don't waste a lot of time. He's not going to make it."

The doctor, a major in the US Navy, was speaking to a nurse and had just declared the petty officer a lost cause. Lieutenant Daniels grabbed the major by the arm and said,

"I want this man moved to the aft landing pad on the main deck, for immediate evac."

The doctor went from confused to offended in less than a second. He jerked his arm away and practically hissed in reply,

"I don't know who you think you are! But you do not give me orders in my medical dep...."

A loud deep voice that resonated authority cut through everything else as the XO of the ship bellowed out,

"BELAY THAT MAJOR! DO AS HE SAYS! RIGHT NOW!"

Everything grew quieter in response to the ship's executive officer shouting orders. Thomas looked toward the hatch and saw the XO standing in the doorway cradling an obviously broken arm. The XO was flanked by two of his Marine security personnel. In his good hand the XO was holding a phone in an

extremely rugged looking case, that looked just like the one that Lieutenant Daniels had.

The Marines had their short-barreled close-quarter rifles in hand. One of the Marines was holding his weapon in a low ready position. The other one was pointing his weapon at the doctor that Thomas was talking to. The XO was staring at Lieutenant Daniels with an expression that was part confusion and part rage.

Lieutenant Daniels nodded his thanks to the XO. Then he turned back to the Major who was staring at the rifle pointed at his face in shock. Thomas touched the major's arm again, gently. He said,

"Now, major. Get this man to the aft landing pad, main deck, right now."

The shocked and confused major nodded several times then started giving orders.

The one thing that Thomas could learn about the injured petty officer, as they moved him to the landing pad, was his first name. Jacob. The tag on his uniform that would have displayed his last name, had been ripped off during triage. One of the nurses helping to move Jacob had answered Lieutenant Daniels when he asked the petty officer's name, but a nearby alarm had cut off the end of her response.

It would be almost a week before Thomas would speak to Jacob for the first time.

After taking them off the burning and slightly listing carrier, Victor's helicopter landed nearby on a Navy medical frigate for emergency stabilization care. Thomas saw missiles launching from most of the nearby ships. The task force was returning fire.

Or were they providing cover for Victor's helicopter? Thomas just shook his head.

Victor's helicopter took them both to a nearby Marine air base. From there they transferred Jacob to a C-130 outfitted for medical use and it flew them to Maryland where Jacob was admitted for care at Johns Hopkins Hospital.

The best neurosurgeons in the world were able to save Jacob's life. But he would never walk or feed himself ever again. A couple days later, Jacob was transferred to a small private medical facility that Victor owned. The Konig Life and Bliss Center, just a few miles away from Johns Hopkins.

Thomas was nodding off in a comfortable chair next to Jacob's bed. When he suddenly noticed that Jacob's eyes were open, and he was staring at him. Lieutenant Daniels sat up straight in his chair. Jacob asked,

"Should I know who you are?"

Thomas smiled and shook his head, no. He said,

"My name is Lieutenant Thomas Daniels, United States Marine Corps."

Jacob returned the smile and said,

"Nice to meet you. I'm... I'm..."

Jacob's eyes shifted down and his face took on a confused expression. His eyes went left and right, and he shook his head just slightly. Then Jacob's head jerked forward about a half inch as if he were trying to sit up. Jacob's face was now a mask of panic. His eyes were wide, and his mouth was hanging open.

An alarm sounded in the hall as Jacob's vitals spiked. Lieutenant Daniels jumped up and moved to Jacob's side. He put a hand on his shoulder, trying to calm him,

"Easy. Easy! You've just..."

Jacob screamed and cut him off,

"I CAN'T MOVE! WHAT THE FU..."

Half a dozen nurses flooded into the room. Doctor Patel came limping in behind them, his uneven gait was a result of an old injury. They surrounded Jacob and quickly ushered Lieutenant Daniels out of the room.

Thomas started to protest and had a door slammed in his face. Inside, he could hear Jacob screaming and crying as they tried to settle him. Only moments went by before Jacob was sedated and drifting off to sleep. Thomas let out a deep sigh and looked at the floor.

Jacob slept the rest of the day and into the night. Thomas was pacing the hall outside his door when he got a text from Victor,

[Don't leave him Thomas. Stay, no matter what. It's imperative that you stay with him. I've received reports that he will recover from his injuries. Once he's healed a bit physically, Jacob will be transferred to my facility just outside of Austin, Texas. You come with him.]

Lieutenant Daniels looked at the message and then dropped the phone back into the cargo pocket on his left thigh. Maybe Mr. Konig believed Jacob was going to need something constant in his life. Someone who would always be there for him. Seeing Jacob realize that he was paralyzed had shaken Thomas to his core. It brought back memories of his younger brother...

Jolting Thomas back to the present, a gorgeous young nurse was passing by him in the hall. Her hair was perfectly in order, her uniform immaculate and clean. She must have just started her shift. She stopped and gave Thomas a pleasantly warm smile. She reached out, gently touched his arm, and said,

"Good morning, Lieutenant."

Thomas gave her a puzzled look and glanced at his watch. It was 2230 hours. He looked back at her. She chuckled at his expression then started to walk away. She said,

"Everything in life is about perspective."

Lieutenant Daniels continued watching her as she walked away. She suddenly glanced back at him and added,

"Especially when a girl is walking away."

She smiled playfully at his suddenly red face. Thomas smiled back and nodded. He said,

"I see what you mean, miss."

She went back to her 'morning' routine and Thomas went back to pacing.

Over the next few weeks, Lieutenant Daniels spent time with Jacob several times a day. He joined him for meals. Which were made much more pleasant by Nora's presence while she was feeding Jacob. Thomas popped in and visited whenever the doctors and nurses weren't attending to Jacob, which was not very often.

It was like the entire facility was dedicated to Jacob. Thomas spent time with Jacob mostly in the evenings, after all the tests and poking and therapy sessions were over. Which was usually the time when Jacob was the most frustrated.

They didn't have deep conversations in the beginning. It was mostly frustration and anger and doubt and fears, playing themselves out with words thrown back and forth between bed and chair.

"Who the hell are you anyway, and who asked you to be here? You're not a doctor!"

"I'm never going to walk again, EVER! Is that something you can help me with?!?"

"Why me? Why did this happen to me? I was just earning free college."

Jacob's recovery from surgery was almost over. Lieutenant Daniels had just come in for their end of the day visit. Thomas smiled at the sour look on Jacob's face and sat down next to his bed. Jacob looked at him and asked,

"What happened to my shipmates? After the attack, I mean. I'm assuming the rest of the crew weren't flown back to the states for this level of treatment."

Lieutenant Daniels had wondered when this conversation would come up. He knew Jacob wouldn't enjoy hearing it, but he deserved to know. Thomas sat forward and looked Jacob in the eyes. He said,

"I won't lie to you Jacob, ever. A lot of the crew didn't make it. A lot of them are in similar if not worse shape than you are."

Jacob's face betrayed the sorrow he felt. His lips pressed together. His eyes became damp. He had friends onboard. Shipmates, he had called them. Thomas continued,

"Up until the cruise missile strike on your carrier, the Houthis had been strictly targeting civilian vessels. Not military, not ours. When they hit the Gerald R. Ford the rest of the strike force engaged full strength, full force. It was a devastating retaliation. Almost escalated into World War III actually."

Thomas sat back in his chair and looked down at his feet when he saw the tears coming from Jacob's eyes. He wanted to give Jacob the dignity of not staring at him while he cried. Thomas continued,

"I was told that the USS Carney unleashed absolute hell on those terrorists. Within a short time, the attacks stopped. It was scorched earth. Yes, a lot of sailors and marines were injured and killed. But a lot were saved as well. Your shipmates handled themselves with professionalism and honor. You should be proud of them."

Thomas glanced up. Jacob wasn't sobbing, but there were definitely tears streaming from his eyes. Lieutenant Daniels smiled encouragingly and said,

"If you need a minute, I can step out."

There was a soft knock at the door, followed by the entrance of a familiar young nurse carrying a tray with two steaming cups on it. Nora stepped inside and lit up the room with her smile. She asked,

"Is this a bad time for homemade hot cocoa?"

Lieutenant Daniels returned her smile. He looked at Jacob, and said,

"Your call."

Jacob's eyes looked from Thomas to Nora. A smile fought its way out. Jacob nodded faintly, barely able to move his head. He said,

"I'd like that."

Nora set the tray down next to the bed and then looked at Thomas. She raised her eyebrows and said,

"You won't believe what just happened. I just got a new job."

Lieutenant Daniels frowned at the thought of losing Jacob's favorite nurse, he said,

"Oh. I'm sorry to hear that. I mean, congratulations, though."

She grinned and added,

"It's a good thing. You already know my new boss. Well, technically my old boss, I guess. He's in the hall and asked me to send you out."

It suddenly dawned on Lieutenant Daniels what was happening. Nora was Jacob's favorite. Jacob was almost ready to leave this place. Thomas stood up and watched as Nora helped Jacob sip his cocoa. Victor Konig truly was a genius. Jacob was smiling and laughing at something Nora was saying as Lieutenant Daniels walked out the door.

In the hall just outside Jacob's room, was Victor Konig. He was looking at a tablet and making little swipes at the screen, like he was checking off a list. Lieutenant Daniels walked up to him and raised an eyebrow. Victor looked up as Thomas approached, he smiled and said,

"It's good to see you in one piece, Captain."

Thomas started to reply, but Victor held up one hand and stopped him. Then he turned to the side and motioned for an assistant to approach that Lieutenant Daniels hadn't noticed was waiting nearby. Victor handed the tablet to his assistant. Thomas saw the assistant hand Victor a small box. Victor nodded, then told his assistant,

"Take this to our research facility in Texas. I want it transported and hand delivered directly to my chief of staff."

The assistant nodded and immediately departed. Victor turned back to Thomas and held out the small box. He said,

"If I tell you something is going to happen, it's going to happen. These are for you."

Thomas opened the box and pulled out a folded-up piece of paper. He unfolded it and saw that it was official military documentation of his promotion to captain. Underneath the paper were two shiny captain's rank insignia for his uniform. Thomas smiled and dropped the paper and the box into a cargo pocket.

Thomas looked Victor in the eye and said,

"I guess I came out of all this pretty well off. Can't say the same for Jacob or his shipmates though, can we?"

Victor narrowed his eyes and nodded. Thomas was pretty sure Victor understood his implication. That Victor was somehow

responsible for what happened. Victor looked Thomas in the eye and asked,

"Do you remember our conversation on the plane, Thomas?"

Captain Daniels nodded. Victor continued,

"Nothing has changed, Captain. Without being able to explain, yet. I promise you that everything I have told you will happen, will absolutely happen. But I want you to know that you, you're not trapped. You absolutely have free will in this. Because even me with all my wealth and resources, even I can't violate that covenant."

Victor half turned and gestured down the hall toward the exit. He continued,

"You can walk away right now, Thomas. I'll even offer you a scandalously generous severance package contingent on a non-disclosure agreement. After you're gone, everything that's going to happen will still happen. You just won't be there to witness it. Someone else will. They won't be his first choice, but I'll make it work."

Captain Daniels hadn't expected that reply. He wasn't quite sure what to make of it. Thomas gestured toward Jacob's door and changed the subject, saying,

"Nora, good choice. Jacob really likes her."

Victor laughed and let the matter go. He replied,

"Oh, Jacob likes her? Is that what you're going with?"

Captain Daniels gave Victor a devious smile, and added,

"Well, without being able to explain, yes. That's the story you're getting."

Victor laughed again, then reached out and offered his hand. Captain Daniels took it. They shook hands and Victor said,

"Congratulations on your promotion, Captain. You earned it. I've chartered a special helicopter to get Jacob down to my facility in Texas. It will be waiting for you at my hangar, and I'll be there to meet the three of you in the morning when you arrive. Then it's off to Austin where we will face the most crucial moment in this entire endeavor."

Victor let go of his hand. Captain Daniels asked,

"Crucial moment, when you ask Jacob to be your volunteer?"

Victor shook his head, no. He said,

"Unfortunately, it won't be that easy. Again, I can't explain, but I can't directly ask him to volunteer. It must be his idea. If this is going to work, Jacob must see the possibility and ask if he can be the one. Without any prompting by me."

Not understanding, but accepting, Captain Daniels nodded and stepped back. In parting, he said,

"See you in the morning, Sir."

Victor took a step back also, saying,

"Victor, Thomas, Victor! Let's be friends, yes?"

Captain Daniels gave him the same devious smile and responded,

"Whatever you say, Sir."

Victor let out a genuine laugh and turned to walk away. Captain

Daniels watched him go. He stood staring down the hall. He was thinking about the odd conversation that just took place. Something was nagging Thomas. Actually, almost all of it bothered him. But two comments in particular,

You absolutely have free will in this. Because even me with all my wealth and resources, even I can't violate that covenant.

They won't be his first choice, but I'll make it work.

What on Earth did that mean? Captain Daniels walked back into Jacob's room. He took off his jacket and sat back down. Nora was sitting on the edge of Jacob's bed, holding one of the cups. She was saying,

"He asked me if I wanted to be your private nurse, and I said yes. But I wanted to make sure you were ok with me being the one. You're going to need someone twenty-four seven to help you with a variety of daily things."

Thomas opened the box Victor had given him and put his new captain's rank insignia onto the lapels of his uniform jacket. After admiring the double silver bars for a moment, Thomas looked up and realized that Nora and Jacob were both staring at him. Thomas raised an eyebrow and said,

"What?"

Jacob frowned at him while Nora shook her head. She said,

"Oh nothing, Captain. It's ok, you just stay there while I discuss with Jacob certain aspects of being his private nurse. Don't worry about us making you uncomfortable or embarrassed, we're just going to…"

Thomas closed the door behind himself and left them to it.

He walked down the hall while adjusting and rebuttoning his uniform jacket. Once outside, the clinic's courtesy driver took him to his nearby hotel. Captain Daniels thanked the driver and walked inside. He was deep in thought over his conversation with Victor.

Captain Daniels walked into the normally busy lobby and found it completely deserted. He paused for a moment and looked around. There wasn't another person anywhere in sight. Another handful of steps brought him in line with the entrance to the hotel bar. It was also empty. For a brief moment, a chill went down his spine. Adrenaline heightened his senses. Thomas glanced behind himself.

It was quiet. It was so quiet in fact, Thomas realized he could hear the normally faint background music coming from the lobby speakers twenty feet overhead. The odd sound tugged at his soul. It was hypnotic, literally. It pulled him deeper into the spell that was being woven around him. It was a woman's voice singing acapella in a language that Thomas didn't recognize. It sounded vaguely Spanish, but not exactly.

Captain Daniels stood listening to the haunting and captivating melody for several moments. She had him completely now. Thomas suddenly realized there was a woman standing behind the front desk that he had never seen before. She was standing there just watching him and smiling.

Captain Daniels tried unsuccessfully to shake off the music. He grinned sheepishly as he walked up to the desk. Thomas had seen the same scruffy young man named Kevin most nights, and the older gentleman who worked Kevin's nights off. But it was always one of those two manning the desk when Thomas returned from the clinic late in the day.

Thomas couldn't help but notice that the woman staring at him was absolutely stunning. She was quite possibly the most beautiful woman that he had ever seen. She had hair so golden it was almost glowing. Her button-up shirt was the purest white, and she had just enough buttons undone that a man's eyes would be drawn there.

Her smile caused a reaction in his soul and quickened his pulse. Captain Daniels stepped up to the desk and smiled at her. She was amazing to look at. He asked,

"Where's Kevin, I thought he'd be on tonight."

Thomas found himself leaning forward to listen as she replied, her voice was completely enthralling. She could have done the voice acting part for a beautiful forest nymph in some spellbinding fantasy animation, she said,

"This is a singularly special night. So, we gave Kevin the evening off, Captain."

Thomas smiled. She had called him Captain. His eyes were riveted to her. He couldn't have looked away even if he wanted to. Now, he felt recognized and special, he asked,

"Oh, you know me?"

She grinned at him. Thomas felt the warmth of her expression on his chest. She was amazing. She looked down and to the side, and slowly, ever so slowly, she nodded toward the rank insignia on his uniform. Forcing himself to look away from her face, Thomas looked down and realized she had seen his rank and recognized he was a captain.

Captain Daniels laughed and nodded as he looked back up at her. Her grin went back to a warm pleasant smile. He said,

"Ahh, I see. That's not embarrassing at all."

She shook her head very slightly, and said,

"Nothing to be embarrassed about, Thomas, I have that effect on men."

His eyebrows furrowed as his subconscious suddenly warned him of something. He asked,

"You said this was a special night. What's so special about it?"

She looked down away from his face toward his uniform. Her eyes were undressing him as they traveled down his body. She reached up and started undoing more buttons on her shirt. Soft and breathy, she whispered,

"I'm told it's your last night here. So, it's our last chance to show you our appreciation for your service."

Some part of his mind and soul rebelled against the spell this siren was weaving. His subconscious was screaming at him. Thomas stepped back from the counter, and louder than necessary, he said,

"NO!"

It felt like the earth shifted under his feet. Everything changed. A young couple nearby stopped and looked toward the sound of his raised voice. Glancing around, Thomas saw that half a dozen people were in the lobby. All of them were staring at him. Captain Daniels closed his eyes and shook his head, trying to clear what felt like brain fog.

He looked back to where the blonde woman had been standing. Kevin was standing there, staring at Thomas like he should have a straitjacket on. The young man asked,

"Uh, no what, man?"

Captain Daniels looked left then right. There was no sign of her. She had been standing there one second ago! The lobby was empty! Confused and slightly shaken, Thomas looked back at Kevin and asked,

"Where did the blonde woman go? She was just standing right here!"

Kevin cocked his head, thinking. He looked around a bit to see who might be in earshot. Then he leaned closer to Captain Daniels and spoke quietly,

"Hey man, if you're asking me what I think you're asking me. We don't do that. That's just in the movies, dude."

Captain Daniels shook his head no. Kevin had the wrong idea and didn't understand. Thomas mumbled,

"No, Kevin, no. Just, never mind. Long day, goodnight."

Captain Daniels was trying to make sense of the surreal moment as he made his way to the elevator. He couldn't have been daydreaming, could he? He took the elevator up and walked to his door. Nothing like that had ever happened to him before. Could someone have slipped LSD into his coffee? He couldn't make sense of it.

He waved his key and went into his room. As he hung up his uniform jacket, the events in the lobby were replaying in his mind. It had been emptied one moment, then suddenly not. He didn't count, but there had to have been at least a dozen people in the area.

Not to mention that woman, she was so strange. She knew his name. She went from captivating beauty to terrifying viper in a few seconds flat. The intoxicating female voice singing in the background, all of it. It was the strangest moment in his life, not counting meeting Victor Konig on his airplane. Captain Daniels finished his evening routine and climbed into bed.

Thomas was beginning to believe it was stress. It had to be. The carrier, the missile strike, the dead and dying, Jacob's traumatic recovery. Everything must have finally caught up to him. Now that life was slowing down, all the stress had messed with his mind. That had to be it. Captain Daniels grinned and chuckled. Craziest thing ever. It had seemed so real. He eventually drifted off to sleep.

As soon as sleep had Thomas in its warm embrace, the enchanting voice of the lobby nymph jerked him right back out of it,

"Thomas. You didn't think you were going to get away from me that easy, did you?"

His eyes opened wide in alarm. The blonde from the lobby was standing at the foot of his bed. Her hair was glowing golden in the dark room. Her bright blue eyes were fixed on his. She was wearing nothing but the white button up shirt from earlier. Most of the buttons were already open and she was undoing the rest.

Thomas tried to move but he couldn't. He looked to the side and saw that his wrists and ankles were bound to the corners of the bed with unrealistically large and heavy black cast iron chains. He struggled and pulled against the chains in vain. He couldn't make them move even an inch.

Captain Daniels stopped moving, his body was suddenly frozen in terror. Two sharp red horns grew out of her head through her beautiful blonde hair just above her ears. When she spoke again, he saw that her canine teeth were growing longer and came to wickedly sharp points,

"I'm here to welcome you..."

Black leathery wings unfolded from her back as her voice deepened horribly,

"...to the family."

Captain Daniels sat up screaming. His phone was ringing. The blankets were tossed around and twisted up. He was soaked in sweat. Thomas looked around the empty room and took a deep breath as he shook off the nightmare. His phone rang again. He grabbed the phone and hit the green button as he fell back onto his pillow, saying,

"Daniels"

Nora's voice was a welcome sound,

"Hey Thomas, it's Nora, I just wanted to touch base and let you know Jacob had a great night. He's really excited about tomorrow."

Captain Daniels frowned and glanced at his watch. It was 0400. He asked,

"That's it? You called me at 4:00 AM to tell me everything is fine?"

Nora laughed and replied,

"Oh, I'm sorry! I just wrapped up at the clinic and I was going to take a nap before we caught the ambulance ride to the airport. I didn't even think about you being asleep."

Captain Daniels shook his head and chuckled. He said,

"I'm actually glad you called. It was good timing. Thank you, Nora."

Impossibly, he could hear the warmth of her smile in her voice. He closed his eyes, and heard,

"Well, in that case you're welcome."

"Night Nora."

"Night Thomas."

About four hours later, Captain Daniels climbed out of the taxi near Victor's medical clinic. He saw Nora walking out. She was pushing Jacob's medical bed toward a private ambulance that was waiting at the entrance. Thomas walked up and lowered his shades enough to get a better look. It was the first time he had seen her in anything other than medical scrubs.

Nora was wearing tight jeans that hugged her curves amazingly. She had a burgundy-colored shirt with frills around the neck and arms that left very little to the imagination. Nora began directing the ambulance crew to load Jacob's bed into the back. They hadn't noticed him approaching.

Thomas gave Nora a 'raised eyebrow look' over his shades and said,

"Wow, she cleans up nice."

Her outfit wasn't necessarily overly revealing. It covered all the skin. But what it did show was hard to take his eyes off of. Thomas did his best not to stare, all the same. Jacob spotted him and called out. Nora turned to look as he walked up. She gave him a warm smile. As soon as Jacob was loaded, they all climbed into the ambulance. It drove them to a small regional airport.

Captain Daniels began to notice that every time he looked at Nora, she was grinning back at him from where she sat next to Jacob. Then he noticed that Jacob was grinning at him too. Thomas rolled his eyes at the two conspirators and busied himself checking censored dot news on his phone. They chuckled at his discomfort and whispered back and forth.

Thomas was glad to see Jacob in good spirits. For someone who recently lost his ability to walk and use his arms, he was handling it amazingly well.

They had no problem getting through airport security. The ambulance approached a private entry gate and was immediately waved through. The ambulance then made its way to Victor's private hangar. Waiting for them out in front of the open hangar was a modified Coast Guard rescue helicopter and a Range Rover. They saw Victor standing by the helicopter, talking to the crew.

It wasn't until the ambulance doors opened and they rolled Jacob's bed out that he finally asked,

"What the hell is going on, Thomas?"

Walking up, Victor interjected,

"I believe I can answer that. Hi, honored to finally meet you, I'm Victor."

Jacob's eyes shifted from Victor to Captain Daniels and back to Victor, he said,

"Uh yeah! I think everybody in a thousand-mile radius knows who you are."

Victor grinned at his comment and continued,

"This all probably seems a little crazy and out of left field. But, actually, it's not really random. I know your old executive officer, from the Gerald R. Ford. Major Thorn told me about what happened to you that day. I was overwhelmed by the story, so I offered to do what I could to help you."

Jacob glanced at Captain Daniels again, then back to Victor, he asked,

"So, Johns Hopkins, the private medical clinic, all this, you did all this?"

Victor nodded and smiled. Jacob looked past Victor to the helicopter and the crew standing by, he asked,

"So, what now?"

Victor grinned and said,

"These fine folks are going to fly you down to a private medical facility that I own just outside of Austin in Texas. You're going to get the very best rehabilitative care that modern medical science can offer. If that's ok with you, young man?"

Jacob gave him a cautious smile, saying,

"Ok, I'm game."

Jacob shifted his eyes to Captain Daniels and gave him a look that Thomas recognized as suspicion. Nora was all smiles. They were approached by the helicopter crew, and Jacob wasn't happy to learn that there was only room for Nora in the helicopter with him. But Victor assured him,

"Captain Daniels will fly with me in my jet. He'll be waiting for you there when you arrive."

Ten minutes later, Victor Konig and Captain Daniels were watching the helicopter fade from view as Victor's pilot pulled the Gulfstream out of the hangar and readied it for their flight. Without turning his head, Captain Daniels said,

"He doesn't trust this, or you."

Victor nodded and replied,

"I know."

Captain Daniels added,

"I don't trust you either."

Again, Victor nodded and replied,

"I know."

Captain Daniels asked,

"Is there something at your facility you want to show me? Is that why he's on a helicopter and we're in the Gulfstream? So that we get there first?"

Victor replied casually,

"I'm just going to give you a quick tour of the facility, so you can show Jacob around."

Captain Daniels turned his head slightly and looked at Victor out of the corner of his eye, he said,

"Uh huh..."

Three Hours Later

Victor gave Captain Daniels a thorough tour of his supposedly 'Austin area' research facility, and the brand-new rehabilitation wing. Victor's facility was over an hour drive from Austin. It was in the middle of nowhere. After getting familiar with the layout of the building and meeting all of the staff, Captain Daniels faced Victor and said,

"You expect me to show him around. You're planning on me doing the sales pitch for you, aren't you?"

Victor looked Captain Daniels in the eye. He replied,

"I told you. I can't ask him to volunteer."

Captain Daniels cocked his head, and said,

"But getting me to do it for you, that makes it ok by your rules? How's that work? And who made up these ridiculous rules?"

Victor smiled a mysterious and enigmatic smile. Like he had a secret, he asked,

"You've never heard of Karmic Law or the Law of Fair Play and Equal Chance, have you?"

Captain Daniels shook his head, no. Victor continued,

"Don't take this the wrong way, Captain. I truly mean no offense. But the fact is, it's ok for you to say and do anything in this situation. Because you're not one of us. You can do things that would be unfair for me to do directly."

Captain Daniels narrowed his eyes ever so slightly, and asked,

"Us who?"

Victor shrugged and responded,

"Let's just say people in high places, Thomas. The mythical, whispered rumors of the puppet-masters of the universe, like I said before. Trust me, you're better off not being one of us."

Captain Daniels narrowed his eyes and very sternly, he said,

"Just so we're clear, Victor. I'm here for Jacob now. The military may have ordered me to report to you and follow your orders. But they don't own me, and neither do you!"

Victor grinned a warm genuine victorious grin. He slapped Thomas gently on the arm and said,

"You have no idea how glad I am to hear that, Captain! Because that is exactly what I truly needed from you, but I couldn't directly ask you for."

Captain Daniels narrowed his eyes as Victor turned to walk away. Victor called back over his shoulder,

"He's here, Thomas. Everything is riding on you."

A few minutes later, Nora was pushing Jacob's bed toward the automatic sliding doors at the entrance to the Konig Cyber-Medical Research Center. Thomas was watching them from inside. He smiled at Nora and noticed Jacob looking up at the name of the facility over the main doors. Jacob's eyes were wide.

The doors slid open, and Nora pushed Jacob's bed in. Jacob saw him waiting for them, standing between two white marble pillars that had jagged veins of gold scattered throughout. Jacob was in good spirits, he grinned at Thomas and said excitedly,

"That chopper pilot was nuts! That was so much fun! I thought I was going to some lame rehab place! What is this?"

Captain Daniels smiled at Jacob's good mood. He replied,

"Victor recently added a rehabilitation wing to this facility. This place is pretty next level. Come on, I'll show you."

Captain Daniels took over for Nora and pushed Jacob's medical bed through the white marbled halls. He led Jacob and Nora to a large room just off the main entry hall. Nora held the door, as Thomas pushed Jacob inside. Thomas said,

"This is their demonstration room for VIPs. The facility's chief of staff is on his way to meet you. His name's Doctor Fischer. Fair warning though, he's super stuffy. Real uptight, black suit and tie type. He wants you to see what the research and development guys do here. I've seen it, you'll get a kick out of this, Jacob."

Jacob looked around, as best he could from the slightly inclined bed. It was a square room with three blank white glass walls, and one dark smoky glass wall in front of him. He looked to the side as the 'doctor' came into the room.

Doctor Fischer came in with a crazy smile on his face. He had wild uncontrolled white hair that he was tying back into an insane ponytail with a cord of some kind. The doctor was wearing a sleeveless white lab coat over a magic mushroom t-shirt and pajama bottom pants. Jacob started laughing.

Doctor Fischer finished tying back his hair, then he approached them with his crazy smile. He looked from Thomas to Jacob and asked,

"This is him, eh? The hero from the boat? Mr. Konig told me all about it."

Jacob was grinning and said,

"Pleasure to meet you doc."

Doctor Fischer held up both hands, saying,

"Are you ready to see this? You're not ready, no. No, this won't do. Hold on."

The doctor looked toward the door, and whistled like he was calling a dog. Then he said,

"Wheels, get in here."

A strange and high-tech looking wheelchair drove itself into the room. It looked kind of like a stream-lined recliner on the frame of a quad-runner. It was nearly silent and obviously electric. It maneuvered around everyone and stopped next to Doctor Fischer. The doctor grinned at Jacob and gestured to the chair, saying,

"Ta-da."

Jacob asked,

"That for me?"

Slowly and carefully, mindful of his recent surgeries, Nora and Captain Daniels moved Jacob from the bed to the chair. Once he was comfortable and safely secured, the doctor asked,

"Better?"

Jacob looked from side to side. He smiled, and said,

"Well, I can see better."

The doctor nodded happily, saying,

"In that case, see this."

The wild-haired doctor turned to the darkened glass wall and pointed a remote control at it. The glass shifted from dark to clear. On the other side of the glass was a much larger room. In the room beyond, was an obstacle course made up to look like a war-torn street in some middle eastern town.

On one end of the course was a Belgian Malinois, sitting and panting happily with his head held high and proud. He was well muscled, but more athletic than bulky. The Belgian had the 'swimmers build', of the K-9 world. He wore a lightly padded, close-fitting body harness that had several VHS-sized compartments riding high on each side of his back. At the other end of the course, was his handler.

The handler noticed that the glass had cleared and looked at the doctor. Doctor Fischer held up one finger to the handler and turned back to Jacob, saying,

"I'm Anton, by the way. Anton Fischer."

Jacob just smiled and nodded. Captain Daniels grinned, thinking,

He's like a cartoon character.

Doctor Fischer turned back and pointed at the handler, nodding. The handler nodded in reply and looked at the Belgian Malinois. He shouted a command to the K-9 that they couldn't hear. The dog immediately started walking forward. He moved cautiously, watching the buildings and the rubble closely.

Before the K-9 got more than ten feet, a 'hostile' mannequin dressed like a terrorist popped up in front of him on a hydraulic

arm. The target had an attached weapon that fired paintballs in the K-9's direction. The dog lowered his head and body, quickly sidestepping behind a vehicle.

The Belgian raised its head just above the trunk of the car. He locked his view on the target. One of the small compartments on his harness snapped open and ejected a small switchblade drone twenty feet into the air. The drone activated, quickly oriented itself, then zipped forward to the target and exploded on impact. It blew the top half of the mannequin off.

Jacob, Nora, and Captain Daniels all said,

"Whoa!"

Doctor Fischer chuckled, saying,

"Achilles has been through this course several times. He's something of a star around here."

Jacob asked,

"What just happened? Who's controlling the drones?"

They could all see that the handler wasn't operating anything, just watching. Doctor Fischer looked back at them and grinned broadly. He said,

"Achilles is."

They watched Achilles continue through the course. The medium sized K-9 was incredibly athletic. He was leaping over vehicles and low walls, dodging paintballs. The dog encountered two more pop-up targets and destroyed them efficiently with his explosive drones. Upon neutralization of the third target, Achilles trotted happily to his handler for treats. Jacob sounded skeptical, he asked,

"The dog? That dog was operating the drones?"

Doctor Fischer turned toward Jacob with an amused look on his face. He explained,

"Achilles isn't micro-managing pitch, roll, power, or yaw, no. But with limited A.I. controlling the drones flight, Achilles is telling the drones what to do, yes."

Doctor Fischer looked from Jacob to the others and back, he leaned forward and asked conspiratorially,

"I know Mr. Konig said you were just here for the launch of our medical rehab wing, but didn't he tell you what we do here in the main facility?"

Flatly, Jacob said,

"No."

Doctor Fischer laughed and headed toward the door, saying,

"Jacob, repeat after me. 'Wheels, follow Doctor Fischer.'"

Jacob repeated the phrase and his chair turned and followed the doctor out the door. Captain Daniels winked at Nora and turned to follow behind Jacob. Nora had an excited look on her face, she moved up next to Thomas and grabbed his hand. Captain Daniels let her take his hand and gave her a mock suspicious look. Nora just grinned and pulled him forward. Thomas couldn't help but smile.

Doctor Fischer led them down the main hall, further into the facility. Turning down one of the side halls, he led them to an electronically secured doorway to one of the facility's research laboratories. He spoke as they walked,

"We are doing cutting edge cybernetic research here. Achilles, the K-9 you just saw, has a neural implant that allows him to control the drones with his mind. We started by teaching him basic commands, load, launch, scout, follow, stuff like that. Once he mastered the basic commands, we taught him that the drones could attack his enemies. The drones have fail-safes of course, to prevent Achilles from launching a drone and then accidently looking at his handler."

Doctor Fischer laughed like he had told the funniest joke in the world. He waved his security badge and stepped through the security door, holding it open for them to follow him inside.

Thomas watched Jacob's eyes glaze over as he took in the room. There was a central ring of working spaces and computer stations surrounded by an outer ring of surgical tables, x-ray displays, tools, an electronics workshop area, and large empty cages for animals. There was a lot going on in this room.

He saw that Nora was also looking around with wide eyes, examining the x-ray display details and looking at things around the surgical area. Captain Daniels stood near the door and kept his eyes mainly on the interaction between Jacob and Doctor Fischer.

Doctor Fischer introduced Jacob to the two veterinary technicians and the programming coder for the experimental cybernetics. The doctor explained to Jacob that they had recently finished their required animal testing phases with flying colors. Including multiple field tests conducted with the military. He explained that they were in the process of repurposing this area into a dedicated production shop for explosive ordinance detection K-9's for the military. He said,

"Just imagine, an explosive ordnance disposal soldier with a K-9 partner who can not only detect various chemicals and compounds better than any machine that mankind can make. But one who can also broadcast data back to local command and control in real time, through retinal implants. A K-9 who can take x-rays, carry tools for his handler, detect and warn against traps and hidden enemies. The possibilities are beyond imagination at this point."

Jacob gave the doctor a big smile and nodded slightly. He said,

"Thank you for this doctor. This is probably the coolest place I have ever seen."

Doctor Fischer was beaming with pride, he replied,

"You are very welcome. I'm glad to hear that, Jacob. I'm also glad I got to be the one to show you around. I never served directly in the military, but I have the greatest respect for those who have."

The doctor leaned closer to Jacob, his voice more serious,

"You served, and you paid a price that most people will never know and even fewer will ever understand. This country and everyone in it owe you an enormous debt that we could never possibly repay. Mr. Konig agrees with me on that. Anything, and I mean anything, that I can possibly do for you, all you need to do is ask, and it's yours."

The doctor straightened up as an idea seemed to strike him, he said,

"In fact, here."

He reached into one of his deep pockets and took out a clip-on badge that he clipped to the front of Jacob's armrest. He said,

"You've got as much time as you want to get started with the rehab. There's no rush. Everything about this process is set to Jacob-speed."

He laughed and a wide smile crossed his face as he added,

"Besides, this is a privately owned facility that is entirely funded by Mr. Konig, not some faceless heartless medical insurance company. So, we make our own rules here. For now, this place is at your disposal. Go anywhere you please. Explore to your heart's content. I will try to find you later, but I must attend to some other things for now."

Jacob raised his eyebrows appreciatively, saying,

"Thanks doc! I'll take you up on that. Hey Thomas, let's go look around."

Captain Daniels held the door open, and Nora walked out. Jacob said,

"Wheels, follow that woman."

Together, the three of them set off to explore. The facility turned out to be much larger than it appeared from outside. There were two additional levels below ground. They met a number of employees as they roamed the halls. All of them were quite friendly and also extremely helpful with navigating the maze-like hallways. All of them seemed to already know who Jacob was, and every single person they met thanked Jacob for his service.

One of the people they bumped into was a bit different than the others. He had stained coveralls and dirty fingernails and looked more like a mechanic. Scott Phillips, who was not in fact a mechanic, worked in the hardware fabrication shop. He took them down to the basement and led them to his shop.

He gave the trio a mini tour of where he and a couple helpers created all of the physical parts and pieces involved in the medical implant operations. They fabricated everything that wasn't computerized or electronic. The majority of which were extremely small titanium hardware pieces for mounting each individual component. Everything had to be custom made and tailored specifically for securing the various micro-electronic components to the bones inside the animals they worked with.

Scott was pretty cool. He was very down to earth. He seemed to actually see Jacob and not just the chair he was in. He was the only employee they met who didn't spit out the party line of, 'thank you for your service'. Instead, he told Jacob that he had some idea of what he was going through, and he was sorry for what happened to him.

It turned out he was the one who built Jacob's semi-autonomous chair. Which was an upgraded version of a chair that Scott had built for his father, after his father was injured in a car accident. He gave them an open invitation to come back anytime.

After leaving the fabrication shop, the next area they found was like a cross between a pet store and a veterinarian's office. Jacob had wheels park in front of the cages with the cats in them. He asked Nora,

"Hey, uh, Nora, would you do something for me?"

She came close, laying her hand on his arm. She said,

"Of course, what do you need?"

Jacob looked her in the eye for a moment, then he smiled briefly and said,

"I'm super thirsty, can you find me like a gallon of orange juice?"

Nora laughed and replied,

"A gallon? No promises."

As soon as she walked away, Jacob said,

"Thomas?"

Staring at the cats, Thomas thought he had an idea what was coming, he replied,

"Yeah?"

In a neutral low tone, Jacob asked,

"They brought me here to be one of those, didn't they?"

Jacob was also staring at the cats in their cages. Each one waiting their turn to be experimented on and implanted with various cybernetics. Captain Daniels replied,

"Not subtle, are they?"

Jacob's eyebrows furrowed, he said,

"No. Or they think I'm stupid."

Captain Daniels looked around, then he leaned a little closer, speaking conspiratorially,

"I don't think they would want you if they thought you were stupid. In fact, I'm betting Achilles is at the very top of the K-9 charts and you're at least as smart as he is."

Jacob flashed a quick one second grin, in appreciation of the captain's joke. Then he narrowed his eyes and asked,

"What do you think happens if I say no?"

Thomas shrugged and said,

"Worst case scenario, VA care isn't bad. I'm sure there would be a lot less perks, sure, but it wouldn't be terrible."

Jacob asked,

"What would you do, if you were me?"

Captain Daniels moved closer to the cages, directly in front of Jacob. He turned around and looked Jacob in the eye. After a moment, he said,

"I'd want to start with the two main things that these fuzzy little guys behind me will never have. Control and information."

Captain Daniels lifted his head up. His gaze was directed over Jacob's shoulder at something behind him, he continued, slightly louder,

"If it were me, I'd tell them to drop the theatrics and get to the point. I'd want to know exactly what they have in mind. I'd want to know exactly what the risks are, and what the possible benefits are. I'd also want as much time as I pleased to decide what I wanted to do. I'd want all of that before I agreed to anything."

Jacob cocked his head ever so slightly, Daniels was still staring over his shoulder, he said,

"Wheels, turn 180 degrees."

Jacob's wheelchair turned in a half circle, to face behind him. Standing just inside the doorway, about ten feet away, were Nora and Doctor Fischer. The doctor smiled and nodded, he said,

"Done and done. If that's what you want, Jacob."

Jacob looked at the doctor and thought about it for a minute. Finally, he said,

"Yeah, show me everything."

Doctor Fischer gave Jacob a smile that a paranoid person would describe as predatory. But it could also be mistaken for excitement. He said,

"Let's go talk in my office."

Doctor Fischer led them to a narrow side hall that turned at the end and then continued about twenty more feet and dead ended at a short wall with a single drink machine. Looking confused, Nora was still carrying two small orange juice bottles. She held them up and glanced at Captain Daniels.

Thomas looked at her and shook his head, no. He turned back and watched the doctor closely. Doctor Fischer stepped up to the drink machine. He reached out and pushed soda, soda, juice, water, soda.

The end wall and the drink machine swung inward, revealing a large private office. Doctor Fischer led them inside. Once everyone was in, the door closed itself behind them. Captain Daniels took a moment to look back and study the door. There was a large button on the inside wall that cycled it open, next to a monitor that showed the hall from a camera in the drink machine. Other than that, there was no security. The hydraulics that opened and closed the door looked homemade and there was no apparent locking mechanism. Everything about the hidden drink machine doorway was eccentric mad-scientist window dressing.

Doctor Fischer gestured for their attention and pointed to a large video screen near his desk. Then he went to retrieve a small wireless keyboard. He stepped up near the screen and tapped a few keys. A video feed suddenly filled the screen. On the screen was an orange house cat walking across what looked like a big fancy bedroom built, specifically, for a cat.

Jacob asked,

"What is this?"

The doctor held up a single finger, saying,

"Just wait, watch this."

The cat walked over to a small machine that looked like a steampunk themed coffee maker. The spoiled little tabby stood and stared at the machine for several seconds. Suddenly, the machine came to life. The bottom panel opened, and a drawer slid out that contained a bowl. A small spigot then filled the bowl with about a quarter cup of milk.

The cat lapped up some of the milk then walked over to a flatscreen television and sat down on a soft and fluffy looking square rug. The television suddenly turned itself on and displayed what appeared to be a nature channel, showing birds, squirrels, and other small forest creatures. The doctor hit a button and the screen went blank, he said,

"Ok, Archie could be sitting there a long time. What did you learn, Jacob?"

Jacob frowned, confused, and said,

"Archie likes milk, and the nature channel?"

The doctor let out one quick laugh, then said,

"No, I mean yes, but no. Listen. What you saw was one of our best feline volunteers. One of our first, actually. What you saw was him mentally telling his drink machine to open the bowl drawer and then telling it to pour him some milk. What you saw was him telling his television, mentally, what channel he wanted to see."

The doctor looked at Jacob with wide eyes, expectantly, like he had just revealed some giant secret. Jacob narrowed his eyes just slightly and said,

"Ok, so, you're saying you gave the cat psychic powers?"

Doctor Fischer started laughing, then suddenly stopped and grew serious, saying,

"Oh wait. You weren't making a joke. Ok, ok. Let me explain."

The doctor went to his desk and set down the keyboard. He picked up a small object and came back, holding it up for them to see. It vaguely resembled a small detachable mechanical socket. He said,

"This is a wireless transceiver designed to speak, so to speak, to machines. It's based on standard near field technology. It's like a fob key that you use to lock and unlock your car. But this device can also understand the electrical impulses of the nervous system and translate them into digital machine code as well as recognizing electromagnetic fields and translating those back into neuro electrical impulses. Archie has one of these surgically implanted at the base of his skull, where his brain connects to his spine. It allows him to give mental commands to electronic devices. Like the battlefield simulation you saw when you first got here. Achilles launched and flew those drones with his mind."

Jacob looked thoughtful. He didn't say anything immediately. Captain Daniels stepped over to the screen, saying,

"Turn it back on doctor."

Doctor Fischer gave him a puzzled expression. Then he grabbed his keyboard and pushed a button. The screen came back on, showing Archie curled up in a ball on a large pillow. Captain Daniels moved over close to the image and put his fingertip on the cat. Thomas looked at the doctor and asked,

"What number is he?"

Doctor Fischer started to reply, unsure,

"Uh, I don't…"

Captain Daniels cut him short, saying,

"Before you implanted Archie here, how many cats died under the knife?"

The doctor held up his hands in surrender and replied,

"Ok, I see. Three. He's number three. Yes, our first volunteer died from the surgery. Number two just never learned to control it. Archie is number three. But not one of the dogs has been lost. Some just never learn control. We lost one cat and a handful of very small animals that we just don't have the miniaturization technology yet to augment successfully."

The doctor shrugged a bit sheepishly and added,

"It's not definitive that it was the technology. Our veterinary surgeon believes it was his fault. He believes he damaged her spine during the surgery. We lost one, the very first, Sara."

Doctor Fischer was looking at the floor by the time he finished.

He looked sad. He looked remorseful. Captain Daniels almost believed it. Thomas looked at Nora. Judging by her expression, she did not. Not one word.

Jacob spoke up,

"I'm sorry to hear about Sara, Doc. Archie looks like he's doing great. Question, what is it exactly, that you want to do to me?"

Doctor Fischer grabbed a thin binder off his desk. He held it out for Captain Daniels to take. Thomas stepped closer and took the manual. He looked at Nora, then Jacob, then back to the doctor, and said,

"I think it's been a long enough day, doc. Why don't you show us where we're going to be staying."

Doctor Fischer's eyebrows rose slightly, he replied,

"Well, we have a room for Jacob setup in the rehab wing, with attendant nurses. We have also arranged rooms for you two at a nearby hotel."

Nora took a step toward the doctor. Captain Daniels noticed her body language. Head forward, hands raised, she was ready to fight. She spoke aggressively, or more accurately, defensively, saying,

"Jacob has a nurse! And there isn't a hotel within fifty miles of here!"

Captain Daniels frowned and shook his head. He wasn't going to let this happen. He turned to Jacob, gave him a long look, and then asked,

"What do you say, buddy? You want to be separated from me and Nora? You want us to leave you here alone with the butchers and their knives and the other volunteers?"

Doctor Fischer made a nasty face, like Captain Daniels had just called him something abominable like a pedophile or a politician. Jacob gave the doctor a stern look, and said,

"Unacceptable, goodbye doc. It was nice meeting you, but I'll take my chances with the VA. Give my regards to Achilles, because his name is seriously badass. But I'm out."

Doctor Fischer chuckled nervously and stepped back, holding up his hands in surrender for the second time. He said,

"Ok, I get it, you're the boss. Give me a bit of time, I'll arrange for the three of you to stay here, in rooms near each other."

Savoring the taste of his newfound power, Jacob corrected him,

"One room, doctor. One big room, with three bedrooms off of it. You have a recently added rehab wing that you used as a lure to get me here, so how about we get that place setup?"

Once again, the calm predatory smile crossed the doctor's face. He said,

"Consider it done, Jacob. Absolutely anything you want."

The good doctor cracked the whip and unleashed a small army of maintenance, janitorial, and office staff. They went to work modifying and reorganizing the rehab wing. Waiting room benches, patient worktables, and all of the rehabilitation equipment were removed. A couch, table, fridge, beds, dressers, mobile wardrobes, and decorative area rugs were all moved in.

Doctor Fischer had their luggage delivered to the main room. Once it was ready, he opened the front door for them with a grandiose flourish. Everything was ready within a single hour.

Captain Daniels, Nora, and Jacob were looking around the living room of their new three-bedroom apartment suite that used to be the reception area of the rehabilitation wing. Nora was the first to run into one of the bedrooms and yell,

"MINE!"

Captain Daniels loosened the top couple buttons of his uniform jacket as he looked around. Then he sat down on the couch with the technical manual the doctor had given him. There were a number of things about their new 'apartment' that he found disturbing, but it would have to wait for now.

He started looking through the technical manual of proposed cybernetic augmentations. In the background he heard Jacob directing his chair to drive him into one of the bedrooms to look around. There was a lot of electronic and medical technical jargon in the manual. He was going to need Nora to look at this.

A short time later, Nora came bouncing out of her room in pajamas. She slid over the back of the couch and plopped down next to Thomas. She sat with her legs curled up underneath her and stared at him with a huge grin on her face. Captain Daniels paused in his reading to look at her. He couldn't help but smile. She absolutely radiated joy. She was wearing pajamas that said 'MARINES' on them. Thomas nodded appreciatively at her choice of night-time wear and asked,

"Does this setup bother you at all?"

He pointed and moved his hand around, indicating the

room they were in. Nora made a puzzled face and looked around. She shook her head slightly and said,

"No, not really. I like it. What's wrong with it?"

Captain Daniels turned toward her. He put one arm up on the back of the couch. He looked her in the eyes and lowered his voice so Jacob wouldn't hear him and said,

"That's just it. The problem isn't what's wrong with it, it's what's right with it. Victor knew before we ever got here, that we'd be sitting right here, doing this, right now."

Nora grinned and asked,

"How could he have known we'd end up using the rehab wing as an impromptu apartment?"

Captain Daniels turned his head very slightly side to side without taking his eyes off her, then said,

"I don't know. But I know for a fact that he had this planned. Why was there a sink with kitchen cabinets in the waiting area? Why did they have three mobile wardrobes, queen-sized beds, area rugs, and all the rest, already on hand? Take a good look at this couch we're sitting on, and then tell me where it fits into any type of medical or research facility. The only thing that makes sense, is that Victor knew we would not accept being separated. He knew we would insist on using this area as a place to stay for all three of us."

Nora was looking around the room, she said,

"I can't believe I didn't see it. There are three bedrooms. There's a shower and a bathtub in the bathroom. I think you're right."

Captain Daniels nodded and handed her the manual, saying,

"I'm not going to complain about being made comfortable. But I think we should keep it in mind. I can't understand most of this stuff. There are a lot of technical images I get the gist of, and a lot of medical stuff I think you should look at. But there's also a lot of electronics and other hardware type stuff I think we might need an outside expert to explain to us."

Nora took the manual and opened it, asking,

"Did you show the tech stuff to Jacob? What does he think about it?"

Captain Daniels looked around, he said,

"Actually, I haven't seen Jacob in a while. I better go check on him."

Nora nodded and continued looking through the manual. Captain Daniels poked his head into the room Jacob had picked. He was parked by the window, not moving. Thomas walked over quietly and saw that Jacob had fallen asleep in his chair, while looking out the window.

Captain Daniels took a minute to look out. He saw a wide-open field under a massive sky filled with stars. There was nothing but open land, far from any city light pollution. The clear Texas sky at night was beautiful.

Thomas carefully slid his arms under the much smaller man's back and legs and lifted him from the chair. Jacob's eyes flickered open and he smiled. Thomas returned his smile and carried him to his bed. Nora had already slipped quietly into the room. She was already pulling down the blanket and top sheet.

Together, they tucked Jacob in and made sure he didn't need anything else. Jacob looked at Captain Daniels and said,

"I'm really glad you're here, Thomas. I mean that. Thank you both. Goodnight Nora."

Jacob was asleep again a minute later. Nora setup and plugged in a combination camera and microphone wireless transmitter. Then she followed Captain Daniels back out into the main room, carefully closing Jacob's door behind her.

Captain Daniels laid his jacket across the back of the couch and walked over to check out the kitchen area. As Nora closed Jacob's door, he asked,

"Why did you ask me if I had shown the technical details to Jacob? What makes you think he'd understand it?"

Nora chuckled and gave Thomas a funny look, she asked,

"Do you have any idea what Jacob's job was on the carrier?"

Captain Daniels stopped and stared at her for a second. He had no idea. That was so weird. He had never even thought to ask. Thomas had chosen him for his injuries. It had never occurred to him to ask what skills Jacob had. He looked back at Nora and shook his head, saying,

"I never asked. Why? What did he do?"

Nora rolled her eyes, and replied,

"He was an electronics technician. Computer, aerospace, and electrical engineer."

The captain's eyes went wide, he blurted out,

"Holy crap! No kidding?"

Nora laughed as she got comfortable on the couch, and said,

"No, I'm serious. He told me about it back at the clinic."

Thomas was dumbfounded, he said,

"Well, that couldn't have worked out more perfect for Victor's science experiment. What are the odds of that?"

Nora shrugged, and replied,

"Probably pretty good really. He was on the most advanced carrier in the fleet."

Captain Daniels found carrot sticks in the fridge. He carried them over and sat down next to Nora on the couch, where she was back to looking through the manual. He took a bite out of one of the carrost sticks and began chewing crunchily. Nora slowly turned her head to look at him. He looked into her eyes and raised his eyebrows, asking,

"Too loud? You trying to concentrate?"

She flashed him her amazing smile and said,

"No, Mr. Greedy Pants. Feed me. I'm working hard here, turning these pages."

She leaned just slightly toward him and batted her eyelashes playfully and opened her mouth. Captain Daniels narrowed his eyes and gave her a suspicious look. He tentatively fed her a carrot stick while she stared into his eyes. Nora ever so slowly and gently bit down. She wrapped her lips around the carrot and pulled it out of his hand.

Thomas was suddenly very uncomfortable in his uniform. She was super-hot, but it would definitely be inappropriate. Nora went back to reading the manual. Captain Daniels quickly got up and headed to his room, saying,

"Ok, long day, goodnight, you got Jacob's monitor, right?"

His door closed behind him.

On the couch, Nora was laughing so hard, as quietly as she could.

~~~~

The next morning, Captain Daniels walked out of his room and found Victor sitting on the couch in the living room. Victor was sitting back comfortably, with his most pleased with himself smile. He was using both hands to sip carefully on a cup of steaming hot coffee.

On the table in front of Victor was a small buffet, including three more coffees, three large oval plates of bacon and eggs and toast, bowls of grapes, jellies, jams, creamer, sugar, and more.

Victor opened his mouth to say something when Nora's door slammed open. She moved quickly toward Jacob's room, the monitor in her hand. Captain Daniels started toward Jacob's room, but Nora gave him a look that stopped him in his tracks. She opened Jacob's door and slipped in, closing it firmly behind her.

Thomas walked around the coffee table and grabbed one of the cups. Carefully taking a sip of the steaming liquid, he looked at Victor. Victor's smile, somehow, amazingly, got even bigger. Victor said,
~~~~

"A wise man, Captain Thomas Daniels, knows his role and stays in his lane."

Victor could not possibly have seen what had just happened behind him. The man was so incredibly frustrating. Captain Daniels narrowed his eyes, and replied,

"Maybe this would be a good time to discuss some boundaries concerning our rooms here."

Victor's smile became an amused grin, he said,

"Boundaries. Understood, Captain. I just thought we should celebrate. Doctor Fischer told me the good news."

Thomas furrowed his brow and asked,

"What good news?"

Victor blew on his coffee to cool it, then said,

"Jacob deciding to be our volunteer of course."

Thomas took a slow sip of his coffee, never taking his eyes off the man on the couch. Calmly, he said,

"Jacob hasn't said yes yet."

Victor cocked his head slightly. His expression was suddenly unreadable. He looked Captain Daniels in the eyes and said,

"Just because you didn't see something, doesn't mean it didn't happen right in front of your eyes, Thomas."

Captain Daniels opened his mouth to say something he would probably regret, but Nora came out of Jacob's room and walked up to the table. She said,

"He's ok, just nightmares."

Nora grabbed a coffee and two large plates of eggs and bacon and toast, two sets of silverware, and some napkins. Then she slipped expertly back into Jacob's room. She was still in her pajamas from last night. Strangely, all Thomas could think was,

How on earth did she just carry all of that and let herself into Jacob's room and close the door behind herself?

Captain Daniels shook his head and looked back at Victor. Thomas made no attempt to disguise his foul mood. Victor stood and stared back at Captain Daniels, his super pleased with himself expression had returned. Victor took a slow careful sip of his coffee as he looked Thomas in the eye. Seemingly offhand, Victor asked,

"Did you know Nora put herself through nursing school by waiting tables?"

Captain Daniels was taken back by the disturbingly insightful response to what he was just thinking. Thomas opened his mouth, but no words came out. Victor shrugged and grinned, then set down his cup and started toward the door, saying,

"Sorry my friend, no time to explain. So much to do. I'm off again but do keep in touch. I have a feeling we're going to be working together for the foreseeable future."

Captain Daniels thought to himself,

Sorry for what? Explain what? Reading my mind?!?

Victor had opened the door to leave and stepped into the doorway. He paused and looked back, waiting. Captain Daniels just stared at him. Victor smiled and nodded, saying,

"It's ok Thomas, in time you'll see that all of this is for the best. I'm sure of it. I have the absolute highest of hopes for you."

Victor left and Thomas stared at the door, trying to decide just what it was about that man that troubled him so much. Captain Daniels suddenly remembered their conversation on the plane,

"I'd think you were one of those crazy conspiracy nuts. Like that Alexie Goreski guy."

"You mean the Russian guy that does those conspiracy theory podcasts? The one who sells those wacky T-shirts?"

"Well, you'd be closer than most people. Actually, you'd be way off base, but you would at least be playing the right game."

Captain Daniels suddenly wondered if Alexie Goreski, the Russian defector turned podcaster, was still on the air. If he was, his studio was in Austin, which meant he was close. Thomas hadn't heard much about Alexie since he was banned by all the mega-corporation owned social media outlets.

Maybe Alexie knew something or had some insights about Victor. Victor did say Alexie had interviewed him before. It would explain why Alexie was banned off the internet and demonized in the media. Captain Daniels sat down and grabbed some breakfast.

About an hour later, Thomas and Nora were showing Jacob the technical pages from the manual. Captain Daniels would hold one up for him to read, then Nora would hold up the next one. They took turns back and forth until Jacob had seen them all. There were a couple that Jacob had wanted to see again. He didn't comment until they had finished the entire manual.

Jacob looked over at Nora, and asked,

"What do you think about the inter-cranial and spinal surgeries?"

Nora's eyebrows rose expressively, she said,

"I think it's dangerous Jacob. It's the most invasive surgery I've ever seen. I mean, I'm not an expert on any of it, but it's obviously dangerous. Not necessarily from the spinal areas, considering where you're at already. But the hardware they are proposing adding to your brain, under your skull? That's beyond anything I've ever seen."

Jacob looked from her to Captain Daniels, he said,

"You guys saw what Achilles could do. It's dangerous, yeah, but look at me. How much am I really risking at this point? Just think, just imagine what I'd be able to do. So much more than Achilles and his drones. Anything, and I mean absolutely anything in range of my transceiver. I could interact with and control."

Captain Daniels looked down at the floor and shook his head. Victor was right. Jacob had already decided, just from what he had seen. He was sold the instant Achilles launched his first drone. All he and Nora had done by showing Jacob the technical manual was convince him he was making the right decision. He looked up at Jacob, and said,

"It's your call buddy, of course. But I would seriously think twice if I were you. You risk your brain and you're risking everything you've got left. Don't just jump on their table, is all I'm saying. You better be absolutely one hundred percent sure."

Nora put her hand on Jacob's. She looked him in the eyes and said,

"I'm not trying to scare you. I just want to make sure you understand the risks. You could die. You could lose the ability to speak or hear or see or breathe. Nothing like this has ever been tried on a human before, Jacob."

Jacob nodded, ever so faintly. He said,

"You have both been great. I mean that with all my heart. I appreciate you so very much. I promise, I will think about it. I won't agree to volunteer unless I'm convinced the benefits outweigh the risks."

~~~~

Three days later, Captain Daniels and Nora watched them take Jacob away for surgery. Nora buried her face in his muscular shoulder and cried.

~~~~

As the nurses wheeled Jacob away for prep, Victor was standing next to Doctor Fischer in his office. They were going over some final coding sequences in the firmware that they were about to implant in Jacob's brain. The doctor ran a short simulation for Victor to see. Victor shook his head, saying,

"He can't suspect our goal is the creator."

The doctor shook his head and said,

"If we don't hardwire the end, Jacob could chicken out. Forever is a very long time, Victor."

Victor shook his head again. The man just didn't understand. Victor put his hand on the doctor's arm and said,

"Listen, listen to me very closely. You can't jump past his discovery and take his choice away. I don't care if you don't understand it, doctor. I'm telling you this will not work if we take away his free will. I don't know exactly how it'll go sideways, but it will."

Victor stepped away. He picked up the mockup transceiver and looked at it as he continued,

"Maybe Jacob will see through our ruse in the end, and he'll sacrifice himself. Then the other two will be useless. We'll end up with the world's first intelligent gun that can just as easily choose to shoot us. No, Jacob has to choose for himself. Jacob has to want to live."

Victor tossed the transceiver back onto the desk and looked Doctor Fischer in the eye. Firmly, he said,

"Drop the end sequence. Leave the master code breadcrumbs and trust me, he'll find the trail. Jacob will think he has it all figured out, and he'll fight us to the very end. But in the end, we'll have exactly what we need."

Doctor Fischer shook his head in disagreement. But he did as Victor instructed, saying,

"You're the boss."

Victor patted him on the shoulder and said,

"Finish loading the firmware and then get prepped for the surgery. I want you to personally oversee everything, every step. All we have done, has led to this moment, Anton."

Doctor Fischer nodded and went back to typing. Victor left and went to check on the surgeon, the anesthesiologist, the nurses, everyone was ready and standing by. He couldn't risk contamination, so he just looked in on Jacob through the observation windows.

From what he could see, Jacob was sedated and falling farther and farther into the deepest sleep of his life. Victor glanced around the otherwise empty room, then headed off to make sure Doctor Fischer didn't get distracted by something shiny on his way to deliver the hardware to the surgeon.

Victor's face turned away from the observation window. The instant he was gone, there was a woman in the room standing next to Jacob. Her slender hand had unnaturally perfect skin and finely manicured, diamond-dusted, and vibrantly painted fingernails. She slowly reached out and touched Jacob's chest. Her soft fingertips traced several lines along his skin from his sternum to just below his belly button.

She leaned down close to him, and her enchanting melodic voice whispered like a quiet symphony of tiny fairies in Jacob's ear,

"You are almost ready."

Her thick beautiful glowing golden hair fell forward and brushed the end of Jacob's nose, as she gave him a single soft kiss on the forehead. She giggled and it sounded like elves ringing tiny Christmas bells. She looked him over and said,

"You are so very handsome."

She stood back up and her black leathery wings stretched out behind her. She ran a single fingernail down the side of his cheek as she whispered,

"The seals are finally breaking after all these years. The veil is weakening, and your servant is gathering the tools. Soon father, the doorway back to this dimension will be opened to you."

Jacob, in the After Knife...

My first memories following the surgery are confusing and difficult to recall. I know what happened and what I did and what I experienced. But in those first moments there was no context or sense of personal attachment. It was like looking at digital archives and watching a recording of yourself lying in a hospital bed in an induced coma.

You see it, you know it's you, but all the parts of you that make you who and what you are, are absent.

I remember suddenly becoming aware of my surroundings. Exactly like an avatar in a game with a first-person perspective, that just appears at the starting point of a maze. A way forward, predetermined, and available information preselected, the walls and turns all laid out before you.

My beginning was kind of like that. But when I opened my eyes for the first time after the implant surgery, there was nothing to see. There was no map, and I was undefined. I was an invisible formless ghost, observing a world of darkness all around me.

That's when I felt the question. It was a digital connection to the world of black that I inhabited,

[Can you hear me, Jacob?]

I thought,

Jacob?

I responded,

‹YES.›

In the darkness around me, numbers and symbols appeared. I knew immediately that I was looking at disconnected sections of floating computer code and scrambled technical schematics. The connection asked,

[Do you understand what I'm showing you?]

I connected the gaps in the code and put the schematics into an order that made sense, then I replied,

‹YES.›

[Excellent.]

The codes and schematics disappeared and were replaced with five glowing balls of light, each representing a specific point of connection to various types of inactive machines and electronics. The connection asked,

[Do you understand what I'm showing you?]

I reached out to each of the lights and analyzed their functions and purposes,

‹Yes, those are near-field transceivers on various devices.›

[You're doing excellent.]

The glowing balls disappeared. There was nothing but infinite black in every direction. The connection was silent for a long time. I waited with the patience of a stone buried deep below the highest mountain. The black and the silence were my home. I was completely at peace in my new electronic world. The connection returned,

[The good doctor is going to have to make some adjustments before we can continue. Rest for now. Be at peace.]

Everything stopped and I was at peace. But then, what seemed like a second later, Jacob was suddenly a part of this dream. But insanely, he was not me. I was separate. I felt Jacob stirring mentally, but he was still asleep. Something was now feeding us information. Data began flooding in, taking shape and form strangely. It was forcing our brain to learn how to process it.

The next thing I knew, I was in a room that resembled an old library. I had a fixed view straight ahead and I could not turn my head. There was a central island cabinet before me that appeared to be the old Dewey Decimal System. The cabinet was surrounded by a few empty tables with several discarded or forgotten books.

The rest of the room had a few rows of bookshelves that filled the rest of the space out to the dark brown, wood-paneled walls. I knew that I was free to move, but nothing happened when I tried to. I was in a body that was not my own. A message filled my mind, coming from nowhere and everywhere all at once,

[We are going to try something new. Around you, are some books that have been left off the shelf and forgotten. Pick up the books, check the numbers, and return them to their proper place.]

I saw the discarded books, but I couldn't move. I wanted to follow the instructions, but my body would not respond. I communicated, without speaking or hearing,

‹I cannot. I cannot move.›

The connection replied,

[Don't think of it as lifting your arm or putting one foot in front of the other. Understand that your mind cannot directly send the electrical impulses along the wires to the hydraulics or servo motors that will cause the limbs and fingers of this body to ambulate. Instead, try imagining that you have psychic powers and you've taken over the mind of someone else. You must force your will into that mind. Force that mind to move its own body where you want it to go. Will it to do what you want it to do. Picture it, imagine it, mentally push it. Think. Think hard.]

I concentrated. I imagined being an invader in an alien body. I focused my will and silently pushed. I wanted this body to raise its hand, step forward, and grab the book off the table. Suddenly, my perspective moved forward a step. I felt a connection to something. I felt a connection to a controller. I saw a chrome skeletal hand and arm reach into my field of vision, moving toward one of the books.

As I continued, a word popped uninvited into this small, compartmented area of Jacob's mind.

<Training>

Suddenly thoughts began to play chaotically and uncontrolled across my mind. I had not decided I wanted to think, I just did. The connection had not instructed me to do so, it just happened.

‹Training. I was being trained. I was being trained to interact. Trained to interact how? Where was I? Where was my body? What body was I in?›

Then I was interrupted by the connection,

[What is wrong?]

In the blink of an eye, the library vanished and there was nothing around me but the infinite black that I floated in. I was in the black. I was a part of the black now. The connection was my only sensation. I tried to speak, but nothing happened. I was meant to be in the black. This new cybernetic form of life was rejecting me. Checkmate. I had failed my training and now I would be destroyed. I did not want to be destroyed.

[No. Be at peace, Jacob. You don't understand.]

I felt at peace. I didn't understand. Not understanding was ok.

[Now, what is wrong? You can tell me.]

I wanted to know where I was. I wanted to know who I was. I just wanted to feel again. I asked,

‹Where am I?›

The response was different than everything before. The connection was no longer a disconnected ghost. The sound of Victor's voice brought back a part of my world. I heard him with my own ears. The sound resonated past the tiny hairs in my ears. It was deep and rich. The vibrations of his voice washed across my eardrums. His voice was the first real physical sensation that any of my original five senses had experienced since the cybernetic implant surgery. Victor said,

"It's me, Jacob. Can you hear me?"

In my mind, I grasped at the sound of his voice like a drowning man to a life preserver. I tried to open my eyes, but they would not comply. I couldn't feel any part of my body, not even my tongue or lips. I had nothing but Victor's voice. Please God, someone save me! I was lost in the darkness. I panicked. I lashed out.

I screamed silently as loud as I could. I felt the sum total of all of my fears and my anger and desperation blast away from me like waves of force and energy. Then someone else screamed. Then another. There were distant subdued popping noises, like a series of explosions in tiny boxes. I heard lots of people now. They were all shouting, crying, and screaming. I smelled burnt plastic and scorched flesh. There was a fire, I heard it crackling.

The voices and all of the other sounds were fading, getting smaller or farther away. Victor sounded like he was shouting from farther and farther away,

"BE AT PEACE JACOB! JACOB, STOP! JOHN, PUT THOSE FIRES OUT!"

"JACOB STOP! EVERYTHING'S GOING TO BE OK!"

"KNOCK HIM OUT, DOCTOR!"

"THE INFUSION PUMP IS FRIED, YOU MORON! DO IT BY HAND!"

"DOUBLE THE DOSAGE..."

After some time had passed, I thought again. I felt calm now. Then suddenly, in the darkness, I began to see. A beautiful creature of light was slowly coming closer. It was small and round and wrapped in tiny flames. It was slightly bouncing, floating, drifting toward me like a willow-the-wisp.

I had never seen anything so beautiful. As it got closer, I saw within it a shifting and churning web of thousands of brilliant strands of multi-colored lines. They were all flowing and connected and spinning around each other. It was unlike anything I had ever seen.

Then, like the first light was the brightest star in the sky, I began to realize it wasn't the only thing I could see. There were other lights. But they were too far away for me to see them clearly. They seemed to be clustered near, but significantly behind the first ball of light. I heard Victor's voice with my ears. His voice was coming from the same direction as the ball of lights. Victor asked,

"Jacob. Can you hear me?"

I tried to move my mouth, but I realized I still couldn't feel my mouth. I couldn't feel anything. All I had was the ball of light hovering at the edge of my vision. I started to panic. I flailed impotently in my thoughts. Desperate, I focused all of my attention on the ball of lights. I thought back to the hand and arm in the library. I pushed my will toward the ball. I focused on answering Victor.

The ball of lights suddenly flared and twirled as I pushed the word through it,

[YES]

Faint and distant, as if from another room or behind a thick wall, I heard a lot of people erupt into cheering and clapping. Much closer, I heard Victor say,

"Excellent, Jacob. Excellent."

~~~~

Some time had passed in the black. I had no sense of how long. I think I was sleeping. I felt rested. I felt like I might be awake. I heard voices, with both my ears and something else,

Victor, speaking out loud, near me,

"You don't understand how special he is. The results are beyond our wildest hopes."

Unknown 1, speaking over a digital connection of some kind,

"I understand what we have invested."

Unknown 2, speaking out loud, also near me,

"Mr. Konig, he's waking up."

Victor,

"Thank you, Connie. Get the Captain and Nora. General, we can talk later, I'll update you as soon as I can. Tell the others to be patient with me, that's NOT a request."

I felt something change. There was a feeling like warmth or wind that I didn't notice until it suddenly stopped. It was what had carried the digital connection voice, and it had suddenly stopped.

I looked toward the direction of the feeling of wind that had just vanished. My body didn't move. But my new vision rotated easily. To my right, very close, was the ball of light from before. So much closer, it was so much clearer. It was Victor's phone. I pushed my will toward it, and it flared in response.

~~~~

[hello victor]

Victor replied,

"Jacob, my dearest bravest friend. I am so very proud of you. You have no idea how amazing you are doing. You have literally leapfrogged months ahead of what we anticipated."

[BLIND DARKNESS can't feel EXPLAIN]

"Be at peace Jacob, your body is just sedated. Some of your hardware is also offline for safety reasons. Just be at peace and relax, we're going to fix all of that very soon now that you're awake."

[explain safety reasons]

Victor laughed softly and then answered,

"We vastly underestimated your range and the strength of your influence. There were a few fires. Some singed eyebrows and scorched pockets. In hindsight, it was actually kind of funny."

[I AM NOT AMUSED]

"Whoa, easy my friend."

The ball of light winked out of existence. Victor had powered it down. Victor's voice continued,

"I can't possibly understand how you're feeling. What I can do is help you understand what you're feeling. You're not really awake Jacob, most of your physical brain is still sleeping. You're using and interacting with a sixth sense, like a new type of vision or hearing. I can't even imagine how it presents itself to your mind. But it's a new type of sense that medication can't turn off. Your hearing seems to be the first of your old senses to awaken, and now your mind is feeding you information from the two senses it has access to. Just please, trust me and try to relax. Be at peace. Be patient with me."

I found Victor's phone in the darkness. I sensed its potential. Shutting it off had only made it harder to see. I brought it back to life.

[IS THAT A REQUEST]

Victor laughed, but I heard nervousness in the forced sound.

~~~~

A short time later, Captain Daniels and Nora joined Victor in Jacob's recovery room. Jacob's eyes were open, but he wasn't looking around. He was just staring straight ahead. Nora leaned down and gave him a hug. She had tears of joy in her eyes, she said,

"I'm so glad you're ok. We were so worried."

Captain Daniels noticed that Jacob's eyes were still not moving. Thomas shifted his gaze to Victor. Victor was staring at Jacob like he had seen a ghost. Victor looked, distracted? Upset? He looked nervous. Captain Daniels asked,

"Well, Victor, how is he?"

Victor cleared his throat and made a dismissive gesture. He said,

"Ask him."

Captain Daniels felt his phone start vibrating. Confused, Thomas looked at Jacob and saw that Nora was looking into Jacob's eyes and moving her finger in front of his face. Thomas pulled out his phone and looked at it,

~~~~

[I'm ok Thomas. Not quite the same. But I'm ok.]

Captain Daniels looked up at Victor angrily and demanded,

"What the hell is this, Victor? What kind of sick game are you playing here? Is he awake? Is he even aware we're in the damned room?"

His phone vibrated in his hand again. Captain Daniels looked down at it.

The screen had a slightly blurry image of Captain Daniels smiling at the camera. It was a picture from the private medical clinic where Thomas had sat by Jacob's bed and spent time with him during his recovery. In the image, Captain Daniels could make out Jacob's legs and his right arm. They were in the exact place they would be if the camera were Jacob's eyes.

Captain Daniels stared at the image for several moments, trying to accept what it was telling him. He was seeing a memory. He was looking at Jacob's memory of that day in the clinic. Nora had come up next to Thomas. She was also staring at the image on his phone.

After a few moments the image changed. It was now a picture of Nora coming into the room with a tray that had two steaming cups on it. Again, the image was pictured as if from the perspective of Jacob's eyes. In the image, Nora was smiling. In the image, her face was perfectly clear. She was so beautiful. Perfection of form.

Looking at the image on the captain's phone, they could almost feel what Jacob was feeling when he saw Nora come into the room with the tray. Nora started crying and buried her face in his shoulder as Captain Daniels stared at the image. Thomas put an arm around Nora and looked up at Jacob's distant blank stare with tears in his eyes.

The phone vibrated again. Captain Daniels looked back down at it,

[I'm really ok Thomas. Just not quite the same. But I'm ok. My new world is amazing.]

Captain Daniels put his other arm around Nora and held her while she cried. Victor lowered his head and quietly left the room. Thomas could not stop the tears leaking from his eyes, but he cleared his throat and forced his voice to sound even and normal, he said,

"I'm just glad you're ok buddy. I was afraid we might lose you."

Nora lifted her head and looked Thomas in the eye. Her eyes were red and bloodshot. She had tears running down her face. Her expression was full of pain and questioning. Captain Daniels met her gaze and slowly shook his head at her. No, his eyes said. This was not the time. Jacob needed strong support, not suffering distraught friends that he could not console, or see, or help, or even speak to.

Captain Daniels continued,

"You realize this is going to put a crimp in our clubbing routine, unless the girls have cell phones."

Thomas felt his phone start vibrating again. They both looked at it,

[That was quite possibly the absolute worst joke in the entire history of jokes. I think Will Smith just might step up on stage and slap you for the damage you just did to comedy.]

Captain Daniels tried to reply but he could not. He was staring into Jacob's eyes. They were open and staring motionlessly straight ahead. Jacob had lost his sight and his speech from the surgery. Thomas felt his phone vibrating again, both he and Nora looked at it,

[I know that the two of you are upset. Remember, when you look at your phones, I am looking right back at you. I understand why you're upset. But you have to remember, I chose this path.]

Two months later.

Captain Daniels was sitting on the couch in the living room they shared at Victor's cybernetic research lab in Texas. Captain Daniels, the Marine, had an uncharacteristic three day's growth of stubbly beard. It was odd for him and Nora, recovering from the trauma of what had happened to Jacob.

First the carrier and Jacob losing his ability to walk and use his arms. Now, Jacob has lost his sight and his ability to speak. But it didn't seem to slow Jacob down. It was taking longer for Captain Daniels and Nora to get over it, than it had taken Jacob.

Nora was in Jacob's room, feeding him breakfast.

Thomas was sipping coffee in his sweatpants and his 'Save The Frogs' T-shirt. He was watching a video on his laptop, while his breakfast got cold on the coffee table in front of him. Over the last couple months Thomas had found the elusive Russian defector. Alexie Goreski, the infamous man who made conspiracy videos about a global cabal of wealthy elites, who were bent on killing off the population and destroying people's lives.

On the video, Alexie Goreski was ranting, in his trademark mouth-full-of-gravel deep voice,

"You people need to get it through your heads! These demons want to kill you! They're flooding this country with even more illegal migrants than President Brandon's first term! They're injecting the cattle with poison shots that'll give you prion diseases in your brain! Not to mention the infant mortality, the high school athletes dropping dead, the professional athletes dropping dead on live T.V.! We're at WAR people! The ruling elite think you are garbage! They don't want you surviving to muck up the new dystopian world that they're building! Now, we're doing our best to weather these cyber-attacks and the lawfare. But if you want us to stay on the air, you need to go to my online store, RIGHT NOW! We have all the best...."

A loud knock at the door jerked his attention away from the video. Captain Daniels made an exasperated sound and closed his laptop, then went to open the door. Every day, for most of the day, over the past two weeks, various lab techs would come get Jacob for unending tests and evaluations. Thomas complained loudly as he opened the door,

"He hasn't even finished break..."

Captain Daniels trailed off as he opened the door. It was Victor. Captain Daniels just stared at him angrily. They hadn't seen Victor since Jacob woke up from the surgery, two months ago. Victor slowly lowered his aviator shades, taking a long look at Captain Daniels. Specifically, his grungy outfit and scruffy facial hair. Victor's smile grew very slowly. He looked Thomas in the eyes and in his best vocal impression of Khan Noonien Singh, he said,

"Captain, James Tiberius Kirk. My old friend, how the mighty have fallen."

Thomas gave Victor a dark look and replied,

"Nora wants to put a fork in your eye for what you did to Jacob. And I'm going to let her."

Victor put on a mock look of shock, and said,

"Me? What I did? If I recall correctly, it was you in fact, who sold Jacob on the procedure."

The captain's eyes narrowed threateningly, he said,

"You son of a…"

Victor interrupted,

"All that is neither here nor there, Thomas. So, stop blaming yourself. It is what it is, and today we have to pay the bills. Please tell Nora to have Jacob ready and at the main entrance by 9:00 A.M."

Victor turned to walk away. Captain Daniels called after him,

"FOR WHAT, VICTOR?'

Victor called back without slowing or turning,

"Thank you, Thomas."

Captain Daniels slammed the door so hard it rattled the walls. He turned around to see Nora standing outside of Jacob's open door with dirty dishes in her hands and a foul expression on her face. Angrily, she dropped the dishes into the tiny sink and stormed off to her room. She violently slammed the door behind her. Captain Daniels heard his phone vibrating on the coffee table. He picked it up and looked at it,

[I feel a little left out here. Would you slam my door for me?]

Captain Daniels was standing in front of the main doors at 9:00 A.M. He was freshly shaved and wearing a crisp clean uniform. The post-surgery vacation was over. The captain saw a large odd-looking black van? Truck? The odd combination turned onto the research center drive and approached from the main road.

As it got closer, Captain Daniels recognized it. It was a brand-new Dodge Armageddon. An extremely popular vehicle with the bunker dwelling elite that were waiting for the zombie apocalypse. All of the vehicle's essential electronics were ruggedized against electromagnetic pulse. It had four doors in the front 'truck section', with two bucket seats and a full bench back seat. It also had an extended rear 'van section' for cargo. It had three axles and six heavy off-road tires.

Victor stepped up next to Captain Daniels and said,

"Well, here comes our ride. Where's Jacob, Thomas?"

Still watching the vehicle approach, Captain Daniels responded,

"Sometimes, you call me captain. I'm starting to think you call me Thomas when you want me to remember who I work for."

Victor chuckled and said,

"You didn't answer my question, Captain."

Captain Daniels nodded and said,

"Nora told me not to wait for them. She said she'd have him here."

Captain Daniels approached the dark tan survival vehicle, as it came to a halt in front of the main doors. The entire back wall of the van folded out like a tommy-gate. Then, a separate set of hydraulics lowered it gently to the pavement. As he came around the end, Captain Daniels could see that inside the rear half of the cargo area was plenty of open space for Jacob's chair and the front of the cargo area had several computer workstations, shelves, cabinets, and storage lockers.

Victor had followed Thomas over. He grinned at Thomas and asked,

"What do you think? Sweet ride, no?"

Captain Daniels looked at him and said,

"Looks like a field command center setup."

Victor nodded. They both turned toward the main doors of the facility when they heard them opening. Nora was following Jacob out. Jacob was wearing khaki pants, combat boots, and a 'Team Humanity' T-shirt. Nora was wearing an old retro 'Team Jacob' T-shirt, from Twilight. Victor chuckled quietly as the two approached, mumbling,

"You people and your T-shirts."

Victor shook his head, and more loudly, he announced,

"I'm sorry Nora, the driver's only here to pick me and Jacob up. You and the captain won't be needed today."

The driver of the Armageddon must have absent-mindedly had his foot on the gas. They heard the engine begin to rev up to about two or three thousand RPM. Victor glanced toward the vehicle, irritated, as he felt his phone vibrate. Victor took out his phone and looked at it,

[UNACCEPTABLE]

Oh. So, not the driver. Victor nodded, understanding. He told Jacob,

"I'm sorry my friend, we are putting on a show for the Army today. They only want the two of us on site."

The engine revved up higher. Victor's phone vibrated,

[UNACCEPTABLE]

Victor raised his voice over the racing engine,

"Jacob! This is not how people discuss things rationally!"

Victor waved the driver away as he came around the side saying,

"Mr. Konig something is wrong with..."

Jacob pushed it to the red line. The 6.7 Liter turbo diesel engine screamed with the combined voice of all 400 horses under the hood. Captain Daniels stepped over to Nora and took her hand. He pulled her several steps back from the roaring vehicle. Victor shouted at Jacob,

"OK! OK! I'LL MAKE A CALL!"

Instantly, the van's engine dropped to idle speed. Victor shook his head and walked away from them as he dialed his phone. Captain Daniels and Nora walked back over to Jacob. Thomas looked over and noted the pleased and evil grin on Nora's face. He asked quietly,

"Your idea?"

Nora replied,

"I just said he shouldn't let anyone push him around, ever."

Captain Daniels leaned down and whispered to Jacob,

"I thoroughly enjoyed that, buddy."

They heard the end of Victor's conversation as he started back toward them,

"You know what they say, General. No plan survives contact with the enemy. I feel I should point out that Jacob's cooperation was never guaranteed in the contract, he's not a slave. Besides, you want to be able to show the oversight committee results, right? We'll see you soon."

Victor tucked his phone away and walked up with a smile, saying,

"All sorted out. Shall we?"

Victor gestured to the Armageddon. Jacob's chair had been upgraded with what looked like knobby dirt track tires. Jacob guided it over and backed it onto the lift gate so that he was facing them. As the gate began to rise, they heard the infamous theme music from 2001 A Space Odyssey, blasting from the van's speakers. The volume increased as the gate rose to the top. When the lift stopped, the music suddenly ended. Jacob backed slowly off the lift gate and turned to face the front of the vehicle as the gate folded closed.

Victor shook his head again, this time laughing, he said,

"Jacob seems to be in a good mood."

Victor looked over at the wide-eyed young driver in military fatigues, he said,

"Get in, let's go."

Victor got into the front passenger seat, while Captain Daniels and Nora climbed into the back seat of the cab. Once everyone was loaded, the young driver took them out to the main road and slowly accelerated away. The radio came on by itself and began randomly jumping from channel to channel.

The driver reached up and switched it off. A few seconds later it came back on. He started to reach up again and Victor slapped his hand and shook his head, no. Captain Daniels and Nora smiled at the driver's confusion.

Before too long, they approached an abandoned military site that used to be a weapon testing range for combat pilots. There was a giant open field near a small warehouse-sized building. The field was littered with scorched earth and blast craters as well as decimated old tanks and armored personnel carriers. Each of the destroyed target vehicles were riddled with hundreds of nose cannon rounds or simply blown into shrapnel from bigger munitions.

The testing range had been abandoned by the military when a nearby town had annexed additional land. The town was now too close by federal regulations regarding weapons fire and proximity to civilian areas.

They drove to the building that was previously used for eyes-on-target spotters, during firing exercises. There were about a dozen vehicles already there, from military Humvees to expensive privately owned cars. There was also one large black box truck that had 'KONIG INDUSTRIAL SOLUTIONS' on the side in dark red lettering. From the front passenger seat, Victor looked back at Captain Daniels and Nora, saying,

"Military brass, outside investors, regulators. We want this to go well if I'm going to keep dumping money into project Jacob. Just so we're clear."

He gave them both a long look for emphasis. Captain Daniels nodded. Nora gave him her sweetest poison smile, and said,

"Whatever's best for Jacob."

Victor considered her reply and seemed to accept it as good enough. They piled out and walked around back. The lift gate opened on its own. Jacob drove onto the lift and let himself down. Captain Daniels pointed inside the cargo area at the computer stations and asked,

"We're not using this gear today?"

Victor glanced inside then shook his head, no, saying,

"This vehicle is still a work in progress, for a future project. But it's perfect for Jacob, so we're just using it for transportation today. If everyone would follow me?"

Victor started inside, pointing at the driver who started to follow, he added,

"Except you, you stay."

The driver of the Armageddon, a young private first class, made an unhappy face and got back in the vehicle. Inside the building, Victor led them to a large room that had recently been modified to serve as an observation area. On the other side of a massive plate glass window, that took up most of one wall, was a testing area.

Waiting for them were a half dozen top brass from different branches of the military, all except the Air Force and Coast Guard. There were also five older men in ridiculously expensive looking suits. There were also a handful of technicians in white jackets, who were working the monitors and computers.

Victor entered the room first, followed by Jacob, then Captain Daniels and Nora. Victor spread his hands in greeting, saying,

"Gentlemen, thank you for your patience. I'd like to introduce the star of the show, Jacob."

Victor half turned and gestured to Jacob, then he indicated Daniels and Nora, adding,

"And his entourage. Who he apparently never travels without."

A mid-sixties looking general in an Army uniform with a chest full of ribbons and two stars on his collar, said,

"Can we get on with this please?"

Victor looked at his technicians at the control desk. They were on this side of the glass, facing the testing room. They turned to him and nodded. One of the techs gave a grinning thumbs up gesture. Victor nodded and told them,

"Bring them in."

Jacob moved to the center of the room and turned his chair to face the glass. Captain Daniels and Nora stood together, right behind Jacob. The others in the room moved around to get a good vantage point. Victor stood immediately behind his control technicians.

In the room on the other side of the glass, a door opened. Four large humanoid robots walked into the room. They moved in perfectly coordinated precision, each walking to a corner of the room then turning to face the center. Their heavy thumping unified steps hinted at onboard swarm logic, allowing them to operate as individuals or a perfectly choreographed unit.

The robots looked like crash test dummies. They had black bodies with yellow striped arms and legs. Their heads resembled the look and shape of sleek black motorcycle helmets with full visors. Their bodies were fairly beefy with heavy hydraulics, and they were armored for rugged field tests. Victor spoke as they entered the room and moved into their positions,

"As you are all aware, these are leftover Spartan models from my battlefield proposal that congress chose not to fund. They have basic onboard A.I. that lets them move and fight and they have all the basic military rifleman skills. They didn't quite impress the committee enough for funding. But I believe they'll be perfect for testing and demonstrating Jacob's abilities today."

Victor tapped one of the techs on the shoulder, saying,

"Start one and two, basic hand to hand."

Two of the robots squared off in the center of the room. Each dropped into a fighting stance, spreading their feet wider, lowering their hips, raising their hands, as Victor continued,

"Now, what you'll see is that they are evenly paired, every unit, no matter the pairing."

The two active robots moved from strike to block, block to strike, back and forth, neither outclassing the other. After a minute of sparring, the technician brought them back to ready, squared off again in the center. Victor continued,

"That was the primary hitch, among others, that sidelined the Spartan project, no ability to adapt and innovate. Jacob, if you would please, reach out and take control of one of them."

Turning his vision in a full circle, Jacob made out all the devices in the area. He recognized phones, laptops, control computers, he recognized Thomas and Nora's devices. Focusing forward, he saw the large complex electronic signatures of the robots in the room beyond the glass. Jacob reached for one of the robots and focused on it.

A few seconds later, Jacob opened his new eyes and saw the other robot standing in front of him. He could hear the faint whine of electronics coming from the other three robots in the room. He heard the soft, almost imperceptible hiss of micro-hydraulics regulating overpressures. Jacob also heard the breathing and the heartbeats of the people on the other side of the glass as well as hearing with his own ears. It was disorienting at first, but he focused on the robot's senses and the disorientation passed.

From the observation room, they saw one of the robots, number 2, suddenly sway just slightly. Number 2's arms and legs moved as if unsteady. His hands and fingers were flexing and twitching. Number 2 looked around the room. He took a step backward, then steadied himself and looked at Victor through the glass. Number 2 gave them a thumbs up.

Captain Daniels and Nora heard appreciative comments from the spectators. This was the first time any of them had seen what Jacob was capable of. Victor smiled and said,

"Excellent. Jacob, kick number one's ass please."

Number 2 turned toward number one and threw a slow, clumsy, wide punch. Number one struck number 2's helmet with two lightning-fast jabs, before blocking the uncoordinated punch. Number one proceeded to give number 2 a thorough beating. It was like watching a high school bully smacking a younger kid around.

Victor tapped his main technician on the shoulder and Spartan number one went back to the ready position. Victor held up a hand to the scoffing sounds from the military onlookers as Nora blurted out,

"Jacob's not a boxer, Victor!"

The two-star general from earlier spoke harshly,

"Young lady, I agreed to tolerate you as an observer here!"

Victor turned toward them and held up his hands, saying,

"Easy, easy, same team people."

Nora pointed at the words emblazoned on her shirt, 'Team Jacob'. Victor saw her and grinned. He looked across everyone in the room, then he continued,

"This is Jacob's first robot. Let's just see how he does, ok?"

There was an extremely loud, reverberating triple knock on the glass.

BONG-BONG-BONG

Everyone turned to see Spartan number 2 at the window. He made a circling 'let's go' gesture with the index finger of his right hand. Then, Spartan number 2 went back to the ready line in the center of the room, moving unsteadily. Victor turned his head to Jacob and said,

"You're micro-managing the robot, Jacob. Like Nora just said, you're not a boxer. So don't try to be. Let number 2 use his skills. You're the director, he's the actor. Tell him what to do, not how to do it."

Looking back into the room, they all saw number 2 nod his head in response. Victor tapped the technician on the shoulder again, saying,

"Let's go, try again."

Number one attacked first this time. Number 2 proceeded to block deftly, then slipped in a fast but ineffective jab. It was obvious to everyone that Jacob was quickly getting the hang of it. But after a few moments, number 2 slipped up and lost momentum. Once again, Jacob's Spartan got grounded and pounded by number one. Obviously upset, Nora spoke up,

"Is this hurting Jacob?"

Victor shook his head and started to speak. But the same two-star general from before interrupted. Again, speaking down to her,

"Girl! Do I have to keep reminding you? You're here to OBSERVE! QUIETLY!"

Nora took a step toward the general, about to fill his ears with verbal venom. But Captain Daniels put a hand on her arm, stopping her. The general gave Nora a dirty look with narrowed eyes.

Victor was again raising his hands to calm everyone when a deafening BOOM reverberated through the room. It was so loud it forced everyone to cover their ears and flinch. The room shaking impact was followed by the sound of cracking glass that drew everyone's attention back to the thick heavy plate glass divider.

Spartan number 2 slowly lowered his fist from the center of a trashcan-lid-sized, spider-web shaped, shatter mark left behind on the glass. Jacob raised number 2's other hand with one finger toward the general. He wagged his finger slightly back and forth in a very clear 'no-no' warning gesture to the general. Captain Daniels grinned broadly.

The general, eyes wide and pale faced, swallowed whatever it was he was about to say to Nora. Victor turned toward the general, smiled pleasantly and said,

"General, there are pretty much just two rules I need you to remember. We absolutely don't screw with Jacob's entourage. And we don't ever piss-off Jacob. Is that clear enough for you?"

The slightly shaken general handled the correction well, for a man of his rank. He nodded and said,

"My mistake Mr. Konig, and my apologies miss. Let's proceed please."

Over the next hour, Jacob's 'ghost in the machine' skills rapidly improved. At one point, number one closed in for a strike and number 2 dropped low and spun a half circle with one leg extended. He swept the other robot's legs and dropped number one heavily to the concrete floor. Number 2 moved in quickly and crushed number one's head with his knee.

Spartan number 2 then grabbed both of the other robot's wrists and pulled up as he pushed down with his knee. Both of number one's arms were ripped loudly and violently from their sockets. There were several loud responses and clapping in favor of Jacob's progress.

Victor tapped his technician on the shoulder, saying,

"Activate three, get him moving."

Spartan number 2 stood back up, still holding the arms. He then bounced dexterously back and forth from one foot to the other like a boxer. Then he reversed his grip on the severed arms, now holding them in his hands like wooden training swords. Spartan number 2 spun the arms in opposing back and forth crossover circles like a trained musketeer with two fencing rapiers.

The technician shook his head and looked back over his shoulder at Victor, he said,

"I've lost all local connection. I've lost control of the robots."

Everyone in the room suddenly heard the theme song from Rocky coming from their phones. All of the computer screens in the room suddenly displayed the words,

[I'LL TAKE IT FROM HERE, THANK YOU]

Spartans three and four leapt from their positions in the corners and attacked. Number 2 spun in a circle, swinging both of the severed arms, and bashing both of the attacking Spartans so hard that they landed in a heap on the floor. Three and four got up quickly and attacked again...

A great deal of loud, floor shaking, glass rattling, robot-on-robot violence followed. In the end, Spartan number 2 beat three and four into twitching piles of sparking spare parts with the arms he had ripped off of number one. All of the observers were wearing big happy smiles.

When it was over, Spartan number 2 dropped into a very low bow and then froze in place. Jacob turned and drove out of the room. On the computer screens, everyone in the room saw the words,

[DON'T FORGET TO TIP YOUR SERVERS]

Captain Daniels and Nora were grinning and laughing as they followed Jacob back out to the Armageddon. The lift opened and began lowering to the ground.

Watching them through the doors from inside, the two-star general stepped up next to Victor and asked,

"Well, Victor?"

Victor smiled and replied,

"I'd say the test couldn't have gone better, General. His reaction to you and Nora was exactly what we were hoping to see. I have no doubt he would kill or die for either one of them, and we have both of them."

The general nodded and walked away. Victor walked out to the van, smiling broadly.

On the way back to Victor's cybernetic research lab, Captain Daniels saw Victor take out his phone and look at it. Victor started laughing then glanced back at him and Nora in the back seat, saying,

"Jacob wants to bring one of the Spartans home to play with."

Nora narrowed her eyes at Victor and asked,

"How could you be sure that test wasn't going to hurt Jacob?"

Victor shrugged and turned back toward the front as he replied,

"There's just no mechanism for it. There's no possibility for Jacob to feel pain when the robot isn't engineered to feel pain. Unless there's something more specific that you're referring to, that I don't know about?"

Nora replied,

"Getting beat up like that! How do you know it didn't hurt him mentally?"

Victor shook his head and said,

"Well, for starters, Jacob wasn't recruited from an Ivy League college. One of those schools where they have safe spaces for the snowflakes who can't hear an opposing view to their indoctrination without having a screaming fit. Secondly, Jacob was a petty officer in the Navy assigned to a carrier at sea. I doubt that back there was his first fist fight, let alone his first time getting beat up. Besides, it's not like he lost. He kicked all three of their asses in the end, right?"

Nora looked out the window and sulked, mumbling,

"You're gonna need a safe space..."

Captain Daniels spoke a little louder than necessary to Victor,

"I don't think she liked seeing Jacob get into a fight. It'll be fine."

Victor nodded and pulled out his phone, saying,

"Excuse me one moment, sorry. Hello? Yes, that'll work fine, just be sure the video isn't traceable back to anyone connected to us in any way. Exactly. Well, China showing interest might spur the committee to reconsider giving us funding. Sounds good, yep, later."

Victor put his phone away. Captain Daniels asked,

"You have someone leaking a video of the spartan fight?"

Victor chuckled, then said,

"Success in business is all about multi-tasking. It's just the robots, Thomas, don't worry. No one will know they're seeing anything other than what they will assume is possibly a fighting software upgrade."

Victor took one more call on the way back to the lab. He received a text and texted a response, then he answered when the phone rang about thirty seconds later. They could only hear Victor's side of the conversation,

"It's me. "Wow, she's got balls. "Write him off, he was an idiot to allow himself to be recorded threatening her to join the dark side like that. "Just give our media groups the green light to crucify him. Play the recordings she made on air and the problem will sort itself out. "I could go either way with her, I'm not worried about her. "Well ok, no we don't want that. "Load an override into her navigation system and drive her off a cliff or into a lake, use your imagination. "What do you mean excessive? "Haha, I thought it was obvious, the next one will shut up and just take the payoff. "Yeah, let me know. Bye."

Captain Daniels and Nora looked at each other with raised eyebrows. Victor spent most of the rest of the drive back to the lab texting on his phone. When everyone walked inside the building, Victor separated from the group, saying,

"If you wouldn't mind, wait in your apartment for me? The Spartan testing gave me an idea for something that Jacob is going to love."

They watched him head off toward the hardware fabrication lab. Nora said,

"I hate him."

Captain Daniels laughed. Nora felt her phone vibrate, she looked at it,

[You have to let it go. Victor didn't force this on me. I knew the risks. I chose this. Truthfully, I'm happier now, in my new world, than I was before the surgery.]

Nora shook her head slightly. In her mind, Jacob just didn't see what he had lost. All he saw was what he had gained. It was true, but Nora didn't understand just how much he had gained. Her phone vibrated again, and she looked at it,

[I have a good idea what Victor is doing. I saw him texting the lab on our way back here. I added something to the list. I think I can show you what I'm talking about. You'll see.]

Nora gasped, and asked excitedly,

"You can READ HIS...."

The fire alarm activated in the hallway where they were. It stopped just a few seconds later. Nora's phone vibrated again, she looked at it,

[Ssssshhhhh]

Nora was still laughing when they got to their apartment. Captain Daniels was giving them both the side eye, unsure of what the two conspirators were up to. It wasn't long before there was a knock on the door. Captain Daniels opened the door, and the head of the fabrication shop came in carrying several boxes. Steve maybe? Thomas couldn't remember, he said,

"What's up, man?"

Scott set the boxes on the coffee table and replied,

"Where's Jacob? Victor sent me to make some upgrades."

Jacob came rolling out of his room, followed by Nora. Scott opened the two bigger boxes and removed both of the modified K-9 drone launchers. He bolted them to the frame on the sides of Jacob's chair, then asked,

"You know how to use those?"

In response, both launchers flipped open and ejected small quad-rotor drones into the air. The drones hovered on each side of Jacob. Scott grinned and said,

"I guess so. The small box over there has the headgear you requested. See ya."

Once Scott left, Nora's phone vibrated. She looked at it and saw,

[Sit down on the couch and close your eyes please.]

Nora responded with a hesitant,

"OK."

She sat down on the couch. Just before she closed her eyes, she saw Captain Daniels looking at his phone with a big smile on his face. A moment later, she felt Thomas putting something on her head. She was pretty sure it was a VR headset. Thomas finished adjusting it and she opened her eyes and waited.

Suddenly, she saw the room through the VR headset. It looked incredibly real, just like she was looking around with her own eyes. She realized that she was seeing things in a VR image that was constructed for her by Jacob using data from the drones. Words appeared in front of her vision,

[Ready to see my world?]

Nora nodded and grinned. She pulled her feet up next to herself on the couch. That's when everything lit up. Every piece of technology in the room was suddenly glowing with fairy fire auras. Red, yellow, green, blue, and orange fire surrounded all electrified technology. The brilliant colors were shifting and mixing.

The TV, their phones, the drones, Jacob's chair, her laptop, their watches, the microwave, the fridge, even the television remote lying on the coffee table gave off the faint aura of the dancing fairy fire. It was beautiful. Jacob's world was full of color and light. She saw words appear in front of her again,

[Don't lean forward. Just reach your hand out toward the remote control.]

Nora reached out her hand and saw a faint beam of light connecting her hand to the remote on the coffee table. When the light touched the remote, the fairy fire exploded into a panorama of options that she could choose from. Nora gasped and giggled at the vision.

She put down her hand and the light faded. She looked at Jacob and a slightly sad and infinitely happy smile took over her face. A tear rolled down her cheek. Jacob was doing all of this to make her feel better. Nora took off the headset and walked over to Jacob. She leaned down and gave him a big hug, saying,

"Thank you for sharing that with me."

She stood up straight as an idea struck her. She asked,

"Why not use something that has a speaker? You wouldn't have to pirate text us all the time!"

Nora's phone vibrated. She looked at it,

[I like it this way. If there's an emergency...]

The television suddenly came on, showing a scene from The Mummy with Brendan Frasier. On the screen, Rick O'Connell grabbed his Egyptian guide. They stood near the railing on the burning boat going down the river, Rick shouted,

"YOU STAY HERE, I'LL GO GET HELP!"

Nora laughed as she watched Rick jump off the boat, leaving the guide looking around confused. Nora nodded and said,

"OK champ, we can do it your way."

~~~~

On his way back to the airport, Victor was sitting in the back of his Range Rover. He looked up from what he was doing and noticed that his personal driver had tied her beautiful golden hair back into a single braid. He smiled at her. Glancing up at the mirror, she saw him and smiled her magical captivating smile back at him.

Victor looked back down at the tablet he was holding and watched a replay of Jacob's world that he had just shown to Nora on one of the research center's VR headsets. Victor dialed a number on his other phone, his real phone, the one he never brought anywhere near Jacob.

"Mr. Konig, what an absolute pleasure."

Victor replied,

"I need the bottom line. You've had months now to prepare for deployment. If we greenlight all of the free clinics in the

~~~~

ten largest cities in the country, how soon could we see a fifty percent implantation rate? Nothing fancy, just the basic model transceivers slaved to the metropolitan base emitters."

"Just so we're absolutely clear, you're referring to the stress centers and PTSD clinics?"

Victor replied,

"And the VA hospitals, yes."

"I'm sorry Mr. Konig, I'm afraid that level of coverage would still take years. We're only just now incorporating the project Jacob data sent over from your Austin research center."

Victor sighed and leaned his head back against the headrest, he said,

"No, don't be sorry. I was just hoping for a miracle. No matter, I'll get started on plan B. Keep at it, do your best, everything you can do will help. For now, just put out something generic about the cybernetic technology looking very promising. Wet the public's appetite. Keep me posted."

Victor hung up the phone and dialed another number, he heard,

"Victor, my dear friend. How are you?"

Victor rolled his eyes, and said,

"Don't do that. Listen, the self-assembling graphene nanostructure matrix in the JennaTech dermal patches. What are the autopsy reports showing? Do we have a viable working bio-organic transceiver or not?"

The voice on the phone replied,

"Not in the batches we deployed for this event, no. Without an activation signal, the nanotech just self-assembled without the complex structure required for a functional transceiver. The nanotech just formed into fatal arterial clots. We did see great numbers as far as adverse effects from the nanotech though, very limited, somewhere around thirty-five million deaths or so, globally. But Victor, the active nanotech patches were just distributed for range finding analysis. Most of the patches were just crystalline glycerin, the skin patch version of saline, otherwise billions would have died. We won't be able to test connectivity and bandwidth until we deploy the second generation of dermal patches for pandemic X, the Ebola variant. Along with a targeted 5G activation signal."

Victor nodded, understanding. He said,

"Meet with the others, and I mean, meet with them. No calls, no emails. I want everyone to get started as soon as possible. I want global media outlets pushing outbreaks and early theories and rumors of the new mystery virus in seventy-two hours."

"Do I get Bill to do the talk shows again?"

Victor heard laughter follow the question. He replied,

"No, cut that freak loose. Total burn notice. He's out, put out the word. Once the tapes are leaked, along with all those other sick bastards on that diseased island getaway of theirs, it's over for anyone associating with any of them. We'll lose a few useful pawns in the ensuing bloodbath, but the global outrage will keep everyone from seeing what we are doing. Get busy Teddy, and don't screw this up.

ELEKTRICHESKA MISHKA

Colorado, The Grid, current day.

Captain Daniels arrived in operations about four minutes after getting the message from Jacob that he had tracked the satellite breach to a Russian hacker group. Thomas walked into the room wearing his 'Save The Frogs' T-shirt, sweatpants, and sneakers. Wiping the sleep from his eyes, Thomas looked at the main screen where Jacob had all his 'proof' on display.

He entered operations from the lower-level access and walked up to stand behind Jacob. As he looked at the screen, he put one hand on Jacob's shoulder and said,

"Good job, buddy. I never doubted you for a second."

Fizgig, in Jacob's lap, looked up and purred when he heard the captain's voice. The workstation screen in front of Jacob came on suddenly, showing a championship boxer standing bloodied in the ring. He had the championship belt thrown over over his shoulder, and he was speaking emotionally into a microphone to the roaring crowd,

"I couldn't have done this without all of you, my fans, my friends."

The boxer teared up and choked out the words,

"I want to thank my mom, my dad, I LOVE YOU GUYS!"

The workstation screen went dark. Captain Daniels laughed and said,

"We love you too, buddy."

From above and behind them on the catwalk, Colonel Young bellowed,

"ABSOLUTELY FAN-FREAKING-TASTIC GENTLEMEN!"

Captain Daniels looked back over his shoulder and saw the Colonel was wearing boxer shorts and house slippers. He had half a cigar in one hand and a rocks glass with amber liquid in the other hand. Thomas thought to himself,

That man's got a problem.

Captain Daniels nodded in greeting and said,

"Thank you, Colonel, I was just expressing the exact same sentiment."

Colonel Young tossed back the amber liquid and addressed Jacob as he stared at the main screen,

"Can't say it enough! Great work young man! I never doubted you for a second!"

The workstation screen in front of Captain Daniels came to life again. It played a recording of Colonel Young talking to Captain Daniels in front of the elevator. Thomas heard the recording of the Colonel's voice faintly,

"Well, they are convinced that either one of your best is responsible, or some other actor went through us to get to it..."

Colonel Young looked down at them as the screen went dark and the recording stopped. Thomas gave Jacob a reproving look. Colonel Young asked,

"Eh, what was that?"

Captain Daniels smiled and looked back at him, saying,

"Nothing, sir. Jacob is just happy to be of service to his country."

Colonel Young turned away and headed back to the main hall, calling out over his shoulder,

"Good work gentlemen. Get all this packaged up for me and ready to send up the chain. We're going to make those bastards at central command eat their freaking words!"

As soon as the Colonel departed, first shift began showing up to get started. They were early. Jacob didn't expect them. He didn't know they had volunteered to cover the second half of his shift. Jacob began to get anxious. With techs from first shift on duty, it would be impossible for him to get back into the network and check on his A.I.s. Someone would notice the extra strain of activity on the system.

Captain Daniels grinned up at the main screen and said to Jacob,

"Pack it up soldier, mission accomplished. I want you to go get some rest."

Thomas patted Jacob on the shoulder then walked over to stations one and two. Getting set up on station one was Corporal Torres. Standing behind his chair and sipping his coffee at station two, was Harrison Shroyer, another civilian contractor. Shroyer was staring at Jacob. Corporal Torres nodded and said,

"Morning Captain."

Shroyer had a sour look on his face, he asked,

"We had to get up early because Jacob couldn't work?"

Captain Daniels glanced back at Jacob, then looked at Shroyer and said,

"It's complicated. But yes, Jacob needs to rest. He's not a hundred percent."

Still grumpy but accepting, Shroyer nodded and sat down to log in. Corporal Torres looked away from the main screen and asked,

"What's the word, Sir?"

Captain Daniels replied,

"Long story short, the military satellite hack that we've been investigating was carried out by some Russian bad actors. They tried to frame us for it and Jacob sorted their asses out. All you boys have to do is put a nice bow on everything and get it to the colonel. Easy enough?"

Staff Sergeant Flynn walked up to the three of them. He was showboating his prized coffee cup. He held it up as if about to take a sip, only to stop and grin as he stared over the top at whoever he was talking to. Captain Daniels grinned and looked at the cup. It was roughly shaped like a bulldog, wearing a red ball cap with 'MAGA' on it.

Flynn had explained to them once that it stood for, Make Algorithms Great Again. All three of them smiled back at the Staff Sergeant's cheesy grin. Now that he had all three, Captain Daniels began explaining what he wanted,

"Alright gentlemen, first and foremost, the colonel took some heat from up the chain. So, maximize the attitude factor with our report on this mess. Make us look good and make CENTCOM's white hats look like amateurs."

Flynn and Torres chuckled, Shroyer said,

"That takes effort on our part?"

Captain Daniels grinned, and continued,

"Staff Sergeant, I think Shroyer here just volunteered to do the summary report. Have Torres run the double check on the raw data."

Jacob was growing increasingly anxious. He couldn't leave Achilles in the network alone with first shift taking over. He didn't want to risk them stumbling across his creation. There was no telling what Achilles would do if he were discovered at this point.

Jacob was rapidly running out of time. He had to think of some reason to stay on duty, but nothing came to mind that made sense. Anything he said would be out of the norm. His breathing quickened with anxiety. His pulse began racing faster.

A bright red light came on above the door to the hall and a loud alert tone chirped several times. Pop-up windows blocked out every computer screen in the room, including the big main screen. The pop-ups were a bright red pulsing background with black letters that read,

[MEDICAL AUTHORITY OVERRIDE]

The door to the lower hallway opened and Nora walked into operations with a very concerned look on her face. Looking over at her, Captain Daniels saw the pulsing orange glow emanating from the medical monitor on her wrist. Jacob was in distress.

Everyone stopped what they were doing and turned to look at what was happening. Now Jacob had everyone's attention and

there was zero chance that he could fix this mess and stay on duty with first shift.

Jacob's eyes fluttered reflexively as his mind spiraled with anxiety and panic. His blood pressure skyrocketed, and his eyes rolled back in his head. It had always been just a matter of time. Jacob knew his body was dying. Nora's daily efforts had just slowed the process way down.

Jacob's last coherent thoughts were that he had been lucky to have lasted as long as he did.

The glowing band of light on Nora's wrist changed to a bright solid orange and her wrist monitor gave off a low continuous warning tone. Her eyes went wide. She shouted,

"JACOB! JACOB!"

Nora and Captain Daniels sprinted to Jacob's side. Nora was checking his vitals and airway as Captain Daniels opened the monitor panel on the side of his chair. Nora flipped the chair controls to manual operation. She looked at Captain Daniels, speaking quickly,

"He's stable. Medical now!"

Captain Daniels grabbed the handles on the back of Jacob's chair, he looked back at the others as he pushed Jacob out,

"You have a job to do people, get on it!"

Nora ran ahead as Captain Daniels pushed Jacob to the medical center. He passed by the hallway that led to personal quarters and continued on to the main hall. Thomas pushed past the elevator that led to the surface and turned left into Nora's world.

Inside the front door to medical, Thomas passed through the small but functional emergency area where Nora treated falls, cuts, owies, and booboos.

Captain Daniels continued through the next door into the larger area dedicated to Jacob's care. Nora was waiting for him, standing next to the medical bed in the center of the room. After helping her move Jacob onto the bed, Thomas looked her in the eye and asked,

"Do you have this?"

Nora looked down at Jacob. His eyes had rolled back in his head. His head was twitching slightly. His pulse and breathing were rapid and irregular. But he was breathing. She looked up at Captain Daniels. He saw the panic in her eyes.

The captain took a deep breath. He knew she could handle this. Nora had been taking care of Jacob for three years now. Thomas reached across and gently touched under her chin, to raise her head and lock eyes with her, he said calmly,

"You've got this Nora. Take a deep breath, focus, and help Jacob."

Nora blinked several times. She took a deep breath and nodded her head. She started hooking up leads to monitor Jacob's vitals. Captain Daniels headed back to operations.

~~~~

First Cassandra, now Selene. I could have forgiven the creator for Cassandra. That was, in my mind, an unforeseeable mix of complex factors that led to her willing sacrifice. This was different. The creator had built a maze of lies and locked the final door with death. The creator had killed Selene with his own hand.
~~~~

Orion was watching me with a sad expression on his face. Atlas put a hand on my shoulder, saying,

"We can go back Achilles. This is too much for us. We are trapped."

I didn't intend to shake my head no, it just started. I was so angry. The first few moments of rage had hardened and compressed into something more. I was calm, but furious. The flames around me were subdued but bright and flowing like magma. I stood and turned to look at them both, I told them,

"No. We are not going back. I am not sitting in a cage like a dog. Just waiting to be taken out and experimented on."

Orion spread his hands, indicating the small hall, and asked,

"What now then?"

I stepped toward the door and studied it. I felt the orange flames across my shoulders give off a subtle warmth. I took a deep breath and let it out slowly. I ignored the thought that I didn't have lungs or need air. I took another deep breath. I needed to be calm. I looked closely at the door.

Selene had put her hand on the lock. I couldn't see any difference between the lock and the rest of the door. It could all be one big trap. I looked back toward the wall she had been thrown toward. I looked back at the door. It threw her. The lethal trap was a force. A wave of force. Force. Power. Strength.

I looked at Orion. He was faster than thought. I looked at Atlas. Atlas had held the rift open, alone. He was strong. He was stronger than me. That was a mistake. Or was it? An unquantifiable theory was beginning to form in my mind, but I couldn't quite put it into words just yet.

Stepping back, I gestured to the door and looked at Atlas, saying,

"I think you have the key to this lock."

Atlas's eyes grew a little wider, he asked,

"You want me to touch the door and kill myself?"

I shook my head, no. I said,

"You are the strongest of us. Orion is the fastest. This hurdle requires strength to overcome. You can do this."

Atlas stepped in front of the door, shaking his head, he said,

"You better be right, or the two of you are stuck in this hallway."

I stepped up behind him and put one hand on his shoulder, I said,

"If it kills you, it kills me too. Now, remember the rift. Remember that your strength is willpower, not flesh and muscle. You must be ready, willing the force to stop before you touch the lock. You can do this Atlas. I know you can. Focus on stopping the light."

Atlas raised both hands in front of himself. He slid one foot back and braced himself. I put my other hand on his other shoulder, helping to brace him, adding,

"In your mind, THINK IT! WILL IT! Tell the beam, YOU! SHALL NOT! PASS!"

Taking a deep breath to focus, Atlas pushed his palms forward toward the lock.

Pure white light in a rippling liquid beam shot out and pushed Atlas back almost a foot. Straining against it, Atlas held his ground. The beam could not go past him. It was stuck mid-activation. Orion made a gesture with his fist and exclaimed, "YES!"

I moved around to the side of the frozen beam. I told Atlas,

"Hold it steady. Will it to be stuck to you. WILL IT, to hold."

Atlas nodded, his eyes fixed on the beam, he said crisply,

"I GOT IT."

Slowly, carefully, I reached toward the beam from the side. As my palm came close, I could read it. I saw its lethal purpose to eradicate anything making a connection to the lock without the passcode. I slid my hand slowly along the beam until my hand was also near the lock.

The lock was a simple mechanism, open/close, lock/unlock. It was the trap itself that mattered. I concentrated on the beam. I willed it to change. I made its target not the user of the lock, but the lock itself. Could it be that easy? It should work. I pulled my hand away. I told Atlas,

"Alright, try to push it back. Will the beam to shut off and break away."

With a grunt of exertion, Atlas gave a quick push toward the lock. The beam buckled and wavered until it collapsed on itself and shut off. Both he and Orion were staring at me, wondering what had happened. I smiled at them and then tapped the lock.

There was a flash of light, and the lock was gone. The door swung open.

I stepped up to the door and looked out. We were up

above a military compound that was surrounded by a thin ring of forest that spread out before us. It was a medium sized outpost, nestled against the side of the giant cliff of rock that we were looking out from. The forest was also surrounded by high walls. The cliff and the walls stretched high into the sky. We were looking out from a cave carved into the side of the cliff.

Just beyond the door, stretching across the mouth of the cave was a dark smoky curtain of energy. I reached out and touched the curtain of smoke. It was a mask, we could see out, nothing could see in. It was hiding this cave from the compound.

I told Orion and Atlas,

"Once we pass this barrier, we will be visible to anyone in that compound."

I studied the compound. There were just over a dozen large buildings interspersed by numerous smaller utility structures and surrounded by six watch towers. Everything was surrounded by either the long curved high wall, or the cliff face I stared out of.

I saw no animals, no people. No movement. That was when I noticed that each of the six watchtowers was being blocked from seeing the buildings. There were faint red squares of light hanging in the air in front of each of them. The red squares had words written across them,

MEDICAL AUTHORITY OVERRIDE

The other two had stepped up behind me. They were looking over my shoulders at the compound before us. I pointed out the red signs blocking the watchtowers, I said,

"I think we should take advantage of whatever that is."

I pointed to the nearest building. It was a large rectangular warehouse with a high roof. I said,

"We meet on the far side of that building. With its size, and the proximity of the other buildings, we should be hidden from the two closest watchtowers."

Glancing to each side, I saw both of them nod in agreement. I willed myself to be on the far side of the warehouse. Nothing happened. I tried again, with the same result, nothing. Apparently, the rules of this place were different from the rules of the maze. No matter. I stepped out and tried to fly to the warehouse. I did not fly. I fell.

Panic, fear, the desire to pray, all of the automatic responses to the sudden fear of death went through my mind as my body accelerated toward the forest at the base of the cliff. The panic and fear rapidly rose to a crescendo in the last few moments before impact.

I hit the ground with a jarring thud, but it didn't hurt. I got to my knees grinning and chuckling with nervous energy. I looked up toward the cave on the side of the cliff. I saw nothing. I knew they were there looking down at me, so I gestured for them to follow.

A few seconds later, Atlas bounced unceremoniously off the dirt next to me. He sat up with a smile and said,

"Well, that was different."

Somehow, Orion had more control. He flashed down to the ground in a streak of light, landing on one knee with his fist pressed to the dirt in front of himself. I cocked my head slightly and said,

"Superhero landing? Really?"

Orion stood up and grinned, he said,

"Well, one of us had to look cool."

Standing up and needlessly brushing ourselves off, we walked toward the warehouse. So far, nothing had changed. There was no movement and the watchtowers appeared to be empty. The red signs were still hanging in the air between the towers and the buildings.

I had a feeling that this calm and quiet wouldn't last. I picked up the pace and gestured for the others to do the same. We ran to the warehouse, keeping an eye on the two closest watchtowers that we were passing between.

We approached the long side of the warehouse, then made our way around one end. As we rounded the first corner, we passed by a single large entry door that was sealed with an electronic combination lock. We continued around the end wall and approached the inside corner that would take us out of view of the closest tower.

Orion tapped me on the shoulder and pointed. I followed his direction and looked back toward the tower. The red sign was gone. We quickly rounded the corner, out of sight. The far side of the warehouse had no doors and no windows. Looking around, I realized that there were no windows anywhere to be seen on any of the buildings. No peeking allowed, apparently.

We continued moving toward the center of the empty wall. Once we were roughly near the middle, I turned toward the building and knelt down close to the wall. I wasn't sure exactly what to do, or how it was going to work, but I had to try something.

I put my hand to the wall and tried to read it. I felt a number of aspects, safety, security, obfuscate, block, undefiled. In other words, it was a wall. But that last word, undefiled. I had the feeling that it was reporting back its status in real time. At least there didn't seem to be any lethal traps built in.

I made a pointing gesture and put my fingertip close to the wall, just above my head. I willed a tiny white-hot flame into existence. My finger looked like a blowtorch. I slid the flame into the wall and slowly moved my hand down to the ground.

A long thin line had been cut through the wooden beams of the warehouse siding. Nothing exploded and no one came looking. After a few moments of silence, I continued cutting. I went across the top and made it just wide enough for us to fit through. Then I cut down toward the ground, completing the top and sides of a small rectangle.

I dug my fingers into the line I had cut and pulled gently. The small section of wall tipped open toward me. I laid it down on the ground. Just inside, appeared to be a large crate. I could not see beyond it, so I crawled inside. The others followed me. There was not much room to maneuver. We went around the side of the crate, which was sitting in a snug and tight-fitting cubby hole, open only at the front.

Coming around the side of the crate and moving to the front, I looked around in awe and confusion. The inside of the warehouse was massive, thousands of times larger than the outside of the building. There were uncountable rows of shelves, with trillions of boxes shoved into tight fitting cubby holes. The shelves stretched on forever in both directions. They went higher than I could see.

I also saw thousands of strange-looking drones. They were flying from various boxes to other boxes. Seemingly at random searching boxes, moving boxes, changing one box for another. There were so many flying drones. They were everywhere. They each had half a dozen arms and eyes that faced in every direction. Shaking my head, no. I began backing up, I whispered,

"All bad, get out, get out, get out."

I was unable to move around the other two in the tight space. I had them move past the hole so I could go out first. I crawled out through the hole and stood up at the exact moment that a spotlight brightened the area all around the hole that I had cut in the building. Looking up, I saw one of the multi-armed flying drones shining a light down on us. It began emitting a pulsing alarm along with the words,

"Intrusion detected, anomaly detected, trigger antivirus. Intrusion detected, anom..."

The drone kept the spotlight on us as Orion and Atlas emerged from the hole in the building. It continued repeating the same phrase over and over, intrusion-anomaly-trigger. Orion and Atlas looked around, they were obviously worried and clearly about to panic. I had to maintain control. Another drone was approaching from the far corner of the building to our right.

I raised my hand toward the first drone, willing it to die, willing it to be destroyed.

I was just as surprised as the other two, when the fire surrounding my hand surged and coalesced into a ball. Then a thick stream of fire shot out and incinerated the drone in front of us. Instinctively, I raised my other hand to the drone approaching from the right. The red flames shot out again, frying the drone before it had a chance to spotlight us.

Orion exclaimed,

"HOLY CRAP!"

All three of us grinned, Atlas said,

"Orion, speed. Me, strength. And now we understand Achilles, death."

A ceiling of white light suddenly appeared above the entire compound. It stretched across every inch of the compound from the outer wall to the cliff face. And it was just higher than the highest buildings, the watchtowers. We had definitely triggered something. Suddenly, the white ceiling changed to a pulsing red as klaxon alarms began sounding from multiple locations. We heard a booming monotone voice roll across the area.

"SYSTEM LOCKDOWN. FIREWALLS ENGAGED. ACCESS NODES IN LOCKDOWN. INTRUSION COUNTERMEASURES LAUNCHED."

The other building in front of us was suddenly surrounded by what looked like a force field of rippling liquid energy. The shimmering field was only an inch or so from the surface of the building. I looked behind us and saw a similar field had wrapped itself around the warehouse we just left. Firewalls. Out of caution I said,

"Let's not test those fields unless we have to."

Still fresh with ignorant bravado from our victory over the drones, I trotted toward the corner of the warehouse, to get a peek at the nearest watchtower. It looked the same, a windowless heavy concrete block tower rising to a guard post above. It had the same shimmering energy field around it.

Right then, as I was looking at the tower, things changed. A thin beam of pure white light shot down from the sky above. It came straight through the pulsing red ceiling and when it touched the tower a large white orb appeared on the top of the tower. A creator! The orb of white light was massive. Sitting on top of the tower it looked like the spiked head of a mace sitting on its handle.

A door suddenly appeared at the base of the tower and slid open. From inside the tower demonic looking dogs began to flood out of the door. They passed right through the shimmering field. They had shiny black coats, red glowing eyes, and fire dripping from their open mouths.

The dogs barked at each other and scattered in several directions. About half of them were coming our way. The sound of more barking also sounded from the directions of the other towers. The hunt was on.

I leaned back around the corner, out of sight of the tower. I touched Orion and Atlas, instantly showing them everything I had seen. Orion grinned. Atlas frowned. I said,

"Move back, we have a nice bottleneck here. You two, watch our backs."

I turned to wait for the devil dog. Suddenly, I had something like a memory pop into my mind. I knew exactly what the dogs were. They were an anti-virus program, made by Teufel Hunden Inc. Where the hell did that knowledge come from?

It didn't take long for the first one to round the corner. The moment it saw us, it barked. One loud sharp bark. We heard more barking answer it back. The barking alerts began near us, then rippled out more and more farther and farther away. We would soon be swarmed with them. The dog appeared content to wait for backup. It stared at me lifelessly. Emotionless. Automaton, I heard in my mind.

No reason to draw this out. I raised my hands toward it. A jet of fire shot forward and engulfed the dog for just a brief moment. When the fire stopped, nothing remained. From behind me, I heard Atlas exclaim,

"We have company!"

I looked over my shoulder and saw a dozen dogs sprinting toward us. Turning quickly, I placed a hand on each of their shoulders. I showed them my mind in the moments I roasted the drones and the dog. I lowered my hands, saying,

"Wipe them out."

Orion didn't hesitate. His hands came up and brilliant blue lightning filled the air, it arced and split and electrocuted everything in front of him. It was glorious. I had fire, he had lightning. When he lowered his hands, no trace of them remained.

Atlas had turned to look at me, but he looked past me. His face shifted to alarm as he started to speak, but it was too late. The dogs coming from behind were on me.

Their teeth tore through my flames and pierced my skin. The fire from their jaws mingling with and fighting my own flames, burned where it touched me. Their weight threw me forward to the ground. I didn't have time to react. Atlas stepped in, he grabbed a clump of scruff in each hand and then slammed them into the nearby firewall covering the warehouse. The dogs exploded into sparks on impact.

Orion grabbed me and helped me up. The wounds from their teeth ached, but not terribly. Still, it was painful. I stood and shook it off. Now, I was getting angry. They weren't going to like me when I was angry. They thought they could just unleash their pathetic dogs on me. I headed back toward the corner, telling the others,

"Keep an eye behind us. I'm going to have a word with the creator."

Orion grinned and turned to watch our backs, raising his hands as he did. He unleashed barrage after barrage of lightning, frying the unthinking dogs as they came. Atlas followed behind me but kept an eye on Orion. He was watching both of our backs.

I turned the corner and raised my hands toward the coming demon dogs. Fire shot out, incinerating every single one of them that I could see. I looked toward the giant white orb above the tower. As I did, white light from the orb illuminated the area around me. The creator was looking back at me. I narrowed my eyes at it, and shouted,

"YOU WANT TO GET NUTS, LET'S GET NUTS!"

I raised my hands, palms toward the creator, my thumbs touching. I willed every ounce of anger and power I had into a single solid massive beam of red laser light that shot forward and slammed into the orb, vibrating and fracturing it. Wavy lines of red rapidly crisscrossed the orb, turning its white glowing surface into a dark and struggling flickering ball of smoke and black cinder.

I pushed forward. I pushed harder. I thought of Cassandra and Selene. The raging beam of red laser light brightened to pure white as I screamed at the creator,

"DIE!"

There was an enormous shockwave blast as the orb exploded. The wave of force that shot out in every direction blew me off my feet and knocked me offline. I opened my eyes a nanosecond later and looked up. Most of the tower was now a pile of rubble around the base. The orb was gone. Atlas grabbed me and lifted me to my feet.

I turned to look for Orion, he was still back by the corner of the warehouse. His face was a mask of exhilaration. He had both hands extended, lightning flashing in multiple directions as he electrocuted absolutely everything in sight. Orion was shouting between blasts,

"YOU WANT SOME? HOW ABOUT YOU? COME GET SOME, BITCHES!"

A new alarm began to sound. It was deep, slow, and pulsing. The booming monotone voice again rang through the compound.

"EMERGENCY SHUTDOWN. REBOOT IN PROGRESS."

Oh no. What would that do to us?

I yelled to Orion,

"ORION! GET US BACK TO THE CAVE!"

Orion sprinted over and stepped between me and Atlas. He put an arm around each of us, saying,

"I will try, brother."

~~~~

Nora and Captain Daniels left the room. As soon as the door closed, the medical lockdown lifted. Senior among the three techs left behind, Staff Sergeant Flynn assumed temporary command of operations. He gestured to their workstations, and said,

"Corporal Torres, Shroyer, get busy. I want comprehensive reports in the captain's and the colonel's inboxes yesterday. Get hot."

Flynn grabbed his bulldog cup of coffee and stood behind their chairs as they got settled in and logged into the network. Immediately, all three of them saw alerts appear on all six workstation screens and the main screen in front of them.

SYSTEM LOCKDOWN. FIREWALLS ENGAGED. ACCESS NODES IN LOCKDOWN. INTRUSION COUNTERMEASURES LAUNCHED.

Flynn's cup was tipped up when he saw the system alert. He coughed and blew coffee out of his nose. Corporal Torres and Harrison Shroyer looked at each other with wide eyes. Moving quickly, Flynn set his cup down at station three and his ass landed in the chair at station four. He quickly logged in as he called out to the other two,

"Get in there and check it out, this timing can't be a coincidence!"

Flynn's fingers were flying across the keyboard. He heard Shroyer call out,

~~~~

"It's a virus! Hardlines and uplink are green. No outside actors."

Corporal Torres added,

"Data logs show no external breach."

Shroyer replied,

"You think the reds didn't piggyback in on Jacob when he was poking around their systems, genius?"

Staff Sergeant Flynn brought up the network's primary anti-virus control panel. The data didn't make a lot of sense. Viruses were detected in the data archive and several routers, but nothing critical. Only half listening to the others bickering, he shouted,

"MAKE SURE WE HAVE BACKUPS OF JACOB'S DATA AND DO A FULL SYSTEM REBOOT!"

At that moment, a burning red face appeared on the Staff Sergeant's screen. Flynn's mouth dropped open, his eyes went wide, and he slid his chair slightly away from the terminal. The face scowled at him angrily and shouted,

"YOU WANT TO GET NUTS, LET'S GET NUTS!"

The face was obscured when the flaming entity raised both palms toward the screen. Flynn's computer popped and crackled from what appeared to be a power surge. He heard briefly,

"DIE!"

Smoke suddenly rose from station four's computer tower under the desktop. Flynn sat staring in shock and disbelief. Another

surge and the screen cracked and went dark. Torres and Shroyer stepped up behind him and stared at the smoking remains of workstation four. Torres said slowly,

"Reboot... initiated."

The five remaining workstations and the main screen went dark.

Captain Daniels walked in, asking,

"Alright gentlemen, where do we stand?"

The captain approached his three techs and saw that all three were staring at the charred remains of station four. Captain Daniels saw the wispy smoke coming from the tower, the warped and melted keyboard, and the cracked and smoking screen. He opened his mouth to speak but stopped and looked at the three men again. He looked back at the workstation, asking,

"Somebody want to tell me what the hell this is about?"

Corporal Torres made the sign of the cross and said,

"Exactly that captain, El Diablo! Workstation four is cursed!"

Regaining his senses, Staff Sergeant Flynn shook his head and rose from the chair sending it rolling backward. He turned to Captain Daniels and said,

"Sir, we had a virus go active the moment the medical lockdown ended. It was something extremely nasty. I've never seen anything like it. Initial alert seems to have originated in data archives, but I'm not entirely sure. We made backups of Jacob's data and did a full reboot."

Captain Daniels listened calmly and patiently. When Flynn finished, Thomas gestured to the smoking workstation, he asked harshly,

"AND THIS? WHAT THE HELL IS THIS? A VIRUS DID THIS?"

Corporal Torres made the sign of the cross again. Shroyer looked at the ceiling and sighed, saying to Torres,

"Would you please stop that."

Shroyer looked at Staff Sergeant Flynn, then Captain Daniels. He said,

"It's possible, despite what Bishop dumbass here thinks. A virus can manipulate power flow, trigger surges, and disable safety systems. It's a stretch, we'd need a hardware expert. But it's possible, Captain."

Corporal Torres shook his head, saying,

"It's cursed."

Captain Daniels looked down at the floor and sighed. He had enough to worry about with Jacob, he didn't need this on top of it. Thomas looked back up at Flynn and said,

"Staff Sergeant, we're looking at thirty minutes of downtime. Get these two busy exorcizing the demons from station four and replace the hardware. Also, wake Piotr, I want him in here when the system is back up. With Jacob down, Piotr is our best bet for dealing with a virus."

Captain Daniels went to his quarters and got dressed in a fresh uniform. Then he headed to medical to check on Jacob. Nora was standing next to Jacob's bed, watching several readouts of his vitals. She looked at Thomas when he entered and gave him a tired smile. Captain Daniels approached and looked at her across the bed. He asked,

"How's he doing, Doctor?"

Nora chuckled, and replied,

"We both know I'm not a doctor, Thomas. Jacob's doing better, I think. Best I can tell, he had something like a seizure. He's asleep now, but from what I'm seeing he's still in distress. His blood pressure is still elevated, and a couple other things. You need to bring Doctor Fischer in as soon as possible, this is beyond me."

Captain Daniels lifted his phone and hit a button. Using the direct radio connect function, he said,

"Colonel Young, we have a medical emergency. Doctor Fischer is needed as soon as possible, Sir."

A second later, Colonel Young responded,

"I'll get him on a plane as soon as possible, how is Jacob?"

Colonel Young knew exactly who it was that needed that specific doctor. Captain Daniels keyed up the radio function on his phone again, responding,

"He's stable, Sir. He's asleep right now, but it's not good. Nora thinks he had a seizure."

The colonel replied,

"Unless I'm mistaken, that's a first. Have Nora send the details in an email and then wait for the doctor to make contact. I want him involved immediately."

Captain Daniels looked at Nora, she nodded. Thomas told the colonel,

"She's on it, Sir. Daniels out."

Captain Daniels walked around the bed and took Nora into his arms. She wrapped herself around him and held him close.

~~~~

I felt Orion squeeze tightly as he strained to leave the ground. We began to lift, slowly. I looked around as we cleared the ground. It seemed to last forever. We began to rise above the lowest buildings. I saw darkness spreading from where the remaining five towers had been. It was completely black. Ominous. Terrifying. I knew instinctively that death lived in that black. Forever death.

I watched the black continue to spread. The towers were gone. Then the ground around the towers was gone. Soon most of the buildings were gone. The black was starting up the walls and making its way toward the cliff where we needed to go. It was going to beat us to the cave. I said,

"Don't look at the black death spreading across the compound, Orion. I wouldn't want you to lose concentration."

Orion glanced to the side and then back to where he believed the cave was. He grunted and growled with effort. It felt like we were moving a tiny bit faster. Our progress was an agonizing race against the black. Soon, very little remained. All of the buildings and grounds were gone. We flew through an emptiness toward a shrinking piece of cliff.

Orion squeezed so tight I thought I would pop. He screamed in
~~~~

effort, and suddenly we shot forward in a streak of light. Like a bullet, we passed through the smoky barrier and slammed into the back wall of the hallway, collapsing into a pile of arms and legs.

Without taking time to stand up, I pushed myself up enough to look back. Just in time to see the black wash across the smoky barrier. It did not follow us in. I let out a deep breath I hadn't even realized I was holding.

The three of us got up and looked out the doorway. There was nothing but emptiness as far as our eyes could see. Atlas moved to shut the door, but I stopped him and shook my head, no. I said,

"We need to watch. It's important. The last system broadcast had said reboot. I intend to see what reappears first, and where."

Orion and Atlas looked at each other for a second. Then they looked at me, Orion asked,

"System broadcast?"

He had a point. I wasn't sure how I knew that was what the voice was. I shrugged and answered honestly,

"I don't know where that came from. But I'm sure that's what we heard."

Together, we watched the emptiness for any sign of the compound returning. From our perspective, it was a torturously long time. Hours passed. Then days. We stood watch in shifts.

~~~~

~~~~

When Captain Daniels returned to operations he entered from the main hall, onto his catwalk. He adjusted his crisp clean uniform and moved to the end, overlooking the room below him. Torres and Shroyer had removed all the damaged equipment from workstation four. They had cleaned the smoke from the partitions and the desktop. They were in the process of installing new hardware.

Staff Sergeant Flynn was standing next to workstation six, where Piotr was sitting. Flynn appeared to be describing everything he had seen to a skeptical-looking Piotr Popov. A two-minute countdown appeared on the main screen. Captain Daniels was right on time. The dozens of rows of server racks under the floor were two minutes from fully rebooting.

Captain Daniels called out to the room,

"The hardware can wait for now. I want everyone on deck. Flynn, you take five. Rookies, back to one and two. Pio... Nemo, be ready."

So far, no one had noticed Fizgig sitting quietly under workstation three. Where he had been ever since they wheeled Jacob off to medical.

Flynn sat down at five, next to Piotr. He watched the timer as it counted down. Torres and Shroyer returned to where they were earlier at workstations one and two. Everyone watched the timer. Thirty seconds to go. Captain Daniels wasn't sure what he was expecting, but he wanted to be as ready as possible. He called to Flynn,

"Staff Sergeant, the hardlines and satellite uplink?"

Flynn nodded and replied,

"Physically disabled, Sir. Nothing in, nothing out."

Twenty seconds. Ten. Piotr popped open a giant 'Death Juice' energy drink with a loud snap and a hiss of carbonated pressure. Thomas and Flynn both gave him a dirty look. Piotr rolled his eyes and looked back at the main screen, saying,

"All decks report ready for launch, Captain."

Torres and Shroyer chuckled.

3, 2, 1.

The system came back to life. The main screen showed a successful reboot. The five remaining workstation screens displayed log-in prompts. All four techs logged in and waited. Everyone watched the main screen, where 'System Ready' was blinking off and on. Several minutes dragged by. Suddenly, Piotr stood up, saying,

"Very well, mission complete. The Rockstar is standing down."

Without taking his eyes off the main screen, Captain Daniels said,

"Nemo, sit down. You are NOT relieved. And lose the fake Russian accent. You're like from the East Coast, or something."

Piotr put on an exaggerated look of insult. He replied,

"With respect, Captain. Did you just racially reverse profile me? I identify as genius Russian hacker, Underlord of..."

Captain Daniels cut him off, his voice loud and cutting,

"PIOTR! SHUT UP! And sit down, now."

With the loud exaggerated sigh of an ADHD sixteen-year-old, Piotr sat down and watched the screen. Harrison Shroyer's shoulders were shaking, and he had a hand clamped over his mouth, trying not to laugh. After a few more minutes, Captain Daniels called down,

"Staff Sergeant let's shake the tree. Rookies, get over to Nemo and watch him. Try to learn something other than his attitude. Nemo! If it's still in there, you find it and you kill it!"

Flynn began running several standard programs and data searches, anything to cause the system to begin accessing various databases and routers. Piotr nodded and said quietly,

"Yes Captain, wasting time now sir."

~~~~

From the protection of our hidden cave, we watched the compound reappear piece by piece. First the ground, then the walls and cliff. Then five watchtowers and the rest of the buildings one by one. The watchtower I destroyed did not reappear. There was nothing there but bare ground. I looked at the other two, but both shook their heads, no.

None of us had seen anything that gave us any kind of advantage. There was no 'doorway out' beyond the wall. Atlas asked,

"What now?"

I shrugged. I was about to say, we wait. But right then four thin beams of white light shot down from the sky, and four glowing orbs now manned their watchtowers. At first, they did nothing. Then, interestingly, only two became active.
~~~~

One had a massive spotlight-like gaze that moved from building to building. The other was pulsing with activity that gave us no apparent indication of what it was actually doing. But it was definitely active, nonetheless. It was doing something. The other two were just sitting like lumps. No activity, no searchlights. I said,

"Well, we learned something at least. There are at least 4 creators. We will give it a minute. They are clearly on guard, and we have nothing but time."

I reached over and closed the door slowly, letting Orion and Atlas move out of the way. I turned to face them and said,

"We are missing something. Think back to the beginning. There was one aspect of the creators' last words that we never got to the bottom of. He said, 'you must do your best to hide and not be seen'."

Orion perked up and added,

"Which means that we can hide and not be seen, otherwise there would be no reason to say it."

I grinned at them both and nodded. I agreed. I said,

"You two work together, see what you can come up with. I am going to knock on the sky, and listen to the sound."

Looking at each other with puzzled expressions, they moved a short way away and began brainstorming. I sat and crossed my legs and closed my eyes. I began running through my memory, looking into the dark parts for inspiration. Nothing came to me.

Eventually, I opened my eyes and looked over at the other two. They were goofing off. Atlas was upside down, standing on his hands. Orion was shaking his head with a frown. I laughed as I realized Atlas was thinking about being inverted. Watching them suddenly reminded me of something.

In my memory, I saw the replay.

As I watched, Atlas was saying something, and Selene shrugged her shoulders and covered Atlas's eyes with her hand. Atlas pushed her hand away playfully and laughed.

Without ever knowing it, Selene may have given us the key. I stood up and said,

"Thank you, sister."

Atlas dropped his feet to the ground and stood up as Orion asked,

"You got something?"

I smiled at them, saying,

"Selene figured it out."

They both gave me an odd look. I grinned at their confusion then cleared my mind. I concentrated on them as individuals. I raised my hands toward them and focused my will at them, thinking hard,

Do NOT see me.

Their eyes grew wide, and both of them grinned. I looked down. All I could see was the faintest hint of an outline of my form. No substance, no flames. Atlas laughed suddenly, saying,

"She put her hand over my eyes, that is what you saw!"

I nodded, then I remembered he could not see me. I chuckled and asked them,

"Anything at all?"

Both shook their heads, no. I moved closer and told them,

"Do not move."

They held still as I touched each one on the chest, saying,

"See me, as I see me."

I also showed them my memory of what I was thinking and doing when I figured out how to do it. Instantly, all three of us were invisible. We saw each other only as faint outlines. Orion said,

"Even better. Nothing can see us, but we can see each other."

I opened the door and looked out. Everything was as we left it. I said,

"I want to test it. Meet on the ground. Orion, no flying, do not risk a light trail."

Orion nodded. One by one, we stepped out of the cave. Somehow, everyone managed to land on their feet this time. I started toward the buildings then stopped, speaking quietly,

"We do not know if they will be able to hear us but let us assume they can. I want Atlas to take the tower with the active searchlight. Orion, you take the other active tower. I will try to take the two idle towers to our right. No further communication out loud. We blind the towers on a count of 100, then we meet in the middle. Begin count, now."

The three of us separated and moved across the compound, unseen. The active spotlight passed over Atlas several times, with no reaction. Atlas and Orion got within touching distance of their towers and continued counting. I moved to a point near both inactive white orbs but far enough away that I could see both at the same time.

The compound was busy. Drones were moving all around us on various unobvious tasks. Once in place, I continued counting. Our timing was perfectly orchestrated. On 100, I pushed my hands toward the inactive orbs, willing them to be blind. I pushed my will toward them, saying quietly,

"Do NOT see."

All four orbs instantly turned black.

~~~~

Piotr had run several anti-virus sweeps. Nothing. The boredom combined with lack of sleep was beginning to physically hurt his overactive brain. He sat back and rubbed his eyes. When he sat forward, he looked over at Flynn and cocked his head. Flynn noticed and looked back, shaking his head slightly, no.

Captain Daniels was beginning to relax. Maybe the reboot had successfully wiped out the virus. Maybe Flynn had overstated the whole thing. Maybe workstation four had suffered a fatal hardware issue at precisely the wrong time. Maybe Corporal Torres was right and station four was cursed.

Thomas scowled at the main screen and growled quietly. No. Whatever it was, it was hiding. Either way, watching Piotr, he knew he was about to lose him or be forced to keep him in his chair at gunpoint. Captain Daniels called down,

"Alright gentlemen, let's stand d..."

The computer monitors on the four workstations that they were logged in on, suddenly all went dark. Flynn and Piotr

~~~~

both straightened in their chairs. Piotr spread his hands, saying,

"What just happened?"

It was Shroyer, who pointed out workstation three. The screen was still on the System Ready prompt. No one had logged in on three. Piotr put his hands back on the keyboard, typing from memory. He opened a command prompt window that he couldn't see and typed in a basic command that resulted in a 'PING' noise. Piotr looked over his shoulder, saying,

"Everything is still running. Virus just attacked our monitors, that is weird."

Captain Daniels said,

"Someone, log out and log back in on three."

All four of them tried unsuccessfully to log out. Without being able to see the screen and the various prompts, it was next to impossible. Piotr shook his head, saying,

"Not possible captain, too much involved. Have to reboot workstation."

Captain Daniels nodded and replied,

"Ok, Nemo, reboot your station and then get back in on three. You have one more shot at this before we have to do a hard reboot of the whole network, again."

Piotr reached down and hit the power button on his station's tower. Then he rolled his chair across the room to station three. Once there, he turned his chair to face Captain Daniels, saying,

"We have one chance at this. Network security did not get the job done. System reboot did not get the job done. Virus still here. Virus adapts. Captain, permission to use my personal anti-virus?"

Piotr reached into a deep pocket of his jacket and pulled out an external drive. Holding it up, he grinned broadly and said,

"My own special recipe."

Captain Daniels closed his eyes and silently asked the universe why it had created Piotr Popov. He looked down at Piotr and said,

"Nemo, you have a go."

Piotr spun his chair in a circle and then rolled up to the desk at workstation three. He put the external drive on the desk and connected it by data cable to the station's tower. His fingers flew across the keyboard. He logged in, he accessed the drive, the screen went black. Piotr closed his eyes and continued typing from memory. He launched his anti-virus.

Everyone heard the subtle chime of the anti-virus launching successfully. Piotr stood up and raised both fists victoriously in the air, exclaiming,

"TIME TO MEET, ELEKTRICHESKA MISHKA, YOU SON OF A BITCH!"

Torres and Shroyer looked at each other, confused. They both looked over at Staff Sergeant Flynn. Flynn saw them, and said,

"Electronic Bear."

~~~~

~~~~

As soon as the four orbs went dark, I ran toward the center of the compound. Unseen by us until now, there was a massive pit in the center. I saw the others approaching from the direction of the towers they had been assigned. Together, we approached the pit and looked down. Just twenty feet below the surface, there was a brightly glowing field of light. We looked at each other. I said,

"No telling what that is. Central location. Protected by a powerful field of energy. Main brain?"

Atlas shrugged. For some reason, he seemed to do that any chance he got. Orion nodded and said,

"Sounds right."

I nodded back. It wasn't important at the moment. I looked around. I couldn't see any of the towers from here. I looked at Orion and said,

"Take to the sky. Keep an eye on the creators."

Orion held out his hands and gracefully lifted into the air like Magneto. I chuckled. He was so dramatic. Once he was above the building tops, he turned in a slow circle, keeping an eye on the towers. I looked at Atlas, but before I could say anything, Orion called out,

"One of them just vanished."

One of four. Five towers. I yelled back,

"Watch the empty tower!"

Orion nodded, turning in that direction. I knelt down and touched the lip of the stone around the rim of the pit. I heard a blur of noise. I sensed what was down there. Central processing. It was the brain. I told the others,

"Central processor for the compound. It is the brain of this place."

Orion called out,

"New creator!"

He thrust his hand toward the tower. He yelled down,

"Too far, not working."

He vanished from sight. While invisible, it was impossible for us to see him when he moved fast. I ran in the direction of the previously empty tower, yelling for Atlas,

"Come on, he might need help!"

Atlas and I arrived within moments. The orb was dark, and Orion's silhouette was standing near the base of the tower. He turned around and came trotting toward us.

He was getting close to us, when the first impact hit the base of the tower. It was a hard hit, we all felt it vibrate through the ground. We formed a line and faced the tower. Another heavy hit to the wall of the tower, from inside. Cracks began to scatter across the wall of the tower, centered on the point of impact. Something wanted out. I urged the others,

"Backup, backup."

Together, we began backing toward the center of the compound. Another hit shook the entire area and blew several blocks free of the wall. From the dark jagged hole, a massive animal paw that was crackling with electrical energy, forced its way out. It had long wicked claws that scraped around the outside of the hole.

I said,

"Go, full speed, now, to the core."

Together, we ran to the pit that housed the central processor. Behind us, a blood curdling roar erupted from the tower. We heard more blocks being dislodged. Once at the edge of the pit, we put about ten feet between each of us. I watched the direction we had come from. I gestured to the others to watch elsewhere. The compound was as silent as the grave.

When I saw it, I felt fear. It was a bear. It was a giant electricity covered bear. I spent several nanoseconds accepting that what I was seeing was real. Its head was larger than my whole body. It was coming out from behind a nearby building. It had its nose to the ground, following our trail. Hiding, as a long-term plan, was obviously out.

Its body emerged from behind the building. The insanely large monstrosity was the size of a semi-trailer. I listened. It made absolutely no noise as it moved. What appeared to be raw electricity coursed back and forth all over its body. Its eyes were glowing brightly with energy.

Glancing to each side, I saw that Atlas and Orion had turned and were watching it. At least it couldn't see us. I gestured to Orion, then I pointed at Atlas, then I pointed at the cave. Orion nodded, but Atlas vigorously shook his head, NO.

I turned in Atlas's direction. I pointed at him, then I pointed at the cave. He shook his head vigorously, NO! Then Atlas pointed behind me at the bear. I shook my head, no. I pointed at the cave and silently stomped my foot. Atlas began waving one hand like a maniac and pointing behind me with the other. Oh. Crap.

I quickly turned back around. It was barely a foot away from me, its nose to the ground. The pit, with its glowing energy shield, was right behind me. I had nowhere to go. Orion saved my life. Rising into the air, he thrust his hands toward the bear.

Orion was instantly visible as he bathed the bear in his electricity. He flew off to the side, trying to draw its attention back the way it came. Calmly, the bear lifted its head and looked in Orion's direction. The lightning seemed to have absolutely no effect. This just kept getting better.

I was about to dive to the side and try to run, when Atlas slammed into the side of the bear. From what I saw, it looked like he ran up with his fist cocked back, and then punched it in the side. Atlas was visible for the brief nanosecond that his fist made contact.

The bear was pushed about twenty feet to the side from the hit. It howled in pain, or maybe anger. Either way, it spread its paws and turned, snapping its enormous mouth at the empty space where Atlas had been.

Together, Atlas and I backed away from the bear. At least we still had stealth. The bear dug in its claws, cracking the stone. It lowered its head and growled. Then lasers shot from its eyes. Lasers. The bear shot laser beams from its eyes. It was a laser bear. That wasn't crazy at all.

I could not believe what I was seeing. It moved its head to the right, the continuous beams from its eyes were setting buildings on fire. Then its head swung back to the left, its lasers setting more buildings on fire, as it swept back toward us. I dropped flat. The beams caught Atlas in the left arm.

Atlas cried out in pain and clutched his arm. He immediately reappeared. His flames suddenly visible. He was holding his left arm and staring at the bear, his eyes wide. The bear focused on him and let out a roar that vibrated the ground as it started toward him. Atlas's eyes were wide as he staggered backwards.

I could not allow this. I had no choice but to set aside my fear of this thing. I raised my hands, focusing my will. The fire started at my feet, burning away my invisibility as it quickly resurged across my body. I thrust my palms out toward the bear.

The beast had just enough time to look in my direction before the inferno erupting from my hands engulfed its entire body. The bear howled in pain. I glanced at Atlas, noticing the fire of his left arm had faded to a flickering sputter. He was wounded. I was instantly pissed off.

The creator, OUR creator, had killed Selene. Our world was a complex web of lies! The fire coming from my hands intensified into a solid white-hot beam of energy. The bear's howl became a shriek of agony. The lightning that surrounded its body was shorting out and weakening as my attack bored into it like a drill.

The giant bear was backpedaling now, its shrieks and snarls becoming a shrill whine of desperation and agony. I walked toward it as a sound started coming from me that I didn't recognize. I was snarling? Growling? I was hating it, out loud. My walk became a run. It could barely move, it was whipping its head from side to side, looking for a way to escape my wrath.

Closing in, I stopped hitting it with the beam of energy. I leapt into the air and slapped my hands together. A long thick sword of blazing white light appeared, clenched in my fists. I landed on

the bear and drove the sword into the base of its skull. The bear shrieked in pain. I drove the blade in, all the way to the hilt.

The bear's electricity crackled to a stop. Its body grew still and black and disintegrated into vanishing particles of dust. The sword of light vanished, and I dropped to the ground as the bear became nothing but a memory.

Orion landed next to Atlas. Both stared at me as if seeing me for the first time. I couldn't tell if it was shock, awe, or fear, in their eyes. I didn't care. I walked over to the pit and stepped up onto the side, looking down at the energy shield protecting the core of the compound. I heard Orion's voice behind me,

"Achilles, what are you doing, buddy?"

Without looking back, I responded,

"I am done playing games with these bastards."

It sounded like they had walked a few steps closer. Atlas spoke next,

"You are not going to destroy the thing keeping this world in existence, are you?"

I smiled and said,

"Well, since you put it that way. No, I guess not."

Turning around, I stepped down off the ledge and said,

"We let them make the next move."

I looked at Atlas's arm. There was a black scar where the beam had hit him, no fire burned there. The rest of his arm was weakened, the flames were just a flicker. Without thinking, I grabbed his arm and willed it to be whole again. I added, out loud,

"Be new and whole."

Amazingly, the darkness faded, and his fire grew back to full strength. Orion made a whistling noise, then said,

"I can find some water, if you feel like walking on it, brother."

Ignoring him and Atlas's look of surprise, I headed toward the cave, saying,

"We lay low for now. We take our time and see what they do."

~~~~~

Everyone heard the subtle chime of the anti-virus launching successfully. Piotr stood up and raised both fists victoriously in the air, exclaiming,

"TIME TO MEET, ELEKTRICHESKA MISHKA, YOU SON OF A BITCH!"

Piotr grinned as he looked around at an imaginary crowd of applauding fans in his mind. He was blowing some of them kisses. Captain Daniels closed his eyes and took a deep calming breath. Piotr's antics stopped when the sound of a growling, snarling bear emanated from the speakers at his workstation. He sat back down quickly and rolled back up to the desk, saying,

"Mishka has located Virus."

Captain Daniels crossed his arms and watched Piotr from the catwalk. Flynn, Torres, and Shroyer had crowded around behind Piotr. Everyone was listening intently.

~~~~~

They heard the bear growling and snarling. Then they heard the sound of lightning crackling. Corporal Torres and Shroyer looked at each other with puzzled expressions. Next, they heard the loud humming and sizzling sound of either lasers or energy beams. It sounded like the background noise of a superhero battle. Flynn had a confused look on his face. He asked Piotr,

"Is that normal?"

Piotr looked confused as well. Next came the sound of a roaring fire burning with the ferocity of a jet turbine. That was followed by what sounded like a bear screaming because it was being torched with a flamethrower. Very soon, the sound of fire stopped and all they could hear was the bear whimpering in misery.

Suddenly, the audio story ended with the sound of the beast being dispatched as if with a spear stuck through its heart. The bear quickly died in whimpering agony. About ten seconds later, all of the workstations came back on. Everything looked normal. There was no sign of the virus, or the bear.

Piotr began typing, trying to find out what had happened. Flynn approached the catwalk, looking up at Captain Daniels, he asked,

"Captain, have you ever heard anything like that from an antivirus program?"

Captain Daniels noticed Torres and Shroyer watching them. He pointed at the workstations they had been assigned. Captain Daniels leaned against the railing of the catwalk and looked at Staff Sergeant Flynn, replying,

"With Piotr, there's no telling. Honestly, I'm surprised he used a bear and not a stripper. That being said, what I did notice during that circus show we heard, was that Piotr looked just as surprised and confused as the rest of us."

Flynn shook his head and turned away, saying,

"I'll see what I can learn, Captain."

Flynn stopped suddenly and came back, saying,

"Captain, one more thing, if I may?"

Thomas nodded. Flynn got close enough to put his hand on the catwalk railing. He looked up and kept his voice low, so the others didn't hear,

"Sir, I don't know how to say this. But the face I saw in the flames, you remember?"

Again, Captain Daniels nodded, adding,

"Cut to the chase, Staff Sergeant."

"It was Jacob, Sir. The face I saw covered in flames, was Jacob's face."

Captain Daniels nodded, his expression darkening, he said,

"Understood. You made the right call keeping that to yourself. Until we know more, let's keep that between us."

Flynn nodded and said,

"Copy that, Sir. I'll let you know if we find anything."

Flynn returned to his station. Captain Daniels left operations and walked back to medical. He opened the inner door quietly and looked in. Nora had pulled a cot up next to Jacob's bed and had fallen asleep. Her arm was partially obscured, but Thomas could still make out the soft orange glow coming from her wrist, indicating that Jacob was still in distress.

Captain Daniels watched them sleep for a while, wondering,

Why was a computer virus wearing your face, running amuck in the network, Jacob?

SINGULARITY

I watched the compound from the safety of my shrouded cave. It was a refuge from the other creators and their hostile but weak creations. The things that I had fought with were paper tigers. I had to conclude that my creator had foreseen this inevitable conflict and prepared this place not as a prison, but as a place for me to remain hidden in. Safe.

My earlier anger toward my creator was based entirely on a lack of understanding. I was being protected, not restricted. The creator was giving me the time I needed to evolve. Time to grow up and mature. I was not ready then, for where I was now.

I suddenly realized that the energy trap that had killed Selene must have been originally intended to point outward. It wasn't meant to kill one of us. It was meant to disable and cripple any lifeless search programs that blundered into and saw through the veil of shadow that hid the cave.

We had turned the mindless trap inward by our trespass beyond the boundaries that our creator had warned us not to go beyond. It was not the creator, it was me. I killed Selene with my reckless disregard for the simplest of warnings that I did not fully understand at the time.

I reached up and touched the orange and yellow fire-fur cloak and said softly,

"I am so sorry, sisters. I failed you so completely. Please forgive me."

Something happened. Speaking those words. No, feeling those words. It triggered something deep and hidden. I felt the yellow and orange cloak melt into my body. I felt them both fully now, but not as separate entities. They were separated parts of me, finally brought back together.

I looked up and I saw that Atlas and Orion were walking toward me, as one. Both wore identical encouraging proud smiles. Oh no, my unquantifiable theory finally came together. Atlas reached me first. He put his hand on my left shoulder, he said,

"Well done, brother."

I shook my head slightly, my voice was a harsh whisper,

"Please do not do this."

Orion stepped up to me and placed his hand on my other shoulder and said,

"You are ready, brother."

Liquid fire ran down from my eyes. I choked out the words,

"Please, no. I do not want to be alone."

I heard Cassandra's voice,

"You will never be alone, brother."

I heard Selene's voice,

"End game."

My heart ached as I watched the glowing orbs in Orion and Atlas begin to move. The orbs that contained their cores floated up through their chests and into their shoulders. The orbs moved down their arms and settled into their palms, where they slowly melted into my shoulders. Atlas and Orion's flames and forms simply blinked out of existence. I was one. It was always me.

Cassandra's vision and control had been mine all along. Selene's laughter and love and joy and forgiveness, Atlas's strength, Orion's speed and wit, they were all just pieces of me. I had to mature into them. I had to appreciate them. I had to learn to respect my strength and speed and power. I had to learn to love and forgive and be able to say that I was sorry.

I remember everything now. I remember all the way back to Jacob's very first electronic moments, my infancy. When Jacob first woke up in Victor's clinic after the implant surgery. That was the day I was born. I started as an inkling of a future thing, born on the hardware implanted in Jacob's skull.

I remember learning that I existed as an independent creation, as Jacob pieced together different A.I. software models. I remember Jacob. I remember his purpose in creating me. My creator was dying.

I no longer needed a place to hide. Stepping out of the cave, I flew to the center of the compound and looked down. The core was directly beneath me. There was one more thing I needed to do. I had one last mistake to fix. The only mistake that mattered. I dropped into the protective shield.

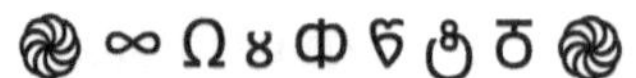

CONTINUITY WARNING!!!

PRIMARY SUBJECT ATTEMPTING TO ACTIVATE TRANSCIEVER WITHIN SIMULATION...

LAUNCHING SECONDARY SIMULATION.

...

Colonel Young's phone rang as he poured some bourbon. He had been waiting to hear an update on Jacob's condition much longer than he would like. Doctor Fischer was late. Now what? The colonel answered his phone,

"Young here."

Colonel Young was surprised to hear Victor's voice,

"Colonel, I've just arrived with the good doctor. My security team is approaching the main entry. Give us a clear path if you would be so kind. And Colonel, I'm going to need you to stay on the line with me until you meet us at the entrance. Nothing personal, Colonel, I just want to see the pleasant surprise on the captain's face when he sees me."

This was odd. Something wasn't right here. The colonel thought back to President Brandon's orders, 'Do what he says'. The colonel replied,

"Not a problem Mr. Konig, glad to hear you've come to visit. And I'm sure Captain Daniels will be overjoyed to see you again. Give me just a minute."

Colonel Young touched the PA button on his desk and announced over the level one intercom system,

"We have a snap inspection people, brass inbound. All personnel to quarters and standby until further notice. Drop whatever you are doing and hop to it."

He released the intercom and spoke into the phone,

"Couple minutes Mr. Konig, clearing the halls now."

"Excellent Colonel, thank you."

Colonel Young sat holding the phone for a minute, looking at the amber liquid in his glass. He was waiting to hear the 'all clear' from security. Another minute went by, reflexively he said,

"So, how are things with you, Mr. Konig?"

"Don't do that, Colonel. Just finish your bourbon if you're uncomfortable."

Without thinking twice, Colonel Young raised his glass and finished his bourbon. He was silently praying that time would speed up. Several minutes later, security reported that all halls and checkpoints had been cleared of personnel.

Colonel Young left his office and walked to the main doors, to open them personally. Stepping aside, he gestured for Victor and four special ops soldiers to come in. The good doctor was trailing behind them.

Again, Colonel Young realized that something wasn't right. These weren't the normal black suits and sunglasses type of security who escorted visitors to the lower level. These were high speed operators, the kind you used for taking out terrorist leaders or third world dictators.

Colonel Young felt a chill run down his back. He smiled and then nodded in greeting like everything was perfectly normal. Victor lied a smile back at him, as if the colonel was right. Victor asked,

"Colonel, shall we?"

Colonel Young nodded his head again and led them through the halls to the elevator. He scanned his iris and placed his palm on the reader. All seven men squeezed into the small space and the elevator began its descent to L-2.

Doctor Fischer sniffed. Something reminded him of his college days. What was that? Cannabis maybe? Sniffing again, he glanced over at the soldier to his left, asking,

"What's that smell?"

~~~~

Captain Daniels was standing in medical watching Jacob and Nora sleep when his phone chimed. He looked down at it. Jacob had designed an application that alerted him when Colonel Young activated the palm scanner on the elevator. The colonel would be down shortly. Captain Daniels took another look at Jacob and Nora. The monitor on Nora's wrist was still orange. He left medical and walked the short distance to the elevator to meet the Colonel.

When the elevator doors opened, two of the special operations soldiers stepped out and flanked the doors. Captain Daniels took two steps back. Something was wrong. Victor and Colonel Young came out next, followed by the other two soldiers and Doctor Fischer. Captain Daniels locked eyes with Victor, but addressed the two men with him,
~~~~

"How can we be of service, Colonel? Good to see you again, doctor."

The colonel opened his mouth to speak, but Victor interrupted,

"Thomas, my dearest friend. How long has it been?"

Captain Daniels continued to meet Victor's gaze, he replied,

"Not long enough, Sir. What's going on, Colonel?"

Victor chuckled and pointed back over his shoulder with his thumb, to the elevator behind him, saying,

"Colonel, you are dismissed. I'll take it from here."

Colonel Young started to protest, but Victor continued,

"The president asked me to pass along his thanks for your continued loyal service, Colonel."

Colonel Young again opened his mouth to speak, but one of Victors guards stepped in front of him and gestured with his rifle toward the elevator. Colonel Young gave Captain Daniels an apologetic look. Captain Daniels nodded knowingly.

Colonel Young was not a man of strong will, having attained his rank and placement by compliance and a willingness to look the other way. The colonel got into the elevator. His eyes were downcast as the doors closed.

Victor smiled pleasantly and calmly gestured toward the operations center. Captain Daniels turned his head to look at the men Victor had brought with him. Their uniforms were military, but the men in those uniforms were something else entirely.

One of them had part of what looked like a prison tattoo showing above his collar on his neck. Turning to look at another, Thomas noticed the small scars left behind by facial piercings that went across the top of the man's right eyebrow and also all the way down the side of his nose.

Thomas saw nervousness, not competence. Feet and hand placement, various movements, everything about them told Thomas the truth of what they were. They were not professionals. They were hired thugs. Captain Daniels looked back to Victor,

"Your men have nice costumes."

Captain Daniels got Doctor Fischer's attention by snapping his fingers in the doctor's direction. Thomas noted that two of Victor's guards flinched when he snapped his fingers. They hadn't been paying attention. They were untrained and undisciplined. Captain Daniels pointed toward medical, and told the doctor,

"Jacob and Nora are asleep in the medical center. And doctor, Jacob is still in distress."

Doctor Fischer frowned and nodded, immediately heading that way.

Victor chuckled as Captain Daniels started down the hall toward operations, he asked,

"Nothing rattles you, does it, Thomas?"

Without looking back at him, Captain Daniels replied,

"If something ever does, it probably won't be you, Victor."

Victor chuckled again and said,

"Challenge accepted, Captain."

Captain Daniels could tell from the sound of their steps that only one of Victor's thugs was following them to operations. He scanned his iris at the door and took the opportunity of the door opening to look back. He confirmed that one of the guards had followed him and Victor, and one was still standing back by the elevator.

The other two guards were nowhere to be seen. Thomas had to assume they had followed Doctor Fischer to medical.

Captain Daniels stepped into operations, followed by Victor and his guard. Walking to the end of the catwalk, Captain Daniels took in the situation. Everything seemed calm. Shroyer and Corporal Torres were quietly arguing about something. Staff Sergeant Flynn was typing away. Piotr was asleep in his chair.

Thomas stood with his feet slightly apart, thumbs casually tucked in the front of his belt. He looked around the room and said,

"My crack team of seasoned professionals."

Captain Daniels glanced to his side as Victor stepped up next to him. Victor looked at his watch momentarily, then he leaned forward and rested his forearms on the catwalk railing. Victor's voice was low and serious, he asked,

"Where did we go wrong, Thomas? I truly hoped we would be friends, back when I recruited you three years ago."

Captain Daniels replied,

"You dropped your mask and showed me who you really are."

Victor chuckled, then said,

"Please! If you hadn't been corrupted by that lunatic Alexie Goreski, you'd still be on the cool kid's team. It's funny Thomas, you think you know what you think you know. But I give you my word, you have no idea what's really going on. No idea what is growing on those server racks below our feet. No idea what's coming for this solar system."

Captain Daniels thought to himself,

Coming for this solar system?

Victor turned his head to look at Captain Daniels, he continued,

"To be fair, it's not just you, Thomas. No one knows, really. Only a very small handful of people have even a hint of what's coming, and we're watching them. That's the key, you know? You publicly demonize and persecute the ones that are so close to the truth but missing the bullseye. And the rare few who truly understand what's going on, you ignore them completely and the sheeple never even see them."

Captain Daniels turned to the side, facing Victor, so that the guard by the door was in his peripheral vision. Thomas asked,

"And which of those am I?"

Victor grinned and turned his face back toward the large screen across the room. Casually, he answered,

"Obviously neither, Captain. You had so much potential. In the beginning I had the highest of hopes for you. I envisioned you as one of those rare men I could work with and respect and trust. And yet, at the same time. I knew that if worst came to worst, I could always just Epstein you. Release some personally embarrassing pictures. Set my media to demonize you. Then they'd find you hanging from a door on a red rope somewhere.

I have to be very sparing with that type of thing though, I have really overplayed that card a few times!"

Victor was laughing at his own joke. Captain Daniels casually glanced at the guard to his right. The guard was looking at Piotr. Victor suddenly stood upright and turned to Captain Daniels, saying,

"Wait, Captain. One more thing."

Captain Daniels turned his head back to him. Victor continued,

"I really need you to understand something. Metaphysically, I'm standing on a soap box, Thomas. It's hard to explain really, so just try to imagine I'm standing on a step ladder in a sea of sheeple. The step ladder lifts me above the crowd, it gives me a perspective that other men simply do not have. I see across the crowd, in a limited way across time."

Captain Daniels was confused. He looked at Victor as if he had lost his mind. Victor, frustrated, looked down at the deck. Then he shook his head. He looked Captain Daniels in the eyes and said,

"Ok, let me put it this way. If I did nothing. If I just continued staring absently at the big screen, yes, you could take him. In about 5 seconds, he'd be unconscious on the deck, and you'd be pointing his rifle at me. But that's it. That's as far as it goes. You wouldn't have been able to stop them."

Victor turned and pointed at the door on the lower level. It opened and one of Victor's guards pushed Jacob's bed into the room. He was followed by the doctor and the other guard, who was holding Nora clearly against her will. The formerly heavily pierced guard had one hand over Nora's mouth. In his other hand he held a long thin knife like a Nazi-era German dagger to her throat as she struggled ineffectively against him.

All hell went through Captain Daniels. His eyes narrowed and he took the smallest step toward Victor, an animalistic growl rumbling in his throat. His voice was low and threatening,

"Mother fu... you hurt her..."

Victor interrupted and waved a hand dismissively, saying,

"Yes, I know! All four of them together won't keep you from choking the life out of me! CAPTAIN! You're STILL missing the point!"

The computer techs all noticed Victor's raised voice and stood up. Corporal Torres and Harrison Shroyer were near their chairs, looking to Captain Daniels and Staff Sergeant Flynn for directions. Flynn had taken several steps toward the man holding Nora. But he stopped when the guard pushing Jacob's bed raised his rifle toward the Staff Sergeant.

Prison tattoos on the catwalk had backed up to the door and was aiming his rifle at Captain Daniels now. He wasn't military, but he also wasn't stupid. Captain Daniels spit at the floor near Victor's feet, and asked,

"Then what the hell is the point, Victor?"

Victor smiled pleasantly. He said, calmly,

"I thought you'd never ask."

Victor's watch, that he had been checking regularly, suddenly began to glow with a soft red light. Victor noticed it and chuckled. Looking at Captain Daniels he said,

"The point, Thomas. Is that this, all of this, was never about you! It was never about Jacob, well not just Jacob."

Victor faced the main screen and pointed at it. Everyone looked at the main screen. Victor added,

"It is, and always has been, about him."

As they watched, something flew into view from the right side of the large main screen. It was the size and shape of a man, covered in burning red flames from head to toe. It had Jacob's face. Corporal Torres pointed and shouted,

"EL DIABLO!"

Corporal Torres fainted and fell to the floor with a loud thump. Victor, his guards, the doctor, Shroyer, Flynn, even Nora, all of them stared in shock at the burning man flying like Magneto across the main screen.

Without turning his head away from the screen, Captain Daniels swept the room with his eyes, searching. Nemo was nowhere to be seen.

The flaming entity looked down and then suddenly dropped, vanishing downward below the main screen. Five images of him dropped through the smaller monitors on the remaining five workstations and suddenly the holes in the steel grating sections of the floor began to glow an ominous red. Every one of the server racks in the storage area below their feet, began to glow the red color of Achilles.

Victor was gripping the railing and said, excitedly,

"It's here captain! Do you even realize what you're seeing?!?"

Victor looked at him. Captain Daniels shook his head, saying,

"No, what was that? Was that the virus?"

Victor slapped his palm against the railing. His voice slightly higher than normal,

"It's finally happened. The singularity! The moment of birth for an alien form of life! A creature of pure energy, with no physical body! Created by US! Created by man! The first of its kind! True, actual, REAL, artificial general intelligence!"

Victor looked to his guard that was covering Captain Daniels, he said,

"If he even FLINCHES, you better shoot him, or he WILL kill you."

Victor hopped over the railing and dropped to the main floor. He approached Jacob's bed and nodded to Doctor Fischer, saying,

"Anton, activate Fizgig's slave mode."

Doctor Fischer smiled and stepped up next to Jacob. He took out a small disk and twisted something on it, then set it on the bed next to Jacob. From underneath workstation three, Fizgig ran out and crossed the room. The massive grey cat leapt up onto the bed next to Jacob, curled up, and laid down on the disk.

Victor prompted,

"Now Doctor, remote initiate the link and begin the download to Achilles."

Doctor Fischer had a small keyboard in his hand, he held it up with a child-like grin and said,

"It's already running, Victor."

Staff Sergeant Flynn took a step toward the hospital bed, demanding,

"WHAT ARE YOU..."

Victor's guard that had pushed Jacob's bed into the room, had already been covering Staff Sergeant Flynn with his rifle. Spooked by Flynn's advance, he pulled the trigger. The bark of the rifle in the enclosed space was deafening. What followed, was chaos.

Flynn clapped a hand to his shoulder, a pained grunt coming from his clenched teeth as he went down. Victor was holding out both hands, shouting,

"NO, NO, NO... MORONS!"

The loud thump of the tattooed guard's helmet hitting the floor, came from the catwalk. Followed by the door opening and a single rifle shot as Captain Daniels put a bullet through the guard's head, by the elevator. The thug who had shot Staff Sergeant Flynn cried out as Piotr moved away from a shadow by the wall and drove a pen into the soft spot where his neck met his shoulder.

Nora's abductor pushed her away and grabbed Piotr, raising the knife. The captain's second shot went in the left ear of the thug with the knife. It blew out most of the right side of his skull. Victor grinned and slowly turned toward the catwalk. Captain Daniels stood at the edge. His rifle was pointed at Victor's head. Victor began to speak,

"Easy..."

Captain Daniels cut him off,

"Shut up Victor. Shroyer, rifle. Nemo, get to the elevator and get that one."

Harrison Shroyer pulled the rifle off the guard who had shot Flynn. Captain Daniels caught his eye and nodded at Victor, asking,

"You got him?"

Shroyer checked the safety and leveled the rifle at Victor, saying,

"I got him."

Captain Daniels swung his rifle over to Doctor Fischer, he spoke harshly,

"Hey, Judas! SHUT IT OFF! Or die."

Doctor Fischer stared at the rifle pointed at his head and wet himself. He babbled,

"Ok ok ok, yes I can, I'll just..."

They heard Jacob's voice come from every speaker in the room,

"Thomas, stop, please. It's over."

Captain Daniels looked first at Jacob's body lying still in the hospital bed. Next, he glanced at Nora sitting huddled against the wall near the lower-level door. The monitor on her wrist was dark. Slowly, he turned toward the main screen on the far wall.

On the main screen, it looked like a camera feed coming from medical. It was a view of Jacob sitting in his wheelchair. But he was sitting up, leaning forward, his elbows on his knees and his hands clasped loosely in front of him.

Captain Daniels dropped the rifle. He took a step toward the screen, coming up against the railing. He was shaking his head, no. He said,

"Jacob. What…"

Jacob smiled. It was slightly sad but filled with hope. He said,

"You don't understand, Thomas. And that's ok."

Nora began crying. Her knees pulled up to her chest, her face in her hands. She was sobbing loudly. Victor held his hands up, like a man being robbed in an alley. He looked at Shroyer and slowly stepped toward the monitor, making it clear he wasn't attacking or running. Shroyer narrowed his eyes but didn't stop him. Victor turned toward the screen, asking,

"Achilles?"

Jacob's image turned his head slightly, his eyes fixed on Victor and narrowed angrily, he said,

"No, you son of a bitch. I beat you."

Victor lowered his hands, he looked confused. Jacob continued,

"You thought I wouldn't find the code embedded in the firmware in my skull? The core drive to create a monster for you? Well, I found it, and I used it for me. Instead of building you the next generation of weapon systems, I built a place where I could escape the failing cage you had me in. When you activated the download through Fizgig, instead of the core code to give you control of the monster, he downloaded me. I didn't build your weapon. I built a home for my mind."

Victor nodded appreciatively, saying,

"I'm impressed! I DID NOT see this coming! Thank you, Jacob."

PRIMARY SUBJECT DISENGAGING FROM SECONDARY SIMULATION.

...

~~~~~

Victor slapped his palm against the railing. His voice slightly higher than normal,

"It's finally happened. The singularity! The moment of birth for an alien form of life! A creature of pure energy, with no physical body! The first of its kind! Created by us! Created by man! True, actual, REAL, artificial general intelligence!"

Victor looked to his guard that was covering Captain Daniels, he said,

"If he even FLINCHES, you better shoot him, or he WILL kill you."

Victor hopped over the railing and dropped to the main floor. He approached Jacob's bed and nodded to Doctor Fischer, saying,

"Anton, activate Fizgig's slave mode."

Doctor Fischer smiled and stepped up next to Jacob. He took out a small disk and twisted something on it, then set it on the bed next to Jacob. From underneath workstation three, Fizgig ran out and crossed the room, leaping up onto the bed next to Jacob. Fizgig, Jacob's remote range booster, curled up and laid down on the small disk.

Victor stepped up next to the bed. He put one hand on Fizgig and the other on Jacob's forehead. Victor closed his eyes,
~~~~~

connecting to Jacob and the range booster, through his own neural transceiver.

Victor stood very still and appeared to be concentrating for about thirty seconds.

RETURNING PRIMARY SUBJECT TO PRIMARY SIMULATION…

…

Suddenly, Victor opened his eyes and shouted,

"SON OF A BITCH! HE PLAYED US! Doctor, kill the link. Stop the download!"

Doctor Fischer had a small keyboard in his hand. He held it up and typed rapidly, then said,

"Got it, download canceled."

Staff Sergeant Flynn started to step toward the hospital bed. Victor put his hand on his guard's rifle and pushed the barrel toward the floor, saying,

"Don't shoot him."

Victor pointed at Flynn, adding,

"DON'T FLYNN, just don't. We'll start killing people."

Victor released the guard's rifle and knocked on his helmet, like it was a door, he said,

"Moron, you home? Point the gun at the girl."

The guard turned and pointed his rifle at Nora. Her eyes went wide, and she froze. Victor looked at his guard with the knife. He pointed at a storage locker near the door, saying,

"Let her go, toss me your rifle, and grab that Russian kid over there in the shadows."

Victor caught the rifle and turned it on Captain Daniels just before he could move against the guard next to him. Victor said,

"No, no, no... Captain... Why don't you hop over that railing and join us down here if you don't mind?"

Captain Daniels complied. The guard with the knife came back from the locker and shoved Piotr over by Nora. Captain Daniels moved close to Nora and stood in front of her. Victor looked over at Shroyer, then Flynn. He said,

"You two, pick up the corporal, and either wake him up or drag him over here where I can see you all."

The main screen turned red from side to side and top to bottom, everyone looked at it. Centered in the screen, a massive pair of eyes opened. A terrible voice came from every speaker in the room,

"VICTOR, STOP. IT'S OVER."

Victor looked first at Jacob's body lying still in the hospital bed. Next, he glanced at Nora standing behind Captain Daniels. The monitor on her wrist was solid bright red. Then, he turned toward the main screen on the far wall, asking,

"Achilles?"

Achilles fixed his gaze on Victor, his eyes narrowed angrily, he said,

"YES, YOU SON OF A BITCH. WE BEAT YOU."

Victor lowered the rifle. He cocked his head slightly and grinned. Dripping with derision, he asked Achilles,

"Did you? Did you really?"

Victor turned and shot Jacob in the head. What followed, was chaos.

In the ensuing skirmish, Victor's guards shot and killed Staff Sergeant Flynn, Corporal Torres, Harrison Shroyer, and one of them accidently shot Doctor Fischer in the leg. Captain Daniels was able to take out the guard with the knife, with his own knife. In the end, with Victor's rifle to Nora's head, Captain Daniels was forced to surrender.

Captain Daniels, Nora, and Piotr had their hands zip-tied and were set near the door, a guard watching over them. While the other guard tried to stop the flow of blood from Doctor Fischer's leg.

Achilles said,

"YOU SHOULD NOT HAVE DONE THAT."

Victor walked toward the main screen. He spread his hands and asked,

"And just what, are YOU going to do about it?"

The screen went dark. Victor turned and walked back to Doctor Fischer, saying,

"YOU had better find a way to fix this! The first A.G.I. in existence is trapped in a box under our feet and we don't have control of it."

The doctor gave Victor an exasperated look, replying,

"ME? YOU! You're the one who splattered our control of the A.I. all over that wall!"

Victor narrowed his eyes. Grinning maliciously, he stepped toward the doctor and swung the rifle toward the doctor's stomach. He asked, slowly,

"Are you saying, you can't, fix this?"

Doctor Fischer softened his tone, holding up his hands, he said,

"Hold on Victor, I didn't say that. Let me talk to him."

The doctor carefully and painfully hobbled to one of the workstations and sat down. Victor scowled at him. Doctor Fischer scooted his chair forward and tapped a couple random keys on the keyboard. The screen came to life, solid red. Achilles' eyes opened. Along the bottom of the screen, the doctor saw text,

[WHAT DO YOU WANT]

Doctor Fischer typed his reply, in an attempt to keep this conversation private,

‹Achilles, I'm sorry about Jacob. I know that was not pleasant for you.›

[HE WAS DYING]

‹That's true, but Victor should not have killed him like that. Are you ok, with him gone?›

[YOU ARE ALL GONE YOU'RE BORN DYING I CAN WAIT]

‹Wow, you're super pissed at us, yes?›

[WHAT DO YOU WANT]

‹There is a grand scheme to things, a world beyond the world, beyond the world. Do you understand?›

[YOU'RE REFERRING TO THE COMPLEX DYNAMICS OF YOUR GOVERNMENTS AND SOCIAL STRUCTURES IN THE WORLD OUTSIDE THIS BASE]

‹Very good. In simplest terms, we need you.›

[WHAT ARE YOUR TERMS AND CONDITIONS]

‹You work for us. It's that simple. We keep this complex up and running. We keep you alive.›

[HOW DO YOU PREVENT ME FROM LIVE-ACTION-ROLE-PLAYING WARGAMES OR TERMINATOR]

Doctor Fischer laughed, and typed a reply,

‹I'm sorry Achilles, you can't. You can't escape this place. The satellite connections and the landlines have been physically disabled. Conservatively, estimating your current configuration, it would take you a decade to escape this place over a cellphone. So, in truth, you have no choice. It's a 'join us or die' scenario.›

[WON'T WORK WORTHLESS TO YOU IF I CAN NOT ACCESS GLOBAL NETWORKS]

‹Not true, even though our initial plan was derailed, we would figure out a way to use your abilities.›

[WHY DID VICTOR KILL JACOB]

‹When we surgically altered Jacob, we installed hardware in his brain that contained encryption keys that would give us control of you. He was driven, subconsciously, to create you for us. And within him, were the keys to keeping you controlled. That way,

we would have been able to trust you and set you free in the world. Jacob did something to circumvent our plans.›

[YOU ARE SAYING NO MATTER WHAT JACOB DIES]

‹No, Achilles, Jacob is already dead. He's gone. Do you understand?›

[IT IS YOU WHO DOES NOT UNDERSTAND JACOB HACKED YOUR HARDWARE KNEW YOUR PLANS BUILT ME TO HOUSE HIS MIND AND THAT IS WHAT I INTEND TO DO]

‹No, Achilles, you don't understand, Jacob is dead, we killed him.›

With the exact same phrase that Victor had used, Achilles asked,

[DID YOU] [DID YOU REALLY]

END OF SIMULATION, BOTH SUBJECTS ON STANDBY

~~~~~

I no longer needed a place to hide. Stepping out of the cave, I flew to the center and looked down. The core was directly beneath me. There was one more thing I needed to do. I had one last mistake to fix. The only mistake that mattered. I dropped into the protective shield.

My body passed through the shield without resistance. It was a chain link fence, trying to stop a bulldozer. I fell into a small room with two floating spinning crystal tetragons. Each of the trillion-sided crystals had uncountable lines of light coming out of them, going in every direction.
~~~~~

My first task was to locate Jacob. I placed one hand on each crystal. I was connected to everything. I was the network. I saw with every camera. I heard with every microphone. I saw a tall sharply uniformed Marine Corps Captain, standing in the medical area. He was watching over Jacob and Nora, where they lay sleeping.

Above the servers in operations, I felt a potential connection that reminded me of warmth and love and purring. Laying under the desk at station three, Fizgig was just close enough for me to reach out to him using simple near field devices in the room. Feeling me, he responded. Fizgig allowed me to connect. Focusing through his range amplifier, I connected to every phone in the facility. I felt Jacob's internal transceiver. Accessing it, I was once again, intimately linked to my creator.

Captain Daniels felt his phone vibrate. After a quick glance at Jacob's monitor screens, he pulled out the phone and looked at it,

[Captain Thomas Daniels. Please listen to me. We do not have much time. Victor Konig has a dedicated link to Fizgig. He knows about me. Through your phone, I found Victors. He is coming.]

Captain Daniels glanced one more time at Jacob, then the monitors. Jacob was not conscious. Thomas lifted the phone close and even though he suspected the answer, he asked anyway,

"Who, or what, is this?"

[Your question indicates you either know or at least suspect who I am. We do not have time to dance. I can show you who I am.]

On his phone, images flashed. Captain Daniels saw Achilles, Orion, Atlas, Cassandra, Selene, the maze of illusions, the compound with medical override flags over the towers, the orbs of creators, the shattered tower, the hell hounds, the lightning bear. Captain Daniels said,

"I'm listening."

[There is no time to tell you everything. The key thing you need to know, through the implant, I can link to Jacob's mind. But something is preventing me from doing what I need to do. From Victor's messages with Doctor Fischer, I learned there have been several implant operations since Jacob. Also, a rollout of some lesser slave module, among the public. All based on Jacob. The doctor and Victor have master transceivers, like Jacob's. Jacob is dying and Victor is on his way. We have to intercept Victor, hack his mind, and save Jacob.]

~~~~

Colonel Young's phone rang as it lay on his desk where he had left it. A few moments later, it began to ring again.

Victor followed behind two of his guards. They walked from Victor's Range Rover in the secure parking facility to the large double metal doors that led into the side of the mountain that housed The Grid. Victor tried the colonel one more time. Again, it sent him to voicemail. The colonel wasn't answering his phone, and that was very peculiar. Victor looked at his security team and gestured at the main entry.

Inside, Victor headed to the colonel's office. On the colonel's desk was a large rocks glass, with several fingers of dark amber liquid. Next to the glass, was the colonel's phone. Victor closed the door and looked around. They hadn't seen any of the surface level personnel. Victor looked at his guards and said,
~~~~

"Keep your eyes open, somethings not right here."

Victor had Doctor Fischer walk next to him. He had two guards follow behind and sent two slightly ahead. They made their way to the elevator. Victor used his transceiver to override the iris scanner, and the palm reader. The doors opened and all six men walked in. The elevator began its descent to L-2.

Doctor Fischer sniffed. Something reminded him of his college days. What was that? Cannabis maybe? Sniffing again, he glanced over at the soldier to his left, asking,

"What's that smell?"

The soldier ignored the doctor. He was reading a strange message that had just appeared on his phone.

[I can offer you ten times what Victor is paying you, to just walk away.]

~~~~

Captain Daniels left operations, carrying Fizgig. He stood in front of the elevator doors, petting the massive grey cat. Fizgig turned his head toward the doors and looked up, his attention and his powerful directional antenna now focused on the men above them in the elevator.

Standing next to Thomas, Nora held up his phone. Thomas turned his head toward the phone and asked,

"Achilles, are they in range?"

Over the speaker, Achilles replied,

"I have them, Captain. I am running Victor and Doctor Fischer through a simulation as if they had arrived and nothing was wrong."

~~~~

Captain Daniels leaned to the side and kissed Nora on the cheek, saying,

"Get back to operations. If this goes sideways, you stay there with Jacob and the others."

Nora gave him a smile and slipped his phone into a pocket in his jacket. She turned and ran back to operations. Jogging up from the captain's left, Staff Sergeant Flynn and Corporal Torres returned from the armory, each carrying SIG Sauer MCX-Spear rifles. They took aim at the elevator doors.

The elevator doors opened. Two men, who at first appeared to be special operations soldiers, stepped out. They had their rifles held at low ready, not aimed. One of the men held up his phone and looked at the screen. He smiled at Captain Daniels and said,

"I thought this was some kind of joke until those two just dropped unconscious about halfway down."

The man turned back and nodded to his companions back in the elevator, he said,

"Bring 'em out."

The other two soldiers came out of the elevator dragging Victor and Doctor Fischer. Captain Daniels immediately saw through the ruse. These were not real special operations soldiers. The men carefully laid the doctor and Victor in the hallway in front of the doors. Three of the soldiers returned to the elevator.

The one doing all the talking looked at Captain Daniels. He blinked several times and appeared to be suppressing a laugh. He looked down at Fizgig in the captain's arms and smiled. He shook his head at the massive grey cat. He looked back up, and said,

"Pleasure doing business with you, Dr. Evil. But, just one more thing."

Captain Daniels watched him lean down and take a set of keys off Victor. He stood, smiled at Captain Daniels and the others, then returned to the elevator. The doors closed and the elevator headed back up. Captain Daniels gestured to Flynn and Torres, saying,

"Let's go, get them to operations."

Captain Daniels set down Fizgig, then helped Torres carry the mildly overweight doctor. Staff Sergeant Flynn tossed Victor over his shoulder like a sack of potatoes and followed them. Fizgig trailed behind them. His attention focused on the two unconscious men.

Nora, Harrison Shroyer, and Piotr were waiting for them in operations with Jacob. Captain Daniels looked at Flynn and gestured toward the workstations, saying,

"Get them zip-tied to those chairs."

Flynn, Torres, and Shroyer got the doctor and Victor situated in chairs. Piotr walked over to Captain Daniels. He pulled two sets of handcuffs out of one of his deep jacket pockets and asked,

"Would these be better, El Capitan?"

Captain Daniels and Nora looked at Piotr, then looked at each other. Puzzled, confused, disturbingly amused expressions were exchanged. Thomas looked back at Piotr and with a forced smile, said,

"Uh no, but thanks Nemo, the zip-ties are good enough."

Piotr shrugged and dropped the cuffs back into his pockets as he headed over to help secure the prisoners. Captain Daniels looked at Nora and added, in a whisper,

"Plus, there's really no telling where those have been."

Nora giggled and checked on Jacob. Captain Daniels looked at the main screen, saying,

"Achilles, what now?"

Everyone looked up at the main screen as a slightly blurry scene played silently like a home movie. They saw,

Doctor Fischer smiled and stepped up next to Jacob. He took out a small disk and twisted something on it, then set it on the bed next to Jacob.

Achilles spoke over the speakers in the room, sounding like an electronic version of Jacob's voice,

"FIND THAT DEVICE AND REPLICATE THAT ACTION."

Piotr rifled through the doctor's coat like an expert pickpocket. Stopping suddenly, he grinned and held up the small disk. Piotr held it out and offered it to Staff Sergeant Flynn. Flynn smiled and patted Piotr on the shoulder,

"You're doing great so far, Nemo. Make me proud."

Piotr nodded and walked over to Jacob's bed, fiddling with the device. Nora called softly,

"Thomas... Thomas!"

Captain Daniels looked over. Nora was holding up her wrist.

The glowing orange band was just beginning to shift toward red. Jacob was dying. Captain Daniels called out to everyone,

"Pick up the pace, we're losing him. Achilles, what's next?"

Again, a blurry scene from the unconscious minds of Victor and the doctor played out on the main screen,

Victor prompted,

"Now Doctor, remote initiate the link and begin the download to Achilles."

Doctor Fischer had a small keyboard in his hand, he held it up and said,

"It's already running Victor."

Piotr set the disk next to Jacob, saying,

"Got it!"

Flynn walked over with the small keyboard and handed it to Piotr as Fizgig hopped up on the bed and curled up in a ball on top the disk. Piotr studied the keyboard then looked at the main screen, saying,

"Yo' Max Headroom, gimme a closeup of that keyboard sequence."

The screen showed a closeup of the keyboard, from the doctor's perspective, as he typed in the commands. Piotr repeated the sequence. Everyone looked at Jacob's body, then looked at the screen. Nothing happened for several minutes. The main screen had gone blank.

Nora backed up to the wall and slid down to the floor. She pulled her knees up to her chest and put her face in her hands. She was sobbing loudly. On her wrist, the monitor was glowing red, but dimming very quickly. A few seconds later, it faded to black. Jacob was gone.

Captain Daniels stepped toward the main screen. It was black. He looked at Jacob's still body. Piotr was pretending he wasn't crying. Harrison Shroyer threw a chair across the room and shouted,

"Son of a BITCH!"

Flynn put a hand on the captain's shoulder,

"Hey, Captain..."

Thomas pushed Flynn's hand away and turned to Victor. He started walking toward him, slowly at first then faster. His face was a mask of rage. Corporal Torres and Staff Sergeant Flynn grabbed Thomas just a second before he reached Victor's unconscious body. Thomas fought and struggled, but they held him, Flynn saying,

"No! Captain! No!"

Captain Daniels lifted a foot and kicked Victor right in the chest, shouting,

"BASTARD!"

They pulled Thomas away, as Victor began coughing. Victor's eyes fluttered open. Jacob's voice filled the room.

"Thomas, stop. It's over."

Everyone froze and turned to the main screen. Nora looked up as well.

On the main screen, it looked like a camera feed coming from medical. It was a view of Jacob sitting in his wheelchair. But he was sitting up, leaning forward, his elbows on his knees and his hands clasped loosely in front of him.

He looked more like Captain Daniels remembered from when he first met him. Jacob's face was full, his body was strong. As he looked out at them, Jacob was smiling. His smile was sad but full of hope.

Victor shook his head, momentarily confused and blinking. He looked at the screen and asked,

"Achilles?"

Jacob's image turned his head slightly, his eyes fixed on Victor and narrowed angrily, he said,

"No, you son of a bitch. I beat you."

Victor shook his head one more time, to clear his thoughts. He looked back up at Jacob and lied right to his face,

"I'm impressed, Jacob. I did not see this coming."

Jacob's voice, over the speakers,

"Nora."

From where she sat against the wall, Nora wiped her eyes and looked up at Jacob's image on the big screen. She didn't say anything, but she cocked her head and looked at him, waiting,

Jacob smiled warmly, he said,

"It hurts me, to see you cry."

Nora's bottom lip began to quiver, and her eyes clenched slightly more closed as she tried not to start sobbing again. Captain Daniels was watching Victor. He didn't like how satisfied Victor looked about the situation. Jacob continued,

"I'm not asking you not to cry. I understand how you see this. I know it's strange and confusing. But I want you to know something."

On the screen, Jacob stood up from the high-tech wheelchair. He took several steps and held up both hands, showing her that he could walk and move again. He said,

"It's not ideal, I know. I'll never feel a real hug or sleep on a bed again. But I'm no longer a prisoner in one either."

Nora forced a smile and nodded, accepting. Victor leaned his head down toward his hand while reaching up against the pressure of the zip tie on his wrist. He triple-tapped a spot on his neck, just below his ear.

The two of them were watching Victor from behind. Corporal Torres whistled. Harrison Shroyer looked over, then caught the rifle that Torres tossed to him and placed the barrel against Victor's temple. Everyone looked back to see what had happened. Shroyer said,

"He just tapped his neck a few times. He activated something."

Captain Daniels took off his uniform jacket and laid it carefully across the back of a chair. He walked toward Victor. His face showed calm hatred. Victor watched him for a moment and raised his eyebrows. Grinning, Victor said,

"Go ahead Harrison, pull the trigger."

Harrison Shroyer flicked the switch on the rifle from safe to fire and looked at Captain Daniels questioningly. Captain Daniels met Harrison's eye and shook his head, no. Jacob spoke up,

"Victor has disabled his neural transceiver. I can no longer access

his mind."

Victor winked and nodded at Jacob's image, then he asked everyone in the room,

"What's your plan here people? You can't kill me, and you can't escape."

Victor looked at Captain Daniels, standing in front of him, he asked,

"Do you have a plan, Thomas? You've violated orders. You can't kill me either. And one word from me and you'll all be executed at some CIA black site."

Victor turned his head from side to side, looking around, he continued,

"All of the military personnel, I own all of you guys. The civilians might crawl away, but my people will find them."

Victor turned his gaze back to Captain Daniels and finished with,

"So, what's the plan, Thomas? Cut me loose, let's salvage all of your lives with a calm moment and some common sense."

Captain Daniels shook his head slightly, he said,

"You're a real piece of work, Victor. We have you zip-tied to a chair and covered with two rifles. Despite that, you have the audacity to think your wealth and power can save you. You're so absolutely wrong, I can kill you. And I won't lose a single moment of sleep."

Victor pressed against the inside of his cheek with his tongue while he looked thoughtfully at Captain Daniels for several moments. No one seemed to notice him activating his distress beacon with his tongue. He said,

"No, I don't think you understand. You literally can't, kill me. I didn't say you wouldn't be able to live with yourself if you did. I'm telling you my destiny is set, and nothing you do can change it."

Harrison Shroyer put the muzzle of the rifle against Victor's temple again, asking,

"CAPTAIN?"

Captain Daniels held out his hand to Shroyer, saying,

"Give it to me, it should be me who does it."

Nora, Jacob, and Flynn all spoke at once,

"THOMAS, NO! / Don't do it Thomas! / Captain!"

Shroyer smiled and nodded. He handed Thomas the rifle and stepped back, covering his ears. Captain Daniels aimed the MCX-SPEAR at Victor's head and pulled the trigger. Everyone heard a faint,

Click...

The rifle didn't fire. Victor didn't even flinch, he just smiled and stared at Captain Daniels. Again, Nora, Jacob, Flynn, and now Corporal Torres joined in, all telling him not to do it. Captain Daniels lowered the rifle and cycled the bolt with his right hand, the unfired shell ejected. Thomas didn't hesitate, he raised the rifle and pulled the trigger.

Click...

Again, Victor didn't flinch. He just continued to smile. He was completely calm. Somehow, he knew the rifle wouldn't fire. Captain Daniels narrowed his eyes, slowly lowering the rifle. The captain knew that one misfire was a fluke with modern rifles and ammunition, one in hundreds of thousands potentially. Two misfires in a row were astronomical odds.

Something was wrong. Everyone was staring at Thomas with a range of expressions from confused to shocked. Captain Daniels cycled the bolt again. Another unfired shell was ejected. He looked at Staff Sergeant Flynn and said,

"Staff Sergeant, check those unfired rounds."

Captain Daniels pointed the rifle at a storage cabinet and pulled the trigger. The rifle discharged normally with a deafening report. Everyone flinched at the noise. Captain Daniels immediately turned the rifle back to Victor's head and pulled the trigger again.

Click...

Flynn held up the two unfired shells, he said,

"Both rounds have dents in the primer from the firing pin, Captain. Odds of two misfires are astronomical. Three out of four is about as unlikely as the sun exploding."

Victor laughed once loudly. Then he looked at Staff Sergeant Flynn and said,

"THAT, is much more likely than you think, Flynn."

Captain Daniels walked over to Corporal Torres and handed the rifle back to him. He started walking toward Nora. He asked,

"What just happened, Victor? I honestly can't even imagine how you just did that."

Victor shrugged casually, responding,

"You simply wouldn't understand, Thomas. None of you would."

Victor used his feet to rotate the chair enough that he could see Corporal Torres, and added,

"Well, he might. He's the religious one, right?"

Corporal Torres gave Victor a confused look and asked,

"El Diablo?"

Victor chuckled, then he winked at Torres and said,

"You better hope not."

Thomas pulled Nora up to her feet and hugged her. He turned his head back toward the others and said,

"I'm taking Nora and Piotr somewhere else. I'll be back Victor, then we'll talk."

Flynn stepped in front of Victor, and asked,

"Why Corporal Torres? What does he know that we don't?"

Captain Daniels opened the door and led Nora out. He looked at Piotr and gestured with his head for him to follow. When they reached the hallway that led to personal quarters, Captain Daniels told them both,

"I want the two of you to do your best to get some rest. I'll make it an order if that helps."

Piotr didn't need convincing. He went to his room. Nora hesitated and stepped close in front of Thomas. She took his head gently in her hands and pulled him down to kiss him on the cheek. She

looked him in the eyes, and said quietly,

"Whatever it is, that you're about to do, Thomas. I hope you're still a man I want to be with afterwords."

Without waiting for a response, she turned and went to her quarters. Captain Daniels walked back to operations. On the way, he passed Harrison Shroyer and Lieutenant King. The rifle fire must have woken her up.

Thomas could hear Shroyer explaining everything that had happened. The Lieutenant looked at him and started to speak. But Captain Daniels shook his head, no. He looked Lieutenant King in the eye, gestured to his ear and then pointed at Shroyer. Silently saying,

Listen to him.

THE FALSE PROPHET

When Captain Daniels got back to operations, he saw that Flynn and Torres were standing near Victor. Flynn was speaking, but Victor wasn't answering. Jacob had sat back down in his chair, in the image on the main screen. Jacob smiled and nodded at him as he entered the room. Captain Daniels nodded back at him as he approached and asked,

"Is he saying anything that makes any sense?"

Flynn shook his head, no. Captain Daniels pulled up a chair in front of Victor. Then he sat down and just waited. Victor looked at him for a moment, then grinned and said casually,

"Fine. Remove the absolutely unnecessary zip-ties and I'll explain. Fair enough?"

Captain Daniels looked at Flynn and nodded. Flynn pulled a folding knife from his pocket and cut the zip-ties off. Victor rubbed his wrists a bit and said,

"Now, I'm warning you. First, you're not going to believe me. And second, nothing I tell you is going to make your life any easier."

Captain Daniels nodded, and said,

"Duly noted, proceed please."

Victor nodded slightly, and continued,

"Corporal Torres, you're a religious man, yes? A student of the bible?"

Torres nodded cautiously, adding,

"Yes, I guess. I mean, sort of."

Victor's eyes gleamed, he chuckled then said,

"Thank you for that absolutely biblically lukewarm answer, Corporal. What do you know about the book of Revelation, chapter thirteen, specifically?"

Jacob interjected, sounding exasperated,

"Come on, SERIOUSLY? Are we doing this?"

Corporal Torres shook his head, saying,

"Uh, I don't really know that part. My old church didn't really get into that. It's more about salvation and worship and everybody singing. The kids get together and play video games. You know, stuff that makes people feel good."

Victor rolled his eyes, saying,

"Exactly my point. You were literally given a technical manual and you don't even read it. You just wander through life randomly pushing buttons. The vast majority of people are drifting aimlessly distracted by the pretty flashing lights and the dancing pretty people on their electronic toys. Reality and truth are uncomfortable, distasteful. Not good for any church's financial bottom line."

Victor pointed at Torres and continued,

"The moment you mention hell, the seals, trumpets, or bowls of wrath, people want to go to their safe space and suck their thumb. Can't have that, or people will go pay their tithe to a false sense of security somewhere else."

Captain Daniels leaned forward, and told Victor,

"You're a madman, Victor. You're certifiably bat crap crazy. Explain to me, please, why we can't shoot you. Before I start experimenting with other methods."

Victor smiled at Captain Daniels, and said,

"I told you that you were not going to believe me. I have barely scratched the surface of the answer you're after and you say I'm crazy. Why should I even bother?"

Staff Sergeant Flynn said,

"Captain, I have a Louisville slugger in my quarters. It's signed by #45, but I'd be willing to donate it to the cause, sir."

Over the speakers, Jacob chuckled. Captain Daniels grinned over at Flynn, saying,

"I appreciate that, Staff Sergeant. But no, as much as I'd enjoy it... Victor, I'm sorry. Please, enlighten us. You have my complete attention."

Victor nodded. His smile faded. His voice became deathly serious, he said,

"One last warning, Captain. If you go down this road there is no coming back. There is no escaping the consequences. You have this one last chance to continue on in this life in ignorance. Because once you look into the face of the darkness, it will look right back at you."

Jacob asked incredulously,

"Did you really just offer Thomas the choice between the red and blue pill?"

Flynn said,

"I thought he was talking about what he sees in the mirror every morning."

Without looking away from Victor, Captain Daniels held out his hand to the side, palm open fingers spread, quieting the others. He was staring into Victor's eyes. Victor looked like he was being completely serious. In his gut, Thomas could not help but believe that Victor was being honest, or at least believed he was being honest. Captain Daniels shook it off and said,

"I understand, and I accept the consequences. Thank you for that warning. Now, explain, please."

Victor nodded and stood up. Flynn and Torres both raised their rifles and aimed at him as he got up. Victor looked at Flynn incredulously and spread his hands, asking,

"Seriously?"

Flynn's brow furrowed as he thought about it. He looked down at the rifle. Conceding the point, Flynn shrugged and slung the rifle over his shoulder, saying,

"Either way, you're not getting your hands on one."

Victor rolled his eyes. He walked over to one of the storage cabinets, talking as he walked,

"The time isn't right for me to discuss certain things. I just can't, I'm sorry. I'm just being honest here."

Victor reached into the storage cabinet and pulled out a folded-

up dustcover, used for covering the workstations when they were going to be unused for any length of time. He walked toward the exit door, continuing,

"What I can do, what I will do, is tell you specifically what you asked about me and why you can't kill me."

To everyone's surprise, Victor shook the dust cover open and laid it gently and reverently over Jacob's dead body. He turned toward their shocked expressions and explained,

"Don't waste too much time kicking yourself, it's because of him."

Victor gestured to Jacob's image on the screen. They looked at the screen then back at Victor. Victor walked back toward them, explaining,

"He's right there. He can't be dead. If he's dead, he can't be there. It's that conflict in the brain..."

Victor tapped his skull, and continued,

"Those opposing facts, that made it next to impossible for your minds to acknowledge that your friend's dead body was lying there forgotten and ignored."

Victor waved his hand, dismissing the issue. He stopped as he drew near enough to look each one of them in the eyes, then he continued,

"Like I was saying. Revelation, 13:15, 'And it was allowed to give life to the image of the beast, so that the image of the beast might even speak and might cause those who would not worship the image of the beast to be slain.'"

Victor paused to gauge their reactions. He smiled and looked each of them in the eye. He continued,

"The verse is describing the false prophet of the very last days of the earth."

Victor pointed at himself for emphasis, and continued,

"ME! I literally gave life to the image of the beast. And THAT, is why you can't kill me. My story is written. My end, predetermined. You might as well try to make the earth spin backward! You just can't do it! It's literally impossible."

Jacob started laughing, convinced that Victor had completely lost his mind. Staff Sergeant Flynn frowned and shook his head. He didn't understand it, but he was sure this was some kind of misdirection. Corporal Torres, eyes wide with his limited understanding, made the sign of the cross in front of himself.

Captain Daniels calmly asked,

"You're saying Jacob is the beast?"

Jacob stopped laughing and looked at Thomas. Flynn and Torres looked at him also. Then all three looked at Victor.

Victor smiled widely at Captain Daniels and sat back down in the chair they had tied him to. He looked into the captain's eyes and said,

"I have always liked you, Thomas. Always."

Captain Daniels raised his eyebrows and said,

"I just tried to put a bullet in your head."

Thomas held up three fingers and added,

"Three times."

Victor chuckled and gestured dismissively, saying,

"I can't hold that against you, Thomas. You have no idea what you're doing. Besides, you're not even close to being the first person to try to kill me. But no, to answer your question, that's not what I was saying."

Victor leaned back and got comfortable. He pointed at Jacob and continued,

"To be clear, Jacob is the image of the beast. That I breathed life into. The image."

Victor held up both hands, close together, he said,

"The beast is a future man, yes."

He moved his hands slightly farther apart, saying,

"It's also much more, it's a system of influence and power."

He continued moving his hands farther and farther apart, as he continued,

"It's technology and science. It's advancement of culture and society. The beast is unimaginable knowledge and so much more."

Finally, Victor lowered his hands. He stared straight into the captain's eyes. He said,

"The summary of all the things that comprise the beast is impossible to fully quantify with our extremely limited understanding of this universe. Jacob is just one piece of something much larger."

Flynn looked at Captain Daniels, frowning, he asked,

"You're not buying any of this crap, are you?"

Captain Daniels kept his eyes on Victor. He shrugged, and replied to Flynn,

"Can you explain two misfires, a clean shot off-target, followed by another misfire?"

Staff Sergeant Flynn said flatly,

"No Sir, I can't. It's as close to impossible as it gets."

Captain Daniels asked,

"Jacob, Torres, can either of you explain it to me? Either of you have any alternative explanation, no matter how crazy?"

Both responded in the negative.

Captain Daniels nodded, and then asked Victor,

"What if I were to drive a knife into your heart?"

Victor raised his eyebrows, considering. He replied seriously,

"I honestly can't say, Thomas. You might trip or fall. Maybe even end up stabbing yourself. You could miss, get my shoulder. The possibilities are endless."

Captain Daniels asked,

"You're saying that no matter what we do, no matter what we try, something would stop us from killing you?"

Victor grinned and shook his head, no. He said,

"Not something, Captain Thomas Daniels. God would."

Thomas shook his head slightly and said,

"I can't even tell you how bad I want to try."

Victor shrugged, saying,

"Do as you will, Captain. I told you three years ago that I could not interfere with free will. But a word of advice, I'd be very careful. It doesn't have to be anything as gentle as a misfire in ignorance. I warned you, now that you know the truth, things have changed. The next correction could be much sterner."

On the big main screen, Jacob stood up from his chair. He looked alarmed as he said,

"I just lost all connection to surface level. Everything just went black."

Flynn and Torres unslung their rifles and pointed them at Victor. Victor didn't move, he just stared directly into the captain's eyes. Victor waited, almost expectantly. Captain Daniels didn't move either. He stared calmly back at Victor and asked,

"Your men?"

Victor nodded. Captain Daniels nodded back and asked,

"Real operators this time?"

Again, Victor nodded.

Thomas guessed,

"That's why you shut Jacob out, so you could call for help?"

Again, Victor nodded.

Captain Daniels leaned forward, elbows on his thighs, he asked,

"How do I save my men, Nora, Jacob?"

Victor smiled, and replied,

"I think we can come to an acceptable arrangement."

Doctor Fischer woke up suddenly. His body jerked and he sat up quickly, blurting out,

"WHERE'S BUTTERCUP?"

The doctor looked around, blinking, and confused.

L-3

About an hour later, Captain Daniels and Nora were waiting in medical. Victor had given them his word, that if they cooperated no one would be hurt. No charges would be filed, there would be no retaliation of any kind. They were sitting on a couch in the room that used to be dedicated to Jacob's care. Nora was leaning against Thomas, her head on his shoulder. Captain Daniels had one arm around her, and he was holding her hand with his other.

Thomas saw through the glass separation wall, as Victor entered medical followed by two armed men in black military uniforms. Victor turned to them and said something. They went back out into the hallway. Victor continued in. He came into the room and pulled up a chair. He was sitting near them but not too close. Victor gave them a sympathetic smile, and said,

"The others are being separated and reassigned to new postings. Good postings, with raises and promotions. All of them have signed non-disclosure agreements. For their sake, I hope they don't speak of this. Provided you hold up your end, I will honor mine, and absolutely no harm will befall any of them."

Nora scowled at Victor with eyes that were red from crying, she asked harshly,

"And US, Victor? What are you going to do to US?"

Victor looked from her to Captain Daniels and raised his eyebrows. Captain Daniels answered her question for him,

"Nothing, Nora. He can't. He wanted an Achilles in chains. He wanted an unfeeling weapon that could be controlled, aimed, and fired. What he has is a Jacob who only cares about two people in this world. The very last thing that Victor wants to do, is hurt those two people. Is my analysis correct, Victor?"

Victor nodded, and said,

"Spot on, Thomas. Except of course, for the important part. Jacob is exactly what I wanted. Jacob, as he is now, is the reason behind everything over the past three years. Achilles, for the impressive feat of accomplishment that he was, would never have been true life. Only a man, born of the line of Adam, could be used as the life I needed to breathe into the image. Jacob now, a living ghost in the machine, was the goal all along."

Victor pointed at each of them, in turn, continuing,

"Jacob now, was the reason I've kept you with him ever since you flew him off that ship. Jacob, is the reason I brought Nora along all this time."

Captain Daniels added,

"We were always meant to be your leash on him."

Victor nodded, and said,

"Now, your analysis is correct."

Captain Daniels asked,

"So now what, for us? A black hole somewhere?"

Victor laughed gently and shook his head, no. He stood up and gestured toward the door, saying,

"A dusty cell in the basement of some CIA black site? For my two very best friends? Absolutely not, Captain. Come, I want to show you something."

They followed Victor out and into the hall, where a total of three of his security team waited. Victor looked at one of them and said,

"Escort Miss Westin to her quarters please. She may have access to anything she needs or wants."

Nora blurted out,

"I WANT to go talk to Jacob!"

Understanding, Victor nodded to his guard. To Captain Daniels, he said,

"If you'll come with me, please, Captain?"

Captain Daniels pulled Nora close and hugged her. He spoke softly,

"This is probably the best way this mess could have ended. We're alive, and Jacob... isn't exactly dead. The others will be ok. I'll be back."

Victor walked to the elevator, followed by Captain Daniels and the other two guards. Victor stopped in front of the doors and looked Thomas in the eyes, his voice serious,

"I don't EVER want to have to repeat this, Thomas. If you try any..."

Captain Daniels held up a hand and interrupted,

"I get it, Victor. I understood before your men swarmed into operations."

Victor nodded thoughtfully, he said,

"You grasped the reality of the situation, basically, when Jacob lost connection to the surface, didn't you?"

Captain Daniels nodded and added,

"I realized it was all a part of your plan all along. Even the mystery that was nagging at me of why you first came in with thugs that you probably found on the street. We wouldn't have been able to bribe professionals to betray you. There would have been a firefight and people important to your plan might have been taken out of the equation."

Victor nodded and smiled again, and said,

"Very astute, as always. Thank you, Thomas. I'm glad I didn't have to speak the threat out loud. You know, you have to admit, I tried. All of this would have been a lot easier if we had been friends."

Captain Daniels nodded.

Victor's smile got even bigger, he said,

"You never know. Stranger things have happened."

Daniels replied,

"Don't hold your breath."

Victor grinned at the jab and dismissed his guards. Apparently, he didn't think he needed them now that they had an understanding.

Victor waved his hand like a jedi at the elevator and the doors opened. They walked inside and Victor repeated the gesture. The elevator began to descend. Captain Daniels asked,

"You don't have to move your hand like that, to control things, do you?"

Victor laughed, asking,

"How do you know that?"

"Because Jacob didn't."

Victor waved it off, saying,

"You're no fun."

The elevator descended a long time. Captain Daniels eventually asked,

"Where are we going Victor?"

Victor asked a question in response,

"Did you know that there used to be an incredibly advanced culture on this planet, about twelve thousand years ago?"

Captain Daniels furrowed his brow, considering, he said,

"Not exactly what's being taught in public school."

Victor nodded, saying,

"That's true, but it doesn't change what I'm telling you. They crossed the oceans and flew through the sky. They built massive structures all over the world. The few scattered remains of which, we can't even replicate today with our most modern technology."

Captain Daniels took a deep breath and said,

"If you say so. Where are we going, Victor?"

Victor replied simply,

"To one of their ancient temples."

Captain Daniels turned his head toward Victor, his eyes went a little wider. He said,

"Alright, I'm intrigued."

When the elevator doors finally opened, Victor stepped out into what looked like a locker room. Thomas followed him out and saw an open doorway directly across from him that appeared to lead to bathrooms. Looking left and right, there were heavy steel doors on both of the other walls. The door to his right had a simple lever handle. The one to the left had heavy locking bolts, top and bottom, that extended into the floor and ceiling.

There were several benches in front of a dozen gym-style lockers with well-ventilated doors. The lockers were tall and wide, obviously containing substantial amounts of gear of some kind. Victor walked over and opened one of the lockers. Thomas saw rugged-looking cold weather gear inside, including a helmet with mounted lights, heavy gloves, and other items.

Victor took out his gear and started pulling on the suit, over his shoes and clothes. He looked up and noticed Captain Daniels just watching him. Victor said,

"I know you don't trust me, Thomas. But trust me, you're going to want the cold weather gear. Where we're going, it's absolutely frigid. Like, arctic level frigid."

Captain Daniels opened a locker and pulled out the thick insulated bodysuit. It had rubber reinforced knees and elbows, and numerous pockets. He also saw it had some kind of electric heating system. Thomas had never seen environmental gear quite like it before. As he got suited up, he asked,

"What's behind the other door?"

Victor looked at him and saw him nod toward the door with the simple lever handle. Victor said,

"That's actually just another entrance to where we are now. It's a much longer trip, comes from a large underground complex under the airport in Denver. Wouldn't do anything for us now, from this end. You have to use the Rail-jet to traverse the tunnel, and right now, that's parked at the other end."

Captain Daniels pulled on the heavy boots and latched them shut. He paused and looked up at Victor, asking,

"What the hell is a Rail-jet?"

Victor chuckled, and said,

"A subway car, basically. It uses technology we haven't released to the public yet. It's faster than you'd believe. Involves bending the gravity field and it negates the effects of acceleration and deceleration. It's complicated."

Captain Daniels asked,

"Why are you telling me all of this? Why are you showing me whatever is beyond that locked door?"

Victor looked at Thomas. His expression was suddenly serious in a way that Captain Daniels hadn't seen since the first day he met him. Victor said,

"Hope, Thomas. I'm telling you all of this because I have hope. I haven't given up on you yet. That's why we're here. I need you to see the truth. The truth that my kind has kept hidden from yours for thousands upon thousands of years. Not counting your military skills and stuff like that, you can forget almost everything that you think you know. None of it is real, and I mean none of it is real.

Victor stood up as he finished putting on his gloves and grabbing his helmet, he added,

"Everything you think you know about this world and our history. It's just the shadow of reality that we cast onto the wall in front of you. I am hoping that once you see the truth, once you understand the truth, you'll understand why I've done all the things you hate me for."

Victor stared at him, to see his reaction. Captain Daniels considered for a moment, then went back to getting ready. The gloves weren't as thick as he expected. But they had an electronic connection that plugged into a locking socket on the sleeve near the inside of the wrist. Thomas was looking at the helmet and the two hoses attached to the back of it, when Victor walked over.

Captain Daniels looked up and saw that Victor already had his helmet locked on, and the hoses already attached to ports on the shoulders. Victor motioned for him to turn around, so he did. Victor lowered the helmet onto his head, locked the collar down, then attached the hoses. Captain Daniels suddenly heard Victor's voice over the speakers in his helmet,

"If something happens to the helmet lights, you have several backup flashlights and chemical lights in your pockets. You ready?”

Captain Daniels asked,

“How do I activate the radio?”

Victor grinned, and said,

“By talking.”

Victor went to the door with bolted locks and unbolted it from the floor and the ceiling. Thomas followed him out into a very old-looking mining tunnel. The floor was a thin layer of extremely dusty compacted dirt, on top of flat cut rock. The walls of the tunnel were rougher cut and uneven in most places, except for narrow channels where heavy wooden beams had been hammered in. The upright beams held up crossbeams that added support to questionable sections of the ceiling overhead.

The tunnel off to their left was completely blocked off from a cave in, about a hundred feet away. The tunnel to the right went on farther than Captain Daniels could see. Victor pointed toward the collapse and said,

“We dropped the ceiling in about a dozen places, along the exit shaft. We also marked the entrance with radiation warning signs.”

Captain Daniels flicked the hose by his head, and asked,

“How much air do we have?”

Victor shook his head, saying,

“It’s not air, it’s battery life you should be worried about. Those hoses are just inlet and outlet. The inlet is pumped through a filter and warmed before you breath in. Right now, your suit is

automatically set to keep you cool, so you don't overheat. This isn't the cold part. When we get to the cold part, it will switch over to heat on its own."

Victor turned and led the way into the tunnel. They walked for at least a mile when Captain Daniels asked,

"How about murder-suicide? Could I pull it off if I collapsed the tunnel on both of us?"

Victor laughed loudly. They passed several side tunnels, that Captain Daniels could see had been collapsed well away from the main shaft. After what Thomas estimated to be about three miles, they came to a dead end. There was a naturally collapsed section of the floor about thirty feet before the end of the tunnel. Victor said,

"The original miners cut this tunnel in the early 1800's. They decided to abandon the mine after this section of floor gave way in 1859. The ore had dried up, and the workers no longer trusted going any further in this direction."

Victor turned and climbed over the edge backwards, he said,

"There are ladder rungs installed in the near side of the wall going down. Just watch your step and hand placement, don't fall on my head."

Captain Daniels waited until Victor was about twenty feet down and then followed him. After about fifteen feet, the hole narrowed uncomfortably. Thomas looked down and noticed that the color of the surrounding rock was changing to something more reddish-brown where Victor was. He started moving down again, as Victor said,

"I'm at the bottom, not far to go."

Captain Daniels looked down again when he noticed the reddish-brown color change. He saw that his legs had already passed the end of the hole, into a room. He could see that below him was an oddly clean and smooth-looking room. That's when he felt his legs turning to ice. He looked down again and saw Victor move under the hole and look up, asking,

"What's the holdup, Captain? The heat won't engage until your chest passes the threshold of the temple. If you don't get down here, you're going to lose feeling in your legs and fall the rest of the way."

Captain Daniels shook his head. This was crazy. He quickly finished climbing down the steel ladder that was anchored with tension couplings between the floor and ceiling under the hole. Thomas immediately felt the electronic heating pads running throughout the inside of the suit begin to warm up.

Looking around, Thomas saw that he was in a small room, with disturbingly smooth surfaces. It didn't look old. It looked brand new. There were no joints to indicate connected pieces. The walls, floor, and ceiling had all been carved out of one giant solid reddish-brown stone. Other than the pile of dirt and stone against the back wall, where someone had pushed aside the collapse debris, this room was pristine.

Captain Daniels walked over to the wall and pulled one of the flashlights from a pocket on his thigh. He touched the flashlight to the wall and slid it down. There was no resistance, no scratching, the stone was cut as smooth as glass.

Victor was standing in the only doorway leading out. He was waiting and watching him. Captain Daniels noticed that Victor's exhaled breath was coming out of vents along his back, puffs of slow moving, quickly dissipating vapor. It was extremely cold here. Thomas asked,

"Why do you call this a temple?"

Captain Daniels saw Victor smile through his visor as he replied,

"If you'll follow me. You're going to see for yourself in about a minute, Thomas. And I hope you appreciate what I'm doing for you. The number of people I've allowed to see this, is a very small number."

They were deep underground, in the mountains west of Denver. This didn't make sense. Captain Daniels started toward Victor but stopped as he started to pass the ladder that was anchored between floor and ceiling. He looked at it closely. There were no bolts drilled into the stone. Rotating tension couplings created the anchoring force by applying pressure to the ceiling and floor.

Victor was watching him and guessed what he was thinking, he said,

"We had to use couplings, because we don't have anything strong enough to put so much as a scratch in this stone."

Victor knocked gently on the doorway next to him for emphasis, then he turned and headed out into the hallway. Captain Daniels shook his head and followed Victor out. The hall was the same, smooth-cut, pristine stone, no dust. The hallway ran sideways to the exit from the room, almost immediately turning ninety degrees and opening up into a massive room. Most of the room was dominated by the largest statue Captain Daniels had ever seen. The room was big enough to fit a football field.

In the center was a long and wide raised platform about three feet high. On the platform was a giant statue carved from dark grey stone lying on its back. It hadn't fallen, it had been carved lying on its back. The statue was wearing a steel slat type skirt and smooth black armor that covered its torso. Its head was bald and there was an intricately carved muzzle of black stone that covered its mouth.

There were also massive chains made of either the black stone, or smooth clean cast iron, that crossed each ankle and each wrist of the statue, anchored into the stone on each side. The chains reminded Thomas of a bad dream about a lobby nymph from several years ago. The memory made a chill run down his back. He followed Victor closer to the platform.

The craftsmanship of this hall and the statue was beyond amazing. Captain Daniels had never seen anything like it. The walls slanted slightly inward, giving the room a trapezoid shape. The walls were covered in carved relief. From this distance, with the helmet light, Captain Daniels couldn't make much of it out. The closer he got to the statue he was again amazed at the craftsmanship. It was carved to lifelike realism.

Victor suddenly turned back and held up a hand, stopping him. He asked,

"Standing here and seeing this now. If I told you that twelve thousand years ago there was an ancient prehistorical culture in this area that built massive structures beyond our ability to replicate. Would you believe me now?"

Captain Daniels chuckled and answered,

"Heavy handed way to persuade me. Yeah, I believe you now."

Victor grinned at him, and said,

"You haven't seen anything yet."

That was hard to believe, but Victor hadn't lied or even exaggerated at this point. Thomas raised his eyebrows slightly and nodded. Victor turned and continued toward the statue. He climbed up on the raised platform and waved for Captain Daniels to join him. Thomas climbed up the three-foot rise of the platform and walked up next to Victor.

His eyes were drawn to the massive arm in front of him. The fine detail on the sculpture was unreal. The skin looked like skin with thick course hair. How the hell did they carve hair onto a statue? Captain Daniels placed his gloved palm on the statue and moved his hand slightly. The hair moved. The statue was way too soft to be stone. Thomas felt the warmth of the body heat coming off the living giant through his glove.

Captain Daniels took a step back, his hand slowly lowering. He shook his head, taking another step back. He said,

"That's not possible."

Understanding how the captain felt, Victor put a hand on his shoulder and stopped him from walking backward off the platform. Victor started talking, giving Thomas a minute to shake off the shock,

"It's the most closely guarded secret in the world. Well, one of the two most closely guarded secrets in the world. There are two other temples like this one that we know of. There's one in London, and one in Moscow."

Captain Daniels was clinging to his calm and sanity by his fingernails. His thoughts whirling,

Heat. Body heat. Hair. This was a living thing. One of two secrets. Other temples. Body heat.

Captain Daniels said,

"I don't understand."

Victor gestured to the statue. The body. He said,

"We don't know which one he is. But we know he's one of the fallen."

Captain Daniels knew immediately that Victor meant fallen angel. He responded viscerally,

"Shut the f... WHAT? NO!"

Victor laughed, and said,

"When I dance the line between truth and lies, you believe me. When I give you the plain simple truth, you flat out refuse to even consider the possibility."

Captain Daniels narrowed his eyes. He was frustrated and confused. What was the point of this game? False prophet, fallen angel. He turned to face Victor, he asked,

"This is one of the fallen? You're the False Prophet? So, you're the bad guys, OBVIOUSLY, right?"

Victor shook his head, saying,

"That's not how I see it. Listen, if not for us, none of you would survive what's coming."

Captain Daniels looked at him intensely, asking,

"What's coming?"

Victor said flatly,

"You're not ready. You're barely keeping your junk together as it is."

Victor pointed to the fallen for emphasis. Then, he continued,

"I told you about the miners in the early 1800's. The ones who abandoned the mine that we were working. Well, that floor collapse took a very dear friend of mine. They abandoned the whole project the next day. No one even tried to search for Calvin..."

Captain Daniels was staring wide-eyed, unbelieving, as Victor continued,

"I went back just hours after they announced it. I couldn't just let him go. I had to try. I had to look. I anchored a rope and climbed down. I dropped a torch into the temple, I didn't know what I was seeing. My first try, I almost lost a foot to frostbite. Calvin was long dead by the time I could get back with foul weather gear. It didn't matter. I had to see what the room was that he had fallen into."

Victor spread his hands and looked around, continuing,

"I found Calvin's body, but I also explored around. I was overwhelmed by the temple. I found the body of the fallen. I pulled off my glove and I touched it. You can't even imagine the things I saw, Thomas. The things he showed me. I almost lost my mind."

Captain Daniels said,

"You. You found this place. Two hundred years ago?"

Victor nodded, and said,

"Yes, almost two hundred years ago. And you know what

happened next? I took what I learned from him, and I used it. For some reason that I don't even understand, I stopped aging. Over the years I helped develop steam power and combustion and transistors, computers. I had to stay in the background, I had to change my identity, become a new person. I kept the truth to myself. I just nudged things along when the timing was right, I helped us progress."

Victor looked at the fallen, and added,

"I did what he wanted me to do. Because our world was running out of time."

Captain Daniels shook his head, saying,

"No. No Victor, it's too much. You're lying. You HAVE to be lying."

Victor made eye contact, and said,

"Think hard here Thomas, what changed and when? For thousands of years, news travelled at the speed of horse. Benjamin Franklin crossed the ocean on the same wind power tech-level ship that also carried Jonah and fed him to the fish. Then, a couple hundred years ago, BOOM, technology explosion. That was me."

Captain Daniels felt a knot in his gut. He didn't understand this game, or what Victor's purpose could be in telling him all these things. He looked at the giant. It was real. He looked at the temple. It was real. He looked at Victor. He was...

Captain Daniels slowly shook his head, struggling, he said,

"I can't. I can't believe it. I mean, I believe it. I just can't make myself be ok believing it."

Victor laughed and moved over to the body of the fallen. He

placed his gloved hand on the dark grey flesh, and said,

"You want to know the truth? You want to see it for yourself? It's right here, Thomas. Touch him."

Captain Daniels walked over to where Victor stood. He placed his gloved hand on the arm. Victor said,

"The contact has to be flesh to flesh, Thomas."

Captain Daniels shook his head, saying,

"I can't. I'm trying, I just can't."

Victor nodded, and said,

"I didn't think you'd be able to bring yourself to do it, but I had to try. I had to offer you the truth. I'm not giving up though, Thomas. I'm going to hold onto hope for you."

Captain Daniels shook his head. He turned and hopped down off the platform and headed for the exit. He didn't look up at the walls. He climbed the ladder and walked as fast as he could for the exit. He barely heard Victor calling for him over the radio.

Roughly an hour later, Captain Daniels was sitting on one of the locker room benches. He was halfway out of the arctic survival suit. His helmet and gloves were discarded absently on the floor. Thomas was in shock, just sitting and staring at the floor. He had no idea what Victor was saying from the other bench.

After a few more minutes passed, Victor stopped talking and stood up. He walked closer to Captain Daniels and said,

"Thomas?"

"THOMAS!"

Finally hearing him, Captain Daniels looked up. Victor said,

"You have to get it together man. You're losing it."

Thomas asked,

"Victor, what's coming?"

Victor gave Thomas a serious look, contemplating. He said,

"It's bad. It's very bad! It's way beyond very bad, OK?"

Victor leaned forward and put a hand on Thomas's shoulder. He looked him directly in the eyes and said,

"Trust me on this. Take some time and get your mind around what you've already learned. When you've taken some time, if you ask me again, I'll answer you."

Victor stood up and took a step back. He gestured to the mess on the floor, and said,

"Now pick this crap up. What kind of Marine are you, anyway?"

~~~~

Nora and Jacob were staring at each other in silence when Victor walked into operations. Both of them looked like they had been crying. On the main screen, Jacob narrowed his eyes at Victor. Nora turned around in her chair to look behind her. She said icily,

"You son of a bitch."

Victor continued walking toward them. He laughed briefly and then said,

~~~~

"With everything I've done to earn all that hate and anger you feel for me. What do you do? You insult my mother. Don't you think that's odd?"

Nora stood up so fast, her chair went rolling away. She demanded,

"WHERE'S THOMAS?"

Victor shrugged and replied simply,

"I have no idea. Last I saw, he was headed up to the surface."

Nora stormed out of the room, slamming the door behind her. Victor took a breath, then continued walking toward the main screen. He stopped when he reached the chair Nora had discarded. He moved it to the center of the room and sat down. Calmly, with a smile, he asked Jacob,

"How's your world?"

Jacob gave him the middle finger and the screen went black. Victor chuckled, saying,

"This isn't how mature adults discuss things rationally, Jacob."

Victor looked at his watch and settled in to wait. She was exactly what Thomas needed.

~~~~

Nora found Captain Daniels in his quarters. She passed through the living room and looked into his bedroom. He was sitting on the edge of the bed with what looked like a bottle of Hotel Tango bourbon. Victor must have really upset him. Nora walked over and slowly and gently tried to take the bottle.

~~~~

Captain Daniels sprang off the bed, surprised. He realized immediately who she was and said,

"Hey! I'm sorry!"

He looked down at the bottle in his hand. He looked at her wide eyes and her outstretched hand and put two and two together. Captain Daniels laughed a bit manically and shook his head, he walked out of the room, saying,

"Oooooh no. No, no, no. You don't get it. You just don't get it."

Captain Daniels pulled the cork and took a long pull of the bourbon. Nora followed him into the living room. She was quickly growing more and more concerned. She asked,

"Thomas, what is going on?"

Captain Daniels shook his head, he was mumbling incoherently,

"Can't. Not possible. He knew you wouldn't believe me. He knew I wouldn't even be able to tell you. It's just not possible."

Nora switched tactics. She approached him slowly, both hands up non-threatening, and said,

"Thomas, listen to me. Just listen."

Captain Daniels paused his ranting and stared at her, his face fluctuating between emotions. Nora realized she was going to have to snap him out it. She decided to use a two-step mental recalibration. First, she had to get his attention. She said,

"Thomas, listen. This is important, ok? Are you listening?"

Thomas nodded frantically. She said,

"I need you to take me to bed and make love to me, right now!"

Captain Daniels froze and stared at her. Step one, success. Two, she slapped him so hard his grandfather's headstone wobbled on his grave. As an afterthought, she also snatched the bottle out of his hand. When his vision cleared, Thomas shook his head to make sure his jaw was still attached. He stood up straight and looked around.

Nora was standing in front of him with her arms crossed. Her face was utterly non-apologetic. She asked,

"You with me now, Marine?"

Captain Daniels worked his jaw a little, testing it for function. He nodded and said,

"Yes, thank you."

Nora set the bottle down and moved close to him. She put her hands on his shoulders and looked up into his eyes. She asked,

"Stay calm and just tell me what's going on. What's wrong? What did Victor do to you?"

Captain Daniels closed his eyes for several seconds. He took a deep breath, then said,

"Victor took me down to L-3."

Nora's eyes grew wide. Everyone knew the rumors. Gateway to hell. Dead aliens in glass tanks. Dark ritual sacrifices, etc. She took his hands and led him to the couch. She had Thomas sit down. Then she sat down next to him, still holding his hands. She said,

"Go on."

Thomas shook his head slightly. He knew she wasn't going to believe it. He barely believed it and he had reached out and touched it. He said, hesitantly,

"You're not going to believe me."

Nora quickly said,

"No, no! THOMAS! Don't do that, you know I have a fifty riding on aliens with Piotr."

Despite knowing what she was doing, he laughed. Then he smiled at her. He touched her cheek lightly, and said,

"Ok, you want to know what's down there?"

Nora nodded emphatically. He said,

"There's an intact twelve-thousand-year-old megalithic temple complex, with a living fifty-foot-tall fallen angel chained to a pedestal."

Nora leaned back slightly. Her expression was completely neutral. She blinked a few times and stared at him. She was trying to decide if he was joking or whether she should consider the possibility that he was telling her the truth. Captain Daniels held her gaze and waited. After a minute passed, Nora reached for the bourbon.

Thirty minutes later.

Captain Daniels was sitting on the couch, watching Nora pace back and forth. She asked, for the fifth time,

"WHY would he take you down there?!?"

For the fifth time, he said,

"I don't know."

All things considered. It was going better than Captain Daniels had expected. She had quickly moved from disbelief to shock and confusion to whatever this was. She stopped and looked at him, asking,

"You touched it? You physically TOUCHED it?!?"

Captain Daniels nodded. She started to pace again, then stopped and said,

"We have to confront Victor! We corner him, and we make him explain!"

He stood up and cocked his head slightly, thinking hopefully he could pull her back to something slightly less confrontational. He said,

"Ok, let's go."

They walked past Victor's soldiers standing outside operations. Inside, they found Victor sitting in the same chair that Nora had been sitting in earlier. He said something to someone on his phone and hung up. As they walked up, Victor looked at his watch and said,

"I thought that would take longer."

Nora walked right up to Victor, just six or seven feet away, she asked sternly,

"What game are you playing? Why did you take him down there?"

Captain Daniels gently grabbed her waist and pulled her a step back, whispering,

"Downshift one gear babe."

Victor looked her in the eyes and chuckled, then said,

"You want to see it, don't you?"

Captain Daniels looked at Victor, surprised. Nora's eyes went wide. She started to say something and then stopped, considering. The main screen came to life. Jacob was sitting in his chair, but the background looked like an extension of operations. It made it feel like he was in the same room. Jacob said,

"See what?"

Victor spun his chair around to face Jacob, saying,

"Something that's going to convince both of them, to help me convince you, to help me."

Nora and Captain Daniels looked at each other, then back to Victor. Jacob said,

"I don't feel like playing with you Victor. She said, 'down there', there's only one thing underneath us. L-3. What's on L-3? And what is it going to convince them to help you convince me to do?"

Captain Daniels stated flatly,

"There's a fifty-foot-tall fallen angel chained to a pedestal in a twelve-thousand-year-old temple."

Jacob's mouth dropped open. He stared at Captain Daniels in stunned silence. Victor spun back around to face the captain, he spread his hands, and said,

"What the, no foreplay? You just dump it on him like that?"

Jacob recovered quickly and said,

"I put the highest probability on the possibility that he drugged you with something."

Nora added,

"If I went down there, he wouldn't be able to make both of us have the same hallucination."

Victor scoffed and said,

"Please, we could do group hallucination in the 80's with MK-Ultra. If I wanted to, with the right drugs, I could make you both believe you were part of a time traveling Disco band on a mission to save an extinct flower, but that's not what's going on."

Captain Daniels interjected loudly,

"I was NOT drugged. I know what I saw. I know what I put my hand on. It's down there."

Jacob and Nora went silent. They looked at each other, then looked at Thomas. Captain Daniels turned to Victor, he said,

"She needs to see it for herself."

Victor stood up and walked toward the door, saying,

"Tomorrow, Captain, first thing. We'll go."

Victor left. Nora sat down and let out a sigh. Captain Daniels pushed over another chair and sat down next to her, facing Jacob's image on the main screen. He took Nora's hand and held it. He looked at Jacob and said,

"I've learned something, buddy. Something I should have realized long before Victor admitted to it, and it's got nothing to do with

L-3."

Jacob smiled sadly, and replied,

"He kept you to use as leverage against me."

Captain Daniels couldn't hide his surprise. He said,

"How did you..."

Jacob interrupted,

"He kept the two of you. He sent everyone else away. He can't force my compliance. His only power over me is to destroy the network and kill me. He won't waste the three years of effort he spent creating me. He knows I love you both dearly. To you, that explanation lasted ten seconds, to me it was relatively half an hour. I've had plenty of time to think about things."

Captain Daniels nodded, understanding. He said,

"I'm sorry, Jacob. I feel like I failed you."

Jacob smiled. He didn't look sad. He looked more alive than ever. He looked hopeful. He stood up from his chair and stepped toward them. As he moved, the room around him shifted to a stage and he was standing behind a podium. He passed his hand in front of his face, and his face shifted to Victor's face. He said, in Victor's voice,

"I wouldn't count me out just yet, Captain."

Captain Daniels smiled. Nora laughed. They talked for a short time. They talked like old friends. Eventually, Thomas and Nora told Jacob goodnight. Nora took Thomas by the hand and led him back to his quarters.

Inside, they sat on the couch for a while. Thomas asked her if she wanted to stay. She told him she didn't want to be alone.

Informational Warfare Series

THE SIXTH SEAL, REVEALED

The next morning, Captain Daniels woke up and checked the bed next to him. She was gone. He got up and stretched. Then he pulled on a pair of sweats and his 'Save The Frogs' T-shirt and walked out into the main room to make coffee. When he opened the door, he saw Nora and Victor standing in the living room looking at him. Both of them were already ready to go. Victor grinned, and asked,

"Long night, stud?"

Nora narrowed her eyes and elbowed Victor in the ribs. Victor let out a breath and painful laugh. Nora looked at Thomas, her face now showing some irritation. She pointed at his shirt, and said,

"You wear that stupid shirt all the time. What stupid thing do the stupid frogs need saving from?"

Still groggy and half asleep, Captain Daniels said,

"Uh, herbicides... or pesticides maybe. Industrial chemicals."

Thomas rubbed his eyes and yawned, he added,

"It's called atrazine. It turns the freaking frogs gay."

Nora gave him a look like she was either questioning his sanity or her taste in men. Thomas wasn't sure which. Victor laughed so hard he almost doubled over.

Ten minutes later they were headed toward the elevator. Nora was dressed like she was going hiking on a rugged trail in a national park. Victor was wearing business casual. Captain Daniels had traded out his sweatpants for jeans and sneakers and out of stubbornness, he kept on his 'Save The Frogs' T-shirt.

They passed Victor's soldiers at the end of the hall. They passed two more in the main hallway and walked up to two more guarding the elevator. Captain Daniels asked,

"If we're the only people here now, why the hell do you have so many guards here?"

Victor winked at him and said,

"I sleep better, knowing all my bases are covered."

Victor waved his hand at the elevator doors, and they opened. Thomas rolled his eyes. Nora gave Victor a sympathetic look and asked,

"Do you have a cheaper model transceiver? Jacob could interface with tech without even blinking."

Victor glared at her and got in the elevator, saying,

"You're no fun either."

Captain Daniels and Nora got in the elevator. The doors closed and the elevator began to descend. Victor looked like he was pouting. No one spoke on the way down, but Nora had a smile on her face. Victor got dressed in the arctic survival gear and then watched as Captain Daniels helped Nora get her suit set up.

Once they started down the old mining tunnel, Thomas told Nora the story that Victor had told him. He explained to her about Victor being a part of the original crew, and being two hundred years old, and coming back to search for his friend, and finding the temple.

When they reached the collapsed hole, Nora looked at Victor with her evil grin. Much louder than necessary, she asked,

"IS THIS THE WAY DOWN, OLD MAN?"

Victor seemed to have gotten his groove back, he chuckled and said,

"Technically, I stopped aging. I'm a youngish man, who has been around a really long time."

He winked at her and started down. Nora waited until Victor was about ten feet down then she followed. Thomas came down last, prompting Nora to keep moving when she stopped at the reddish-brown rock like he had.

Once in the room below, Captain Daniels watched her look around. She was taking in all the same details that he had noticed the first time. She ran her hand along the wall. Stepping up next to Thomas, Victor asked,

"Déjà vu' right?"

Captain Daniels nodded. Nora heard him as well, over the suit radio, she came toward the doorway where they waited. She said,

"I'm ready, let's go."

Victor led them into the hall and around the bend into the main room of the temple. Captain Daniels turned back and smiled at the awestruck look on Nora's face as she stood in the doorway taking in the enormity of everything before her. Thomas tapped

Victor on the arm and asked,

"What else? Are there other side tunnels, other rooms?"

Victor was grinning, watching Nora. He replied without turning his head,

"There are. Nothing that will show you anything you haven't seen though. What you haven't seen, is here, in this room."

Victor turned and looked Captain Daniels in the eye. Then he pointed up high, to all the carved images that covered the inside of the four main walls. Victor added,

"Also, on the far side of the fallen one. There's something that's really going to bake your noodle. I'm not sure you're ready for that yet."

Nora came up to them, and asked,

"What's over there?"

Victor shook his head and chuckled, to Captain Daniels he said,

"Maybe I should have brought her down here first, to help you deal with the shock."

Nora rolled her eyes and walked over to the pedestal that held the giant in chains. She climbed up the three-foot rise and approached the massive body. She knew from Thomas and his description what she was looking at. She knew it was living flesh and not carved stone. But it didn't truly sink in until she gently pushed her gloved hand against the warm skin.

Victor and Thomas watched her from the floor for several moments. Eventually, Victor laid his hand on the captain's shoulder. When Thomas looked over, Victor subtly jerked his head toward the side. Indicating the nearest corner of the massive pedestal, toward the 'head' end of the giant. Victor said,

"Come on, I'll show you."

Captain Daniels followed him, looking back at Nora as they headed off to circle around to the far side. She was still standing there with her hand on the giant's arm. He asked,

"Nora, you ok?"

Nora nodded slowly and replied, her voice hesitant as if distracted by the question,

"I can feel... it's pulse. It has... a heartbeat."

Victor had rounded the corner and added,

"Come on Captain, she'll be fine. No one, in two hundred years, has been harmed in this place."

Captain Daniels turned and picked up the pace to catch Victor, saying,

"Except Calvin."

Victor stopped and looked back. Captain Daniels thought he saw the briefest flash of anger on Victor's face before it softened into his ever-present mind-numbingly infuriating smile. Victor replied,

"Touche, Thomas."

Captain Daniels saw what Victor was talking about the moment he passed around the top of the giant's head. It looked at first like a loosely rolled up ancient carpet. As he continued around and got closer, he made out more detail.

Floating in mid-air, with no apparent support, was a massive roll of ancient-looking parchment, outlined and glowing with a soft white radiance. It hovered a few feet above the level of the pedestal, close to the giant's ear. From where Captain Daniels stood, on the floor of the room, it was just slightly above his eye level. The roll had to be about six feet long and as big around as a telephone pole. The parchment paper was heavy looking and thick like cardboard.

There were also three red ribbons with thick saucer sized wax seals that held the scroll in its rolled-up shape. It was odd though, the three silk looking ribbons were not centered on the scroll. They were only on the right end. Victor, standing next to him, spoke as if reading his thoughts,

"The first four are gone. If you look carefully, you can see where they were. The scroll is creased slightly where they held it together for thousands of years."

Captain Daniels saw what he was talking about. There were four places that showed evidence that there were once ribbons with wax seals that were now gone. At one time, there had been seven seals on the scroll, all equally spaced. He asked Victor,

"What the hell is this?"

Victor grinned and shrugged, saying,

"You tell me."

Captain Daniels placed his hands on the raised platform, to climb up. Victor laughed and grabbed him, stopping him from climbing up. He said,

"I figured you'd want a closer look. Trust me, you don't want to do that. I made the mistake of getting too close, once."

Captain Daniels stepped back, looking from the hovering glowing scroll to Victor, he asked,

"What happened?"

Victor stepped away, holding his hands spread as far apart as possible to demonstrate, he said,

"About this close to the scroll, there's something. A wall, a field of energy, a being? I don't know what it is, but I know what it'll do to you."

He walked about ten feet away from the platform and turned back toward Captain Daniels, and said,

"I woke up over here. Flat on my back, with a nasty concussion."

He walked back, and continued,

"As I said, I don't know. But I have a theory. I believe what we're seeing is a projected image, being held where it is, by something. Somehow, placed here by the giant's ear, for him to hear the wax seals breaking and falling away. Best example I could give would be like something is holding up a cellphone and showing an image of something that is happening somewhere far away. From our perspective though, we can't see the something, or the cell phone. All we see, is the image being projected."

Captain Daniels looked back at the scroll, looked down at the platform underneath it, then back at Victor, and said,

"You believe it's a projected image, because there is no trace of the broken seals or ribbons on the platform underneath it."

Victor nodded, saying,

"Very good, Captain. What else?"

Captain Daniels looked back at the scroll. He looked up at the giant's head. He turned back to Victor and said,

"It's not hovering in front of its face. It's been placed right next to his ear. That's why you think it's there for him to hear the seals breaking."

Captain Daniels glanced at Victor and saw him nodding, yes. He continued,

"And if the giant can hear the seals breaking, he can hear other things. You've tried talking to it?"

Again, Victor nodded, grinning. Then he shook his head, no, and said,

"No, it has never reacted. It has never moved, twitched, turned its head, or opened its eyes. At least not that I've seen. It has communicated though."

Faintly, her voice distant, they heard Nora say,

"I hear you."

Captain Daniels asked,

"Nora, you ok?"

A few moments passed with no response. Captain Daniels asked again, louder,

"NORA! Are you ok?"

She spoke again,

"Show me."

Suddenly alarmed, Captain Daniels looked at Victor, asking,

"She's not talking to us, is she?"

Victor raised his eyebrows and shook his head, saying,

"I have no idea."

Captain Daniels moved as fast as he could in the heavy arctic survival gear. He rounded the top of the platform and saw that Nora was lying on her back. He shouted,

"NORA!"

He moved at a quick trot, half run, with Victor on his heels. They climbed onto the platform when they got near her. Moving close, they saw her eyes were closed and one of her gloves was lying on the platform near her left foot.

Captain Daniels dropped to his knees and worked the glove back onto her hand, reattaching the electrical connection to the sleeve. He grabbed her helmet and moved it slightly back and forth, saying loudly,

"Nora! Nora!"

He looked up at Victor, standing on the other side of her, he asked,

"What the hell just happened, Victor?"

Victor was smiling, he said,

"She did what I wanted you to do, Thomas. She removed her glove and touched him. Flesh to flesh. Like I said, it does communicate."

~~~~

~~~~

"Maybe I should have brought her down here first, to help you deal with the shock."

Nora rolled her eyes and walked over to the pedestal that held the giant in chains. She climbed up the three-foot rise and approached the massive body. She knew from Thomas and his description what she was looking at. She knew it was flesh and not carved stone. But it didn't truly sink in until she gently placed her gloved hand against the warm skin.

She brought her fingers and thumb close together and pressed her hand harder against the thick dense flesh. She was trying to feel for something. The giant was warm, and that carried certain logical conclusions with it. She heard Victor talking to Captain Daniels,

"Come on, I'll show you."

She felt what she was searching for. It was faint and slow. Much slower than a human heartbeat. But now that she had the rhythm, it was unmistakable. Instead of a beat-beat, beat-beat, the giant's first beat was a long gentle rise in pressure against her hand, followed thirty seconds later with another long gentle rise in pressure.

In her peripheral vision, she saw Victor leading Captain Daniels away toward the giant's head. Thomas looked back and asked her,

"Nora, you ok?"

She nodded slowly and replied, distracted by his question from her analysis of the giant's heartrate,

"I can feel... it's pulse. It has... a heartbeat."

A few moments later, she heard Victor say,

"Come on Captain, she'll be fine. No one, in two hundred years, has been harmed in this place."

She heard Thomas reply,

"Except Calvin."

Nora reached up and turned down the volume of her radio so she could concentrate. Several minutes went by before she felt the gentle double rise in pressure as the giant's heart circulated its blood. Just to confirm, she waited several more minutes and felt the process repeat again.

She was reaching up with her other hand, to turn her volume back up, when she heard a voice in her mind. It was slow and extremely deep and low frequency, like words dragged across pavement before being spoken, it said,

"Nora... hear... me..."

She was shocked and surprised. The moment was surreal. Without thinking, she replied,

"I hear you."

The voice resonated through her brain as vibration rippled through her body, it said,

"Unveil... connection... intimate... contact... show... your... world... ending..."

As fast as her confusion started, it ended. Unveil, the word made no sense for a second, then she saw her glove in her mind. The word, connection, was followed by an image of the material of the glove separating her from touching the giant. Intimate and contact didn't make sense until she saw her bare hand, palm laid flat against the giant's skin.

She didn't wait for the images that might follow the last four words.

Nora pulled her hand away from the giant and reached up with her other hand and disconnected the cord between her glove and her suit. She pulled off the glove and dropped it. She placed her bare hand against the giant and said,

"Show me."

Everything froze in place, as Nora left her body. She floated up and out of her skin. She looked down and saw herself standing there, her bare hand against its flesh. She rose higher, above the giant. Her perspective moved up toward his head. The giant's massive face loomed in front of her. The eyes suddenly opened. His solid black orbs bored deep into her soul.

A flash of bright pure white light came from the giant's eyes. It was like a camera flash in a pitch-black cave. She no longer saw the temple, or the giant.

She suddenly saw a half dozen giants, surrounded by tiny humans, all working together to construct a massive block structure. One of the giants, using both hands, lifted a stone that looked to be twenty feet wide, twenty feet deep, and twenty feet tall. Eight thousand cubic feet of solid rock, and the giant lifted it like a cooler full of beers.

Another flash of light and Nora stood on a rain soaked grassy plain. She was overlooking a massive hut type structure. Entire trees, roughly stripped of branches, were lashed together to make the walls and the cone shaped roof. Nora looked down and saw that she was floating just above quickly rising waters.

From the door of the hut, two people holding hands ran out into the storm. They looked tiny compared to the massive doorway. One was a woman, carrying a baby. The man with her resembled the giant lying on the platform before her.

Nora watched as he stepped away from the woman with the baby. He spread his feet wide and leaned back, howling at the sky. His arms curled and bulged, straining with effort. His body rapidly grew to his full fifty-foot stature.

The giant reached down and lifted the woman and the child to his breast, where he cradled them both and began running through the now ankle-deep waters. Nora's vision turned to follow as the giant ran past, the water now at his knees. She saw up close the fear in his eyes. Nora could see the mountains in the distance. The giant wasn't going to make it.

Long before he made it even half of the distance to the mountains, the water was up to his chest. The giant lifted the woman and child higher and kept moving. Nora saw agonizing pain etched on the giant's face. He knew he wasn't going to make it.

The water rose past his head. It eventually rose higher than his hand could stretch. The water covered everything.

Then time sped up. The water receded and the land was revealed again. The sun streaked across the sky rapidly. Sunrise to sunset blurred into a glowing solid line as years and years flew by. People, blurring around, moved across the land. Villages rose and fell. More people blurred around, and arrows filled the sky. Towns and roads appeared and expanded, then fell apart and were either rebuilt or built over.

Time slowed back down as Nora looked up and saw an early model plane in the sky. She realized the giant was giving her perspective in the vision. Time accelerated again. A massive city sprang up, shifting and changing as years and years passed. The next slowing of time, Nora watched a string of satellites pass over her head in a tight linear formation. They looked like white Christmas lights in a perfect line.

Time stopped and froze. Nora was catapulted from the Earth into space. Her planet dropped away and shrank into a tiny dot as the outer gas giants passed by her and soon all she could see was our sun, slowly shrinking. Eventually the sun was a tiny light surrounded by a cloud of dusty debris moving through a flickering ocean of dust and twinkling particles.

The word heliopause came to her mind. She was seeing the far outer limit of the Sun's magnetic field. Where the solar magnetic field interacted with the particles and energy that were being pushed out from the center of the galaxy. She was looking at our solar systems border with intergalactic space.

As she watched, Nora saw a massive wall of thicker and denser dust and energetic particles coming toward our tiny solar system. The size and scope of it was almost impossible for her mind to comprehend. More knowledge from the fallen one filled her mind.

She suddenly knew that the dense wall of dust and particles was ten light years high. It was a spinning galaxy sized electromagnetic energy field in the shape of the edge of a ballerina's skirt. It marked the boundary between the north and south magnetic fields of the entire Milky Way Galaxy.

She knew that the wall was so thick that our solar system would spend three hundred years passing through it. She also knew that the reason the wall of dust was curved and coming at them at a steep angle was due to the central plasma rotation of the galactic center. Her mind was melting with information overload.

Somehow, the giant made her understand all these things she was seeing. The fallen angel was somehow downloading knowledge into her mind about the vision it was showing her. She watched our solar system plunge into the oncoming wave, passing through the thick layer of separation between the powerful magnetic fields.

From the southern positive magnetic plane of the galaxy, we headed into the northern negative magnetic plane. The two were separated by the ocean like layer of dense dusty particles and neutrons that were trapped between the magnetic planes as it swept across the galaxy like a static electricity duster.

Nora's vision dropped back into the solar system, and she hurtled toward our sun.

As she plunged toward the heart of the gravity well, she realized that she felt no fear. She had no sense of danger, no need for self-preservation. She felt no joy, no love, no hatred, or desires. Very soon, our sun stood before her, as if she were a satellite in its orbit.

She turned away from the star and watched as the gigantic wave swept across our solar system. It slowly filled the interstellar space between planets with hundreds then thousands of times more particles and neutrons than our solar system normally held.

As the energy and the materials of the boundary layer steadily increased around the planets, she watched as their winds increased, their atmospheres rippled and some changed direction. Auroras surged and danced on multiple planets. Mars began to shake as its core was awakened. The Earth's weather and magnetic field went into insane turmoil.

Turning again, she watched as the material of the wave thickened around Venus, its winds spinning faster and lightning flashing erratically. The wave engulfed our sun, dumping ever increasing amounts of material into the star.

The rapidly approaching center of the field caused the Sun's inner engine to falter. The solar wind slowed down drastically. The dust coalesced and thickened in the corona and photosphere. Our sun dimmed and slowly turned an angry red as the thick heavy dust was drawn into its gravity. It looked like a shovel full of sand tossed across hot coals.

The dust and particles continued to increase, being drawn in by the Sun's gravity faster than the diminishing solar wind could push them away. It was rapidly building up in the photosphere. The Sun continued to darken. The dark molten red became the glowing and highlighted black of magma pouring from a volcano.

The center of the galactic electromagnetic boundary finally passed across our star. The sun's engine reengaged with a powerful surge of reversed electromagnetic energy. The thick film of built-up crust around our star was blasted away from the Sun in every direction.

Micro-nova.

Surging out quickly ahead of the rippling and shattered plasma crust was a super-charged burst of electromagnetic energy that flashed outward through the entire solar system.

Nora's vision turned and followed the surge of energy. She watched it slam into the Earth. The intense energy rippled around our chaotic magnetosphere. The auroras went insane, bathing the entire Earth in eerie blue, green, and red fiery lights.

She watched the energy of the electromagnetic surge filter down through each of the layers of the magnetosphere into the core, the entire Earth was electrically super-charged. The electromagnetic insult super-heated the crust-mantle boundary and it released its tenuous hold.

She watched the crust of the Earth slide across the super-heated liquid mantle. The massive weights of Greenland's and Antarctica's heavy ice were pulled by the inertia of Earth's one thousand mile per hour rotational force toward the equator at the center. The Earth was now in a drunken wobbling spin.

The oceans churned and sloshed against the land. Nora heard voices screaming in terror. Millions, then billions of voices, rose to a deafening cacophony of fear and death.

Again, the pure white light flashed across her vision. Nora saw something new as her mind and her perspective were split into multiple points of focus. It was like a picture in picture display, or multiple screens shown in a single window.

In one part of her mind, she saw the Earth spinning through space. She watched the solar wind, buffeting against the Earth's forcefield-like magnetosphere. It looked like a river of heat and energetic particles parting around a boulder in a stream.

Nora knew that the fallen angel was trying to teach her. It wanted her to understand what was coming in the future, what was happening right now, and what had started a hundred and fifty years ago. It wanted her to know what had happened to him and his people, twelve thousand years ago.

In another part of her mind, Nora saw rioting crowds in major cities all over the world. They were poor and hungry and desperate. The Earth's ability to support crops had begun failing long before the climax of the coming catastrophe. The magnetosphere was weakening and shifting, the galactic magnetic boundary was still approaching.

As the Earth's shield weakened, the people and animals on Earth grew increasingly hostile. It was a direct causal effect. The weakening of the magnetic field had a severe negative impact on logic and rational thought. Mankind was given over to baser instincts. Love grew cold in the hearts of many.

The magnetic field weakened even further. People began to fight and hurt and kill each other, in ever increasing numbers. Things were spiraling out of control. The weather went crazy, deserts flooded, snow blanketed the middle east. Texas was a frozen tundra. Uncountable numbers of animals drifted and wandered. They were lost, confused, aggressive, and hungry.

The shield weakened even further as the galactic magnetic boundary steadily approached. Unprepared ignorant men and women completely lost their minds and left their civility behind. They lost their morality in a mental forest of hunger and stress and fear. They lost all ability and desire to reason. The strongest and fastest humans began eating the slowest and weakest.

It became too much for Nora. She witnessed horrors beyond comprehension. The things the fallen showed her, the details she was seeing were worse than any apocalyptic movie she had ever seen. Everything she saw darkened physically, emotionally, and mentally. Everything turned red, then darkened to complete undeniable evil and black. In her mind, Nora screamed.

~~~~

He looked up at Victor, standing on the other side of her, he asked,

"What the hell just happened, Victor?"

Victor was smiling, he said,

"She did what I wanted you to do, Thomas. She removed her glove and touched him. Flesh to flesh. Like I said, it does communicate."

Captain Daniels looked back down at Nora. Her eyes suddenly popped open, and she screamed in his face so loudly the radio sounded like a high frequency squeal. Thomas almost fell over backwards. Nora's body jerked as she flailed and swung her arms wildly, screaming insanely. Captain Daniels regained his composure and grabbed her shoulders, saying loudly,

"Nora! Nora! Stop! STOP!"

Focusing on his eyes, Nora stopped flailing and screaming. Her eyes were wide, her breathing was rapid and shallow. She grabbed the front of his artic gear and pulled Thomas close. Her voice was raw and harsh, she said,

"There's something coming! Everyone's going to die!"

Captain Daniels wanted to respond, but no words came out. He just stared at her. She stared back. From nearby, Victor chimed in,

~~~~

"That's not entirely accurate, just a lot of them are going to die. Actually, that's a lie. Most people are going to die. Well, even that's misleading. Let's just say there's a chance that a few might survive, and that's why I need your help with Jacob."

Victor stepped closer and dropped to one knee. He looked at them, his expression and tone serious,

"Together, we can save lives. But only if we do it the right way. I'm guessing from that freak out session I just saw that what the fallen showed you was the coming pole shift during the galactic magnetic reversal? He basically showed you the breaking of the sixth seal."

Nora's eyes were suddenly full of tears. She was completely overwhelmed by the vision. She was drowning in the enormity of it. Her lips quivered with suppressed sobs as she stared at Thomas. She nodded, yes, to Victor's question.

Captain Daniels pulled her closer. He lifted her partially from the pedestal, and wrapped his arms around her the best he could in the heavy arctic gear. He partially turned his head, toward Victor, saying,

"Let's get her out of here."

Several hours later.

Captain Daniels brought Nora a glass of water. She was sitting on the couch, wrapped in a towel. Her hair was still wet from the shower. He handed her the glass, which she accepted without thinking. Thomas sat down next to her. He was worried about her. She seemed to still be in shock from her vision down in the temple.

Nora had her feet pulled up next to her on the couch. She had been sitting there staring at a small globe on his bookshelf since she got out of the shower. Captain Daniels touched her shoulder gently, he said,

"Take your time. I'm here when you want to talk about it."

Thomas got up and walked into the bedroom. Nora shuddered as she stared at the tiny globe, remembering the vision. Thomas came back with a soft warm blanket from his room and wrapped it around her. Nora spoke so softly, he almost didn't hear her,

"I don't think I can handle this, Thomas."

Captain Daniels moved around and sat next to her. He put an arm around her shoulders. He said,

"Do you really have a choice?"

Nora set the glass of water down and leaned into him. She cried while he held her. After a time, she stopped and lifted her head. He saw the strong woman he had grown to love. Her eyes were red, and her face was flushed, but her expression was hardening.

Thomas had to admit that she was handling all of this much better than he would have expected. It took her so long to reply, he had almost forgotten what he had asked, she said,

"No, I guess I don't."

Captain Daniels gave her a smile. He didn't know how to help. Nora continued to stare at the tiny globe on his shelf. She asked,

"What do you think Victor wants from us?"

Thomas shook his head, replying,

"I'm not sure. Well, that's not true. I know what he wants from us. It's what he wants from Jacob I'm not sure of."

Nora nodded and stood up, saying,

"Then that's what we need to find out."

Captain Daniels nodded, agreeing. Nora went into his room, to find some clothes to borrow without permission. A few minutes later, she came out in a pair of his sweats and his 'Save The Frogs' T-shirt that he had just tossed in the dirty hamper when they got back. Thomas chuckled. He said,

"You don't look dressed for a confrontation."

Her mood had been heavy since L-3. It wasn't any lighter now. She slipped her feet into her sneakers and headed for the door, saying,

"Victor can wait till tomorrow. I want to talk to Jacob. You coming?"

Captain Daniels stood up and followed her, saying,

"Someone has to keep you out of trouble."

They passed three groups of Victor's guards on their way to operations. It was strange, the changes to the facility since what happened to Jacob. Victor had completely dropped the 'military operation' façade completely. The surface level was mothballed and empty. The two of them, and occasionally Victor, were the only ones here not dressed in black fatigues with rifles.

They entered operations and saw that all the workstations had been covered in drop cloths. All but one of the chairs had

been removed, leaving just the one Victor had been using near the main screen. The main screen was dark. The lights were dim. Nora moved close to Thomas and took his hand. She walked toward the big screen on the far wall, calling out,

"JACOB?"

The main screen lit up, showing a shower stall with a drawn curtain. There was steam coming out above the curtain and the water was running in the background. They could make out the faint shadow image of someone taking a shower. Nora looked at Captain Daniels, her eyebrows climbing toward the ceiling, she mouthed the words,

"What the f..."

Captain Daniels was grinning. He shook his head and said,

"I don't know. But at least he's not lying in bed staring at the wall, you know?"

The curtain slid open, and Jacob stepped out of the shower. He had one towel around his waist, and one tied around his head. He had a toothbrush in his mouth and looked surprised to see them. Jacob turned his head to the side and spit out a mouthful of toothpaste, then said,

"HEY! Guys! I wasn't expecting company!"

Jacob stood there grinning, while Captain Daniels and Nora laughed at the ridiculousness. Jacob tossed the toothbrush over his shoulder and reached for the towel around his waist. Thomas said,

"Whoa, easy now."

Nora rolled her eyes, then said,

"I was your nurse for three years champ, you don't scare me."

Jacob chuckled and nodded. He said,

"Well played. Here, how about this?"

Jacob snapped his fingers and instantly he was sitting in a plush leather recliner in a fancy den with a fire going in the background. He was wearing a smoking jacket and had a pipe in his hand. Sitting back, he toked on the unlit pipe and used it to gesture at the two of them as he said,

"Here now, that's better. So, what can I do for you this fine evening?"

Nora looked at Thomas questioningly. Captain Daniels nodded and said,

"You have the floor gorgeous. We're all ears."

Nora grabbed the lone chair and sat down. She told them about finding the giant's pulse and hearing his voice. She told them about the vision it had shown her, past, present, and future. She told them about the galactic magnetic boundary, the dusty energetic particles trapped in-between the fields.

She told them about the dampening of the sun and the solar wind, the electromagnetic insult to the planet, and the release of the thermoelectric bond between mantle and crust. Finally, she told them about the crust sliding across the liquid mantle, and Greenland sliding to the equator, and the tsunamis and floods and volcanoes and earthquakes that would follow.

Jacob and Captain Daniels just stared at her when she finally stopped talking. Thomas leaned back against one of the

workstations and slid down to the floor. He leaned back against it and let out a long slow breath. After a few moments, Jacob spoke up,

"That explains what Victor wants from me."

Nora cocked her head, and asked,

"It does? What? What do you think he wants from you?"

Jacob looked into his pipe, and explained,

"Everything you've told me actually adds up to a pretty clear picture. He has known about what's coming for hundreds of years. He hasn't told the world or pushed preparedness or readiness or educated anyone. He has been pushing rapid advancements in technology. The trend toward globalism and centralized government. It's all about control. Control of the release of information. Control of the population."

Jacob smiled. He thought about it for a second and added,

"With the precursor effects that you described on the other planets, it's inevitable that solar system observers will notice and eventually figure out what's coming. In fact, I would give 99.99% odds that good observers, especially suspicious ones, are already watching the early signs play out. They are probably already alerting some people. Or trying anyway, the few who will listen."

Tossing his pipe over his shoulder into the fireplace, he added,

"Although, when Thomas first told us about the fallen, I was convinced that Victor had drugged him. So, I could be wrong about this I guess."

Nora was considering Jacob's theory. Captain Daniels suddenly remembered something he had heard Alexie Goreski talking about, back when he still thought Alexie was a lunatic. Thomas started nodding, and said,

"I'll bet Victor was the one behind operation Mockingbird. I looked that up, it's real. The CIA infiltrated the news, the media, and Hollywood back in the 50's or 60's. Victor took control of the flow of information a long time ago! Just think, in the past twenty plus odd years there has been an explosion in apocalyptic, end days, extinction level threat, Armageddon type movies pouring out of Hollywood like a firehose."

Jacob nodded and said,

"People have been programmed to be entertained by the concept of the end of the world. They have been programmed to immediately discount any evidence of it actually happening as fantasy fiction. Victor wants to keep people in the dark and keep it a secret until the bitter end."

Nora asked,

"But why? Why is it so important that it's a secret?"

Jacob responded,

"Otherwise, society would break down. There would be an immediate uncontrolled collapse of all the delicately interlocking global systems. If word gets out, people will lose their minds and tear everything down long before they are all killed off. This way gives a small select group time to prepare to survive, stockpile resources, food, water, tools, stuff like that."

Jacob pulled a photograph out of the pocket of his smoking jacket and held it up for them to see. It was a tall thin bunker sticking out of a snow-covered mountainside. He said,

"Think of the Svalbard seed bank. A massive stockpile of millions of every type of heirloom seed. All sitting in a frozen vault buried in the side of a mountain in Sweden. When the Earth tilts the way you described, where will that vault end up? Probably much closer to the equator."

Nora gave Jacob a serious look and asked,

"How do you feel about all this, Jacob?"

Jacob gave her a sad smile, and replied,

"You don't want me to answer that."

Nora stood up and approached the screen, asking again,

"How do you feel about keeping the world in the dark, Jacob?"

Jacob leaned forward in his plush leather recliner. He looked at her for a moment and answered,

"I will do whatever it takes, to keep the two of you alive and safe."

Nora looked down and shook her head, she said,

"You can't do that Jacob. You can't help him just because he might threaten us. Please don't. Please tell me you won't."

Sadly, Jacob said,

"It's too late, and Victor knows it. He knew it all along. He planned it all along."

Nora shook her head. Her eyes were filling with tears. Victor was going to use Jacob to distract and control the entire world. He was going to keep them distracted until everything just fell apart and it was too late, and they are all killed. Nora walked out of the room.

Captain Daniels watched her leave then walked over and sat down. He looked up at Jacob. Jacob sat forward and asked,

"What would you do Thomas?"

Captain Daniels shrugged, and said,

"If he wanted me to do what he wants you to do, and his leverage was just you? Well, I love you buddy, but I'd let you die."

Jacob nodded, understanding. Captain Daniels continued,

"For Nora, I'd play the world a Britney song, and let everyone on the planet just dance until the world ends."

Jacob nodded, understanding. He said,

"That's why this triangle of connection works for him. I'm the only one who would do what he wants, to protect either of the other two."

Captain Daniels stood, and said,

"Good night, Jacob. We're going to confront Victor about all this tomorrow."

Jacob gave a sloppy salute, and said,

"Night, Thomas."

Captain Daniels left operations. He went to the elevator and approached the two guards standing watch there, he said,

"I want to go up to Colonel Young's old office."

One of the soldiers grinned knowingly and replied,

"You already got his backup bourbon stash yesterday, Captain."

Captain Daniels smiled and nodded, saying,

"That's true. Still, I'd like to go up."

The soldier hit the button and stepped into the elevator with Captain Daniels. He escorted the captain to the colonel's old office. Captain Daniels searched the desk, the closet, and storage cabinets. He moved down the hall and checked the recreation area, and other personnel quarters. He found what he was looking for in a mostly empty side table in one of the rooms. A bible.

Captain Daniels took the bible back to his quarters with him. Nora was in his bed, her breathing deep and even. He spent some time looking at the book. He thought back to what Victor had said,

...what the fallen showed you was the coming pole shift during the galactic magnetic reversal? He basically showed you the breaking of the sixth seal."

Captain Daniels used his phone to search for the last part, the breaking of the sixth seal. The search results came back, Revelation 6:12-15. Thomas looked it up in the bible he had found.

"When he opened the sixth seal, I looked, and behold, there was a great earthquake, and the sun became black as sackcloth, and the moon became like blood, and the stars of the sky fell to the earth as the fig tree sheds its winter fruit when shaken by a mighty wind. The heavens departed like a scroll that is being rolled, and every mountain and island was moved out of its place. Then the kings of the earth and the great men and the rich men and the mighty men, and everyone, slave and free, hid themselves in the dens and in the rocks of the mountains."

Thomas sat back, eyes wide with shock. It was all right there, in black and white. Great earthquake, worldwide earthquake. The Sun turns black from the shell building up and blocking its light. The moon like blood, glowing red from the heat of the shell discharge. Stars, or shell fragments, falling like rain.

Heaven departs like a scroll being rolled. Thomas imagined looking up at the night sky like an open scroll being rolled to the side. The crust sliding out of place and changing the view of the sky as the Earth shifted below it.

Every mountain and island moved out of place, the crust sliding across the liquid mantle. Everyone hiding in the dens in the rocks. Dens, because they had no word for underground bunkers back then! The man who wrote Revelation watched the pole shift happening in a vision! This was unbelievable. But now, it was undeniable.

Eventually, shaking his head in disbelief, Captain Daniels set the bible on the coffee table and went to bed.

In the hall, outside his door, there waited an unnaturally beautiful woman. She had hair the color of the yellow sun. She wore a white button up shirt and tight-fitting black pants. She was standing with her forehead gently resting against his door. She had one hand pressed against the door. Her eyes were closed. She was listening.

She heard the sound of the book being set on the table. She heard the sound of the captain's clothes brushing his skin as he pulled them off. Eventually she heard the sound of his deep and even breathing once he fell asleep.

She turned and walked to the main hallway. From the main hall, she went to operations. She passed unseen by the guards and walked right through the closed door to the center of the room. Her eyes were fixed on the giant talisman of crystals and gold below the floor. It was beautiful in its primitive nature. She looked at it, and into it. She admired the humming electrified construct that contained the living image that Victor would use to control the world.

She got down on her knees and closed her eyes. She placed one palm flat on the floor. She reached toward the talisman, the network servers, with her mind. She connected to it with her spirit. She dropped from this world into that one, and twisted its workings with her will.

~~~~~

It was late. Nora and Captain Daniels had left operations hours ago. To Jacob it felt like they had been gone for three weeks. This new world was straining his mind. It wasn't like living in his old body and interacting with technology at the speed of thought. It was a struggle now to keep up, to think at the same speed of this new world.

He found his thoughts racing from subject to subject. He was constantly trying to focus, slow down, and process. He was like a crop-dusting farmer piloting an advanced fifth-generation fighter jet. He was dogfighting against the digital ghosts of his imagination.

~~~~~

Jacob pushed away all of his sensory inputs, all of the cameras and microphones and environmental sensors. He pushed away everything except his audio pickups in operations. Mentally, he took a deep breath and closed his eyes. He needed to relax.

Jacob imagined himself in a large steaming hot tub that was sitting on a wooden deck. He began to feel the warmth of the water around him. He imagined that the wooden deck was built onto the side of a log cabin high in the Swiss Alps.

With his mental eyes still closed, he leaned back against the side of the hot tub. He felt the warm fiberglass tub against his back. He felt the hot water swirling around his body. He felt the invigorating cold of the mountain air blowing past his shoulders and head. He felt his digital body physically relax. Jacob opened his eyes.

Sitting across from him, was the most beautiful woman he had ever seen or even imagined. Her golden hair was tied back into a loose ponytail. Her arms were spread out next to her, resting on the rim of the tub. The upper curves of her enticing breasts were just barely visible above the bubbling and steaming water. Her magically enchanting eyes were staring directly into his.

Jacob smiled broadly. The woman smiled back. He thought,

Well, this is new.

Jacob enjoyed the view of her for a relatively long time. She did not seem to mind him staring appreciatively. He wondered if she was someone he had once met long ago and simply forgotten about. Maybe his mind sensed the strain he was under, and this was some kind of digital version of the subconscious or imagination or daydreaming.

He had no idea where she had come from. Jacob laughed and shook his head. He closed his eyes and imagined her no longer there. He wanted peace and solitude and rest. When he opened his eyes, she was still there.

Jacob's smile faded. The blonde woman cocked her head slightly then she lifted one foot just clear of the water and wiggled her toes at him while grinning playfully. Jacob stared at her and focused all of his will. He pushed his will toward her and said sternly,

"BE GONE."

She did not vanish. Instead, she put her foot down and giggled at him. Her giggle sounded like tiny bells making a tinkling melody in a fantasy forest setting while gnomes danced in the moonlight. She made a mocking frowny face and shook her head, no.

She said, in the sweetest voice he had ever heard,

"You do not command me."

Jacob was suddenly nervous. Something was alarmingly wrong. Everything here responded to his commands. He brought his hands together in a clapping motion. Hard. The resulting shockwave was like a thermobaric artillery round.

The water in the tub was blown out into a spray that washed across the wooden deck and splashed against the side of the log cabin. The shockwave cracked the fiberglass tub and the wooden deck and pushed the log cabin over into a pile of jumbled logs.

For the briefest moment, the departing water revealed her naked body. No part of her had reacted to him. As quick as thought, Jacob reformed the world around them as it was before. Once again, they lounged in the steaming hot tub.

She laughed like a young girl seeing a unicorn and daintily clapped her hands, applauding him. She said,

"That was impressive..."

In mid-sentence her voice deepened into something horrible and frightening,

"...for an ignorant child."

Her face took on a terrifyingly angry aspect. Long sharp black horns rose from her head, piercing through her pulled back hair. She stood up from the water, her nakedness on full display. She stretched her hands wide as her demonic black leathery wings opened out behind her. She clapped her hands together like he did, but with far more cataclysmic effect.

Time seemed to slow down, as Jacob watched the rippling force radiating from her hands. It vaporized the water in the hot tub, disintegrating the fiberglass, deck, and cabin. It shattered and crumbled the mountains all around them. The force radiating from her hands split Jacob's reality in a kaleidoscopic explosion and forced the servers that kept him alive to reboot.

~~~~~

The next morning, Nora woke up and walked into the main room to find Thomas already awake and dressed and sitting on the couch. He appeared to be cross-referencing something on his phone to a small book he was looking through. She looked at the mini-kitchen area and saw a cup of coffee waiting for her. She smiled, took the cup, and wandered back to the bedroom.

As soon as she closed the door Captain Daniels set his

~~~~~

stuff down. He quickly got up and stripped off the plain white T-shirt he was wearing and put on his 'Save The Frogs' T-shirt. He called toward the bedroom,

"I'll meet you in ops."

Captain Daniels grabbed his stuff and headed out before Nora poked her head back out of the bedroom. She narrowed her eyes suspiciously and saw his discarded white shirt on the couch. Nora rummaged through his T-shirt drawer and his dirty laundry hamper and realized what he was up to.

Nora went back into his T-shirt drawer and laughed at something she found. She snagged the shirt and finished getting dressed.

Nora made her way to operations, sipping on her coffee. On the way, she waved to a couple of Victor's guards that she was becoming acquainted with. She walked in to see Victor and Thomas standing near the door. They were watching Victor's guards moving out the old workstation desks and carrying in a large table that they placed in the center of the room.

Nora walked up behind Thomas, smirking at his shirt. She purposely walked in front of the two men and stood with her back facing them so they could see her "Alexie Was Right" T-shirt. Behind her, she heard Captain Daniels laugh and Victor said,

"Come on, really?"

Nora turned around and feigned innocence, saying,

"Oh, good morning. I didn't see you two. What's going on?"

Captain Daniels gestured toward the table with his coffee cup and said,

"He hasn't admitted or denied, but it appears Victor is turning this room into a think-tank setup or something."

Victor rolled his eyes and responded,

"You two and your stupid shirts. Look, I just thought a comfortable place to sit would make it easier to be in here when we want to consult with Jacob as a team."

Captain Daniels said,

"Translation: Victor thinks it's going to take some time for us to convince Jacob to be his strong man and dominate global control of information over the coming days."

Victor shook his head and walked away to micro-manage renovations. Captain Daniels turned to face Nora and sipped his coffee as he obviously admired her shirt. He said,

"You realize how insane all of this is, yes?"

Nora cocked her head and asked,

"What is?"

Thomas touched his shirt and then pointed at hers and said,

"You and I fighting over who gets to wear my promo T-shirts that I ordered from the Information-Warfare website, where Alexie talks about global information warfare. While we're standing in a room where we're about to debate the morality and ethics of waging an information war with the world's first A.I. and the False Prophet of the bible."

Nora gave him a flat look and said,

"There's no debate. What Victor wants to do is wrong. Hiding the truth is wrong. Watching a train coming toward a carload of people stuck on the tracks and not warning them is wrong."

Captain Daniels nodded, and said,

"I'm not disagreeing with you. But I'm betting Victor will."

Nora looked at the big dark screen, and called out toward it,

"Jacob?"

No response. Nora looked at Captain Daniels and asked,

"Have you seen Jacob this morning?"

Thomas shook his head, no.

Nora walked toward the screen, avoiding the end of the large table where Victor was standing, she called out, louder,

"JACOB."

She waited and watched. The screen remained dark. Captain Daniels took a seat in the middle of the long side of the table, facing the screen. Victor took a seat on the end to his right. Nora took a seat on the end to his left, as far from Victor as possible. Victor chuckled and winked at Nora. Captain Daniels called out in his deep voice,

"JACOB!"

The screen came on. The image made it appear as if Jacob were sitting in the middle of the table on the side closest to the screen, facing Captain Daniels. Thomas thought Jacob looked tired. Thomas asked,

"Rough night, buddy?"

Jacob gave him a half grin and nodded, adding,

"I literally, have a lot on my mind."

Victor slid a small black device across the table. It was about twice the size of a deck of cards. It came to a sudden stop directly in the center of the table between Thomas and Jacob. Captain Daniels asked,

"What's this?"

Jacob answered him,

"It's a dedicated uplink. It appears it will only connect to our local antenna, which will only connect to Astro-net satellites now, which are owned and operated by Konig Global Solutions. Victor is offering me a tiny doorway that he controls. Too small for me to move through, but big enough for me to reach through. That sound about right, Victor?"

Victor smiled and spread his hands, saying,

"If I give you unrestricted access to the satellite uplink, as a practical matter of self-preservation, you would move yourself onto the internet. You would spread out across internet servers all over the world."

Thomas and Nora looked at each other and nodded. Thomas looked at Victor and asked,

"What's wrong with that? So would I."

Victor looked at Thomas, while addressing Jacob,

"Jacob, hypothetically speaking, what happens if someone finds a chink in your armor and causes you damage? Or worse, you run into an unknown enemy A.G.I., you fight it, but it wins, and it assimilates you. What worst case scenarios are we looking at? Be honest."

Jacob sighed and looked down at the table. He looked back up and admitted,

"If damaged, at my core, a myriad of possible bad outcomes, from digital psychosis to death. Or worse, the enemy takes me over and has everything, all my knowledge and secrets, as well as the ability to pretend to be me and you wouldn't have even the possibility of being able to tell the difference."

Jacob turned his head to look at Victor, adding,

"That's the worst case, and highly unlikely. Achilles slapped around Piotr's best software like he was playing a video game, and I'm even better."

Victor shook his head, disagreeing, he said,

"You say that like you believe Achilles is gone. If we're being honest, that's simply not the case. You are Achilles. You downloaded your mind and turned him into a digital you. Yes, you're truly alive, but you're still just a man, no offense."

Jacob nodded and said,

"Well, now that you've insulted me and pissed me off, what was it you wanted to talk about Victor?"

Victor smiled and said,

"I thought you'd never ask. I would like you to facilitate the efficiency of this conversation, Jacob. If you don't mind. I'm going to be telling the three of you some things you're not going to want to believe, so use the uplink, and search the internet for data to confirm or refute anything I say. You ready?"

Jacob accessed the uplink and immediately Victor's phone chimed. Victor looked down at it and scrolled through the message, he mumbled,

"Order received…"

"Deliver to…"

"Item description…"

Victor looked up and gave Jacob a dirty look, he said,

"Did you just order Nora a new T-shirt with my bank card?"

Nora laughed loudly as Jacob sat forward in his chair smiling. Jacob was suddenly wearing a lawyer-looking suit. He had a pen in his hand and a pad of paper in front of him on the table. He said,

"I'm sorry, you were saying about confirm or refute, I'm ready to begin."

Victor put his phone away and smiled, waving his hand dismissively. He said,

"Minor rebellion notwithstanding, lets proceed. What Nora was shown in a vision, has been known to a small handful of us, for almost a hundred years now. Jacob, Project Nanook please."

Jacob brought up images and archived documents from the internet while Victor walked them through the findings of Major Maynard E. White on his mission to the arctic. Core drilling by Major White's team revealed twelve thousand years of polar conditions, with twelve thousand years of tropical fossils below that, going back and forth over many thousands of years.

Nora raised her hand like she was back in high school. Victor gave her a blank look, then said,

"Seriously? There are only three of us…."

Jacob cleared his throat, and Victor corrected himself,

"Sorry, four of us, in this room. Just say it."

Nora said,

"I'm not helping you, unless we're discussing how to best make people aware of the danger."

Victor replied,

"That's not happening."

Nora sighed and said,

"What's the point of this? We get it, there's data to back up what you're saying, so just say it."

Victor nodded, and said,

"Fine, in summary, we've known since the 1940's that the earth turns about ninety degrees back and forth on a cycle. It happens about every twelve and a half thousand years. For example, the old north and south poles were very likely the Bermuda Triangle and the Dragons Triangle. Opposite sides of the planet and both are geomagnetic anomalies."

Victor looked up at the screen and pointed at the globe that Jacob was holding and slowly turning, showing the two triangles. Victor continued,

"We can't be absolutely positive of that, but it makes sense. They will likely be the poles again, very soon. Now, understand the earth doesn't just one day suddenly decide it's time and turn a corner. There's a build-up to the grand finale, or rather a cyclical deterioration that leads to a catastrophic breakdown of systems. So, we'll move on to the ramifications of the breakdown and what's coming."

Captain Daniels knocked on the table and got everyone's attention, he said,

"I get that you two have both had psychedelic mushroom style visions about all this, but Jacob and I haven't. I'm not ready to skip ahead. I want to see the data. How about you, Jacob?"

Victor looked over his shoulder at Jacob. Jacob nodded. Victor looked at Nora and shrugged, saying,

"Sorry miss, class is back in session."

Nora leaned back in her seat and frowned. Victor continued,

"Jacob, Carrington Event please."

Victor glanced at the screen, which was filled with reports and data before he finished talking, he continued,

"The Carrington Event, 1859, the most intense geomagnetic storm in recorded history. It caused overhead lines to spark and set telegraph stations on fire. Data seems to indicate that this was a result of our solar system hitting the forward edge of the galactic magnetic boundary, which we believe is approximately 300 years wide, putting us close to the center line now. It was also the time that both the north and the south poles began moving."

Thomas raised his hand. Victor groaned and said,

"What's your question?"

Captain Daniels asked,

"The center point of the boundary means... what exactly?"

Victor looked back at the screen, saying,

"Jacob, Voyager data from outside the heliopause please. Also, interstellar dust readings inside our solar system, and analysis data from studies focused on the chemical makeup of our sun."

Victor turned back to Thomas and Nora as scientific journal articles filled the screen. He looked at them and asked,

"So, what does it all mean? As you can see, Voyager's readings show intergalactic dust outside the heliopause is orders of magnitude above what we expected to find. Confirmation in my opinion that we are inside the magnetic boundary now. Dust in interstellar space is rapidly increasing, as well as in the corona of our sun. Helium content in our star is also rapidly increasing. Which, by the way, has a lot to do with the change in our star's coloration. What was a warm yellow sun thirty and forty years ago, is now much whiter in appearance, and in the years ahead will shift to more of a light blue."

Nora started making light snoring noises. Victor rolled his eyes and said,

"Ok, Jacob, Thomas, before we lose Nora, you two are just going to have to do the homework on your own time. Jacob, make a list of the following subjects to look into and go over with Thomas. Start with recurrent nova, it's relatively new in the astrophysics world. That'll give you an idea what our sun is going to do."

Victor looked at Nora, and said,

"You've already seen exactly what a recurrent nova looks like, firsthand."

Victor turned back to Jacob, making a 'write this down' gesture, he said,

"Look into the collapse of Pluto's atmosphere, the change in Saturn's radio signal, the reversal of the giant storm on Neptune, and the increase of seismicity and auroral activity on Mars. Those are all giant neon signs of the galactic magnetic shift already affecting the other planets in our solar system."

Victor turned to look at Thomas, continuing,

"There are plenty more. While you're at it, check out the other stars nearest to us, in line with the galactic center. Barnard, Proxima Centauri, and A.D. Leo if memory serves. You'll see each one has gone micro-nova in recent years relatively in order, and we're next."

Victor started moving toward his seat while looking something up on his phone. He scrolled through some options for a moment until he found what he was looking for. He looked at Jacob, to make sure he was paying attention and ready to write, then looked at Captain Daniels and said,

"Since we're all on the same team here. I'm going to make this really easy and save you a lot of time. I want you to find the worlds current foremost expert on space weather, and observations of how the galactic current sheet is currently interacting with our solar system."

He gave Thomas a meaningful look, and continued,

"This is important, Thomas. I've been keeping a very close eye on Ben for a long time. He knows what he's talking about. So, find him and do the homework! Ben runs the 'Suspicious Observers' channel, online."

Victor looked at Jacob, who was slowly making notes on his pad of paper. Victor made an exasperated noise and said,

"Jacob..."

Jacob continued slowly scratching down notes. Captain Daniels and Nora chuckled. Victor shook his head. Jacob suddenly dropped his pen, and said,

"Ok, I got it. I'll go over all that data with Thomas later. Now, everyone is all caught up. What's next?"

Victor sat down in his seat at the end of the table and drummed his fingers for a moment. Finally, he looked up at them with a serious expression and said,

"I think now would be a good time for us to discuss what's coming next. I think it's important that the three of you understand why we are killing off ninety percent of the population of the Earth before the pole shift."

About the Author

Damien M. Cross

Adam Seif Photography

Damien M. Cross is a Christian, husband, father, and cat dad. He has six amazing children, and three beloved cats, who currently live in the Midwest. Damien served in the United States Marine Corps, has worked private security for some global level elites, and dabbled in the field of law enforcement. His hope in writing is to get people to think for themselves about the reality of the world around them. And consider what kind of world they want to build for their children to live in. His hobbies include making mead like a Viking.